The Paris Predicament

Lexi Haddock

Chrysalis Press

Cover design by Stephanie Anderson, Alt 19 Designs

Published by Chrysalis Press, an imprint of Kat Biggie Press

978-1-955119-59-7 paperback

978-1-955119-60-3 ebook

Printed in the United States of America

For Nick

1

October 2001

I STARED at the clock as if I could make time fast forward by my will. The clock chimed loudly, announcing the thirty-minute warning before I'd walk down the aisle. An unpleasant buzz vibrated in my belly. Was this what cold feet felt like?

My mother's hands trembled slightly as she delicately arranged the soft tulle fabric of the veil around my bare shoulders. "Perfection," she said, giving me a once-over before placing a delicate kiss on my cheek. "You look like a princess!"

Her words pulled me back into the moment. Admittedly, I had transformed quite nicely. "Ironic, isn't it? I guess even hippy chicks can look good on their wedding days," I said, smiling at her. My sleeveless silk dress, with a form-fitting bodice and flowing, but not Scarlett O'Hara-level full skirt, made me feel like royalty. I was rarely the type to describe myself as such, and definitely not one to wear dresses regularly, but this gown made me want to dress up in luxurious fabrics daily—a thought that suddenly made me question how well I knew myself. I twisted slightly to look at the overall effect of the veil with the dress in the mirror. The smoky makeup made my dark eyes shine like a raven's wings, and I turned my head to admire the up-sweep of my long dark hair, which was usually down. I had to admit, I liked it.

A wave of excitement along with a bit of nausea coursed through me. I lifted my bouquet out of its vase on the vanity next to me and took a deep breath of its sweet scent. I tried to calm myself down as I admired the perfect hydrangea in the center, the same navy as the bridesmaids' dresses, encircled by stunning white roses. I hoped this feeling in my gut was just nerves as I replaced the flowers in the vase on the vanity.

My mother beamed at me, although I saw her chin quivering. Her gray-streaked hair was pulled up in an elegant bun, and her silver dress accentuated her pale blue eyes.

"Keep it together, Mom! If you lose it, we're all going to be a mess! And that makeup job is too good to waste!" I said. I hugged her, and she squeezed me tight.

As we dropped our embrace, my mom nodded, and Callie appeared with a tissue box. My mother plucked one and gently dabbed at the corner of her eyes.

"You're absolutely stunning, Lila," Callie said, giving me a gentle hug from behind.

I placed my hand on top of hers and made eye contact in the mirror.

"I'm so glad you're here," I whispered.

This is the perfect day. All my besties from childhood and college, and Callie, who was the newest addition to my inner circle, but one of the most important, gathered in one place to celebrate me and Matt.

"I wouldn't miss it for the world!" Callie said, squeezing one more time before dropping her arms.

Callie and I had become close friends when we stumbled upon each other in Paris, where we'd both been living and working. While I had returned to the United States, she had met a French man just days before she was supposed to come home, and, in an epic fairy-tale fashion, ultimately stayed in France with him. She and Julien had recently tied the knot, but they had made the trip over from France for my special day.

Navy blue was definitely her color. Her eyes sparkled and her dirty-blond hair had grown much longer over the last almost two years. The stylist had woven Callie's hair into an intricate knot at the base of her neck, leaving a few tendrils framing her face.

The recent events of September 11th had scared many of my international friends away from traveling, which made it even more special that Callie, Julien, and his best friend Philippe had made the journey. We were still missing the third piece of our girl trio—our French friend Emilie—who had been unable to travel over for the wedding, but I had chatted with her earlier that day and she'd given me all her best wishes. I touched the earrings I wore, which she'd sent so that she could be present in some way.

"It's almost time," Callie whispered in my ear.

My heart raced. I excitedly twisted my engagement ring around my ring finger. Soon it would be paired with my forever band. The light caught the stone, and it shimmered brilliantly. After four years together, Matt had proposed six months ago, and we'd decided not to have a long, drawn-out engagement. I had sufficient time for the most important tasks: find the perfect dress, taste enough cakes to ensure I'd picked the best of the best, and decide on the flowers—a perfect blend of roses and hydrangeas—and my mother had taken care of the rest. She'd been dreaming of this day since I was born, and I gladly allowed her to tend to the details that were most important to her.

"Ladies, join us in a circle!" Amy, my maid of honor and

childhood best friend, announced. She started handing out small shot glasses. "I have the perfect speech prepared!"

Of course she did. She'd always been the life of the party, from our earliest grade school slumber parties where she led our Mountain Dew chugging contests, all the way through our sorority events in college.

Amy, looking gorgeous with her blonde curls cascading around her shoulders, blue eyes sparkling with mischief, held out her glass, waiting for everyone else to follow suit. I prepared myself for an epic toast, hoping I wouldn't blubber all my makeup off.

Amy looked around, ensuring she had everyone's attention, then raised her small, plastic shot glass higher, and said, "Here's to the men we love. If the men we love don't love us, then BUMP them, and here's to us!" She knocked back her cup and gave a little cheer.

My eyes widened. Not what I'd been expecting. I doubted this was Amy's first shot of the afternoon.

Callie snickered. She caught my gaze, raised her glass, and said, "To love!"

Thank you, I mouthed.

This time everyone lifted their cups, cheering, "To Lila and Matt!" and "To love!" The mint liquor both burned and refreshed on its way down.

As we scattered to powder noses, reapply lip gloss, and adjust our dresses, a knock sounded at the door.

"I'll get it!" Callie volunteered, darting over and cracking the door open. She glanced back at me, pointed to her ring finger, and exited the room to be with her husband, Julien. I scuttled over, eager to say hello to him as well.

Peering out of the doorway, I noticed Philippe, Julien's closest friend. He looked different from the last time I'd seen him. No glasses, longer hair than when we'd met, and he had donned a suit rather than his usual jeans and T-shirt look. As I approached, the three of them stopped whispering furiously and turned to me. "You certainly clean up well!" I said. I leaned into Philippe, air kissing him on one cheek and then the other, while trying to avoid transferring the cake of makeup on my face to his.

Philippe addressed me in English, his French accent thick. "Happy day of marriage!"

So *cute*! "Thank you!" I replied. "I'm glad you're here."

Philippe stiffened, looked down at the floor, and shuffled his feet. *Had he always been this shy?*

Julien leaned forward to kiss me on the cheek. "Lila! You look amazing! We're so happy for you." He turned quickly to Callie, reaching for her hand.

Philippe messed with a button on his suit, and silence settled over us. As they looked at each other, their expressions revealed something other than joy. Prickles shot up and down my spine as I wondered what was causing them to avoid eye contact with me.

I didn't love this vibe. "What's going on?" I asked, looking from one person to the next, my heart rate climbing.

"Um, uh, nothing. I just wanted to see my beautiful wife before the service started," Julien stuttered. He looked to Callie for confirmation, and she nodded, a little too emphatically. Philippe busied himself picking invisible lint off his jacket.

Chalking the weirdness up to my own wedding day jitters, I nodded. "Well, I can't say I blame you for that," I said, throwing an arm around Callie. She focused her eyes on the plush carpet, rubbing at a stain with her foot. I tilted my head at her, squinting my eyes. She kept silent, still staring at the ground. What in the world was going on?

"We're going to go back downstairs now," Julien said, turning to Callie and planting a quick peck on her cheek. He squeezed her hands. "I'll see you soon," he said. Again with the bizarre glances between the two of them before Julien turned away, followed closely by Philippe.

What was going on? Why were they acting so weird?

Laughter from the bridal dressing room caught my attention. My bridesmaids were giggling as they finalized their makeup and grabbed their bouquets. At least they were behaving normally. I didn't have time to ask questions before Callie quickly reentered the room, bypassing me, and hustled over to my mother.

That's weird.

I stared at the two of them as they huddled up, whispering. Occasionally one or the other glanced back in my direction. My mother grabbed Callie's arm, looking back at me with a wild-eyed glance. Another chill rolled up my back.

I hiked up my heavy dress and marched over to demand answers. "Mother?" I never call her mother. I cocked my head, asking the question without words.

"I'm sure it's nothing, ladybug," she said, reaching over to fluff my veil. "Finish getting ready. I'm going to find your father." She kissed me on the cheek and darted from the room.

"Callie, you guys are freaking me out. What's happening?" I cupped Callie's chin in my hand and forced her to look at me.

She chewed on her lip, and I could see the wheels turning furiously. Callie and I were always honest with each other, but her pained expression reminded me of New Year's Eve 1999 when she'd lost it in a grocery store in Paris over her exasperation at her imminent departure and the life she'd thought she would have with her ex-boyfriend, Vic. She'd been so angry at how he'd treated her and how her plans had gone wrong. Neither of us had any idea she'd meet Julien a few hours later, completely changing the course of her life.

Her smile didn't quite reach her eyes. "I'm sure it's nothing," she said.

"That's what my mom just said! Tell me!" I said. "It doesn't feel like nothing."

Breathing in deeply, her face still very pale, she exhaled slowly. "I don't want you to worry about something that may not be important." She took another deep breath. "I shouldn't say anything. But if it were me, I'd want to know."

"Want to know what?" Amy shoved her way in between me and Callie.

"Shhh." Callie turned to Amy and brought her index finger up to her lips in the *Be quiet!* signal.

I stood still, except for my knees, which began to shake in worry. What on earth could have happened? Did my dad have another heart attack? Had the priest not shown up? No musicians? The cake? We'd had no shortage of scares in the last month, and I feared the worst. "What's happening? Tell me! Is my dad okay?"

Callie finally met my gaze. "Don't worry, your dad's fine," she whispered. "I'm sorry to scare you like that. But, Lila, no one's seen Matt yet."

All the air escaped my lungs, and I crumpled into a chair next to me, fear crippling me.

"Why would you say that?" Amy crouched down at my side, taking my arm and helping me stand again, her arms wrapped protectively around me.

"It could be nothing. His dad isn't here either, so maybe they were just stuck in traffic! I don't want to scare you if it's nothing. Matty is always late!" Callie exclaimed, her voice getting higher and higher. "Cheese and biscuits!" I heard her whisper. That was her signature expression when she was trying not to curse.

Panic started to rise in my chest, but I took a beat, inhaling in and out a few times. According to my bridesmaid Liz's boyfriend, the boys had had a late and eventful night, not returning until after 4 a.m. I'd begged Matt to do his bachelor party on Thursday, like I'd done my bachelorette party, so that he wouldn't be a wreck today, but they'd insisted they would behave. Apparently, they had not.

"Has anyone tried to call him? Where's my phone?" I said, moving to where I'd placed my things and clawing through my bag.

"Julien already tried before he came up here," Callie said.

"I'm going to try again." I dialed his number and waited, breath caught in my chest, as the phone rang once, twice... five times and went to voicemail. "Matty? Where are you? We're all worried about you. Please call me back." I hung up and dialed his number three more times. No answer.

Despite my attempts to calm myself, emotions slammed into me—anger, sadness, disappointment. Even annoyance at Callie. I looked over and saw her distraught expression. She looked crushed, standing with her arms wrapped around her torso. I broke away from Amy and pulled Callie into a hug.

"Thank you for telling me. Even if he's just running late, I wouldn't have wanted you to keep this information from me."

She squeezed me back tightly, whispering. "It's probably nothing." Her hand rubbed soothingly up and down my spine.

"I have a horrible feeling that it's not *nothing*," I said grimly.

2

MY BRIDESMAIDS IN TOW, I shuffled down the stairs as quickly as I could in my suddenly very heavy and constricting dress and into the ballroom that was set up for the ceremony. I stopped at the doorway, observing the beautifully decorated room. The floral centerpieces my mom had insisted on, hydrangeas and baby's breath with spray roses, gave the perfect elegance to each of the round tables where the guests sat, waiting for the processional to start.

I stopped short of actually entering, not ready for anyone to see me yet.

Mayhem. To say hell had broken loose was an understatement. My father stood at the front of the room, where Matt and I should be standing right now, demanding answers from Matt's dad, who had apparently arrived *sans* Matt. The groomsmen stood in a loose line behind him. The small priest had wedged himself between the two men, apparently trying to keep them from arguing, and my brother Andy had his hand on my dad's arm, obviously trying to calm him down. Andy's efforts seemed to be in vain, and I watched as he pushed the brown locks off his face in what I knew was his telltale move when frustrated. My mother was off to the side with the wedding director, arms waving frantically, probably trying to figure out how to direct guests and support staff. My bridesmaids, except for Amy and Callie, squeezed around me to stand in the back of the room quietly.

Amy, however, marched into the middle of the makeshift center aisle, hands on her hips. I stood transfixed, waiting to see what she would do.

She turned to face the groomsmen and gestured angrily at Matt's brother and three closest friends, who looked like they wished the floor would swallow them whole. She pointed her finger at them, and I heard her yelling something about tracking him down. This was a scary side of Amy we only saw on the rarest of occasions. Despite her petite frame of a whole five foot three inches, Amy could step into almost any situation and almost instantly take command. She'd shown her sillier side earlier with the toast she'd given, but her no-nonsense side was fierce. Grateful to her for taking charge, I leaned against the doorframe, trying to make sense of my situation.

As if having an out-of-body experience, I saw everyone whispering to each other. I imagined they were trying to figure out whether to help or leave or wait for a few minutes in case Matt showed up. I held onto the hope that Matt would saunter through that door at any moment, give his lopsided grin, and explain that it was all a mistake. I'd spent four and a half years of my life with him, and he didn't even have the guts to show up on our wedding day. How could he do this to me? How could he do this to our families and friends?

My mom's cousin and her three daughters stood off to one side, dabbing their eyes with tissues. I barely knew them, so their sadness seemed trite. My childhood piano teacher sat on the bride's side of the room, studying the program. She must be a hundred and fifty years old by now. It touched me that she was here, even though it didn't look like she realized there wouldn't be a wedding today. My old friend Tommy, who used to live down the street and mowed our yard for fifteen dollars a pop before my parents realized they could just force me or my brother to mow it and save the money, stood with his arm protectively around a very pregnant woman, who I assumed to be wife number two. Tommy, my brother Andy, and I had spent many of our childhood evenings climbing the giant trees in our neighborhood, pretending we were on the Millenium Falcon. I, of course, was always Princess Leia.

Our flower girl, Andy's three-year-old daughter, had dumped her basket of flowers out and was gleefully kicking the rose petals around, making a mess of the center aisle that had been prepared for the walk it looked like I would not make today.

The oddest thing of all was that, for some reason, the pianist continued playing. Amy turned in her direction and yelled, "This isn't *The Band Played On*! Will you please stop the music?"

Silence immediately fell across the room as the pianist's fingers stopped stroking the keys. If my life were a movie, we'd have all heard the sound of a record screeching to a halt.

The world spun around me. I took a step into the room and stopped.

"Dad?" I whispered. He didn't hear me. "Dad!" I shouted. All eyes turned in my direction. Except my dad's. He was still gesturing wildly in the direction of Matt's dad, who stared at the ground, hands shoved in his pockets, shoulders slumped. My heart went out to him for having to endure the wrath of my bulldog father.

Lifting my shoulders, I stood, as tall as I could muster, hand desperately clenched around the bouquet. Why on earth had I brought my flowers?

"Dad!" I yelled again, and he finally turned my direction.

My eyes locked with his and he dropped his arms to his sides, looking defeated. "Lila."

I took a few steps forward, my eyes scanning the room slowly, humiliation growing with every second. I made eye contact with a few guests. Some gave me small smiles of encouragement, but there were many looks of pity. Anger surged through me, and I wanted to scream at all of them. It was none of my guests' fault, but the person I wanted to rage at was not here.

My mother touched my arm. Concern clouded her face. "We can send everyone home!"

"Why would we do that, Mama? All this food is here, everyone is gathered. We have a DJ and a bar."

Finally, I addressed the room. "I'm sorry, but it doesn't appear there will be a wedding today." My chin started to quiver, and I turned to my mom for support.

My mother squeezed my arm and nodded. She took over. "However, we have a fully stocked bar, and a large amount of food that is about to be served, so we invite you to please enjoy lunch, and not let all that go to waste. You can move through the side door into the reception hall." She pointed at the door. I leaned into her, grateful that she had taken over.

The guests moved slowly into the other room, and I stood there shaking, unsure of what to do next as my bridesmaids circled around me and my mother.

"Do you want to go into the reception hall, or do you want to..." my mother's voice trailed off, unsure of what other option to give me.

While the thought of joining my guests at the reception for my failed wedding seemed utterly unappealing, I wanted to find Callie. I moved toward the reception hall, trailed by my mother and father and the rest of the pack of bridesmaids, except for Amy.

My great-uncle Bob stood near the cake table. I gazed at the beautiful pound cake, smoothly iced with buttercream frosting and supporting a perfect little bride and groom on the top tier. I'd so looked forward to lovingly smashing a piece in Matt's face. Now I wanted nothing more than to drop the entire cake on his head. My great-uncle glanced between the cake and the commotion around him, a confused look on his face. He turned in my direction, adjusted his hearing aid, and yelled, "Lila dear, is it time for cake?"

Laugh, cry, or scream? Which should it be? In an overly dramatic gesture, I threw my arms up toward the heavens and hollered, "Let them eat cake!"

The catering staff, bewildered expressions on their faces, turned to the lead caterer for directions. Within moments, she'd organized several attendants, who hurriedly worked to slice and plate up the pieces.

I marched over to the DJ, who stared at me as if I was a zombie bride coming to eat him, and snatched the microphone. "Everyone, food will be ready in thirty minutes in the garden," I announced. "You may as well enjoy it or it will go in the garbage. In the meantime, help yourself to the cake and the bar is open!"

For a moment, no one moved. Amy looked around and yelled, "You heard her people. Get cake!" If this had not been my own botched wedding, I probably would have snickered at the sight.

Dang, she's good at ordering people around.

Scanning the room, I found my would-have-been-mother-in-law sitting at a table in a corner, her face in her hands. One of Matt's aunts was rubbing her shoulders. Mrs. McKenzie was a lovely, kind woman. She adored me, already considering me her daughter. I walked in her direction. At the sight of me, she bolted out of her chair, panic on her face, probably assuming I would respond to her as my dad had to her husband. That was not my intent at all. I reached out my arms for a hug, and she pulled me in, squeezing me against her.

"I'm so sorry, sweet Lila," she sniffled into my neck.

"This isn't your fault."

She held me tight for a minute longer before stepping back. "What are you going to do?" she asked.

"I don't know. I can't stay here, but I don't want to go back to my place."

"The hotel suite is already paid for. Maybe you can take some friends there. It's a nice room. You may as well use it." She patted my shoulder, a very slight smile on her lips.

"That's a generous offer," I said. It was both tempting and weird. Take my friends to the wedding suite Matt and I should have used to seal the deal? Where we should have spent our first night as husband and wife? I wrinkled my nose. The idea seemed a bit gross and painful. But then again, I knew I could not go back to my apartment alone and face the place we were going to live together with all the memories that lingered there. And I didn't want to go to my parents' house or any of my friends' places. Maybe it could be a fun place to crash for the night? How weird was it that I was even considering it?

With a parting hug and a promise to stay in touch, I excused myself, searching the room for Callie. I hadn't seen her since we'd come downstairs, and if I was going to the hotel room, I wanted her to come with me. Looking around, my eyes stopped at a group of my college friends who stood hovering in a corner, avoiding eye contact with me. Amy stood in the middle, gesturing wildly with her hands, and I wondered what she was telling them. Probably assigning tasks and duties or giving strict instructions on what they could say and how to behave. Something about seeing all of them huddled together inspired an (in hindsight absolutely terrible) idea. Marching over to the table where my bouquet had been placed, I grabbed it, and continued over to where my friends were huddled up. They looked over sheepishly at me.

"We've paid for a big party, and you all should enjoy it. Starting with someone taking this bouquet." I raised the bouquet high for them all to see and turned around, my back to them. "Ladies, heads up!" I yelled and launched my bouquet over my head in their direction. It hit my friend Sam square in the chest and fell to the floor, somewhat symbolically, as a visual representation of my marriage. Sam just stared down at it.

No one moved. Everyone just stared at the flowers on the ground as if they might be infected with a deadly virus. This was getting worse by the moment. I couldn't blame them. Who would want a bouquet from a wedding that had never happened?

My face heated. Why had I just done that? Clutching the skirt of my dress, I bolted for the door of the reception hall, careful not to trip. I finally found Callie, who was standing near the exit of the building with Julien and Philippe. Their eyes widened as I barreled past them and beelined it to the waiting limousine.

"Just married, my ass!" I yelled, yanking the streamers and decorations from the back of the limousine. "Aaaargh." I bent over, hands on my knees. A small crowd had followed me out of the reception hall, but no one moved or said a thing, as if they'd been frozen in place. My mother and father stood at the top of the stairs, mom blotting away her tears.

"No. No!" I muttered to myself. This was not how I was going to spend the evening of my would-be wedding.

Callie approached and gently put her arms around me. She pulled me in as I stood there, arms hanging limply at my side. No tears came. I was numb.

Glancing up, I made eye contact with Julien. "You!" I pointed at him and Philippe. "Get in!"

3

No one moved. The chauffeur looked confused as I grabbed Callie's hand, waited for him to open the door, and practically shoved her in the limo after he did so. Julien and Philippe stood firmly rooted, so I hollered at them again. "Get in!"

Reluctantly, they followed my command. I paused for a moment and turned to the driver. "Wait here just a minute."

I hiked up the skirt of my dress and huffed back into the hotel, past the guests, some of whom still stood in shock, and others who seemed socially engaged as if this were an everyday occurrence, and through the reception hall where a good number of guests still sat at the tables eating. Thankfully. I'd hate to see all of that food go to waste. I hustled past them to the garden. I had no desire to stop and speak with anyone while on this mission. Finally, I stopped in front of the bar. The bartender, a young guy probably my age with spiky brown hair, an eyebrow ring, and a tattoo of flames that licked up his neck and stopped just under his jawline, stared at me with a bored look.

Seriously? This had to be the most interesting event he'd worked in a while. Unless this was a regular occurrence?

"I want a case of the champagne!"

Without batting an eye, as if he'd been waiting for this, he turned and lifted one of the wooden crates. "It's really heavy!" he stated, setting it on the bar.

"Then follow me." I turned on my heels, reversed direction, and tried to stealthily slip back past the guests, bartender and champagne following closely behind me. However, being the one person in the room with a billowing white dress, all eyes followed me, waiting to see what would happen next.

We should have provided popcorn, I thought.

My mother intercepted me near the exit. "Lila, what are you doing? Where are you going?" Her eyes, filled with worry, glanced from me to the bartender and back.

I snickered. "Don't worry, Mom, he's not coming with me."

Relief flooded her face.

"I really need to get away from here. I'm going to the hotel suite with Callie, Julien, and Philippe."

Worry lines popped up on her forehead. I watched her struggle for a moment, opening and closing her mouth several times as she tried to get out words. I could almost hear her internal dialogue as she debated what advice to give me, but alas, her parenting playbook had no chapter for what to do when your daughter is left at the altar.

The bartender sighed, clearly annoyed with this little pause.

"I'll call you later. I promise. Tell Daddy I'm okay." I didn't remember the last time I had referred to my father as daddy, but that's what came out in the moment.

Her forehead creased further, but she nodded and hugged me quickly, kissing my cheek. I breathed in her perfume, remembering times she'd comforted me as a child. She'd always surrounded me with her love and comfort, and for a moment, I didn't want to leave the protection of her arms. I guess we all want our mommy when things go south. Releasing her, I turned, scooped up my skirt again, and descended the stairs. A silly thought crossed my mind, as I imagined myself being a real-life Cinderella running from the ball. *Should I flick off one of my shoes for full dramatic effect?* Glancing back at the bartender, I decided against it. He'd likely trip on the shoe, tumble down the stairs, break all those incredible bottles of imported French pink champagne, and sue us for every cent. The shoe stayed on.

We reached the limo, and I pointed to the back hatch, plucking a bottle of champagne from the crate, then grabbing a second one as he placed the box in the trunk. After all, there could be traffic. The bartender gave me one final side-eye glance before shaking his head, turning to go back up the stairs, and vanishing inside. The limo driver closed the trunk and opened the door of the passenger compartment for me.

Leaning inside, I handed the two bottles to Callie before climbing into the nearest seat. I pulled in my dress, arranged it around me, and looked up to see the other three staring at me with wide eyes.

Unable to suppress it, I burst into uncontrollable giggles. I started gasping for breath, as I tried to get out words around my fit of laughter. I looked across to Callie and Julien, and at Philippe on my left, who all looked back and forth at each other, unsure of how to respond. I finally got enough of a breath in to look at Philippe and say, "Welcome to America, my friend! I bet you don't do weddings like this in France?"

He shook his head solemnly, sending me into another fit of laughter, this time joined by the rest of the crew.

The driver lowered the dividing window and cleared his throat. "Where to?"

"Take us to the hotel!"

He glanced up in the rearview mirror in surprise, certainly not expecting us to follow the original plan since there was no groom. Seeing that I was not joking, he nodded, closing the privacy divider.

"I need a drink!" A bottle of champagne was already prepped in the ice bucket, which I pulled out and tried to wrangle the top off. My hands kept slipping. Philippe, avoiding eye contact, gently took the bottle from me. His brow furrowed as he worked the cork out, careful to pry the lid off gently without popping the cork into the ceiling of the car or someone's eye. I noticed that as he concentrated, he stuck his tongue out a little on the left side of his mouth.

"Lila, are you okay? Should we be leaving like this?" Callie shared a worried glance with Julien before looking back at me.

"Would you rather stay?" I asked. She shook her head back and forth, grabbed the glass of champagne Philippe had just finished pouring, and took a large gulp. Her free hand gripped Julien's hand tightly, as if she was waiting for a terrifying roller coaster ride to begin. Maybe she was.

"I'm okay," I insisted, although rather unconvincingly. "A couple glasses of champagne, and I will be fantastic!" She glanced back at Julien, and the two of them shared a silent exchange, neither of them looking convinced by my fake enthusiasm and the large, fake smile plastered on my face.

Callie nodded, and busied herself by grabbing the champagne flutes from the small bar in the back of the limo. Philippe poured more champagne and handed me the second glass, giving me a small smile as he made eye contact.

"Salut!" I raised my glass to the group. "Santé," the boys replied, lifting their glasses and taking a sip. Callie raised her glass, her brown eyes full of emotion as she looked at me and took another big gulp of champagne.

I promptly knocked back the whole glass, passing it to Philippe for a refill. "I mean, there was no way I was going to stick around there. So when Matt's mom offered me the suite at the hotel tonight, it seemed like a good idea?" I shrugged. I was completely winging this one. After all, I was supposed to be standing at the altar, forever linking my life to Matt. What exactly does one do when the groom doesn't appear?

No one answered my question as the limousine departed the parking lot. I stared out the rear window at a few guests who were milling about outside. Some people waved as we departed, and others just watched in silence. Humiliation coursed through me. Sadness certainly had her piece of the emotional pie. But mostly I was just in disbelief. Could this be a nightmare? Was I really in my bed, the night before my wedding, dreaming about the worst case scenario? I reached up and touched my face, then the fabric of my beautiful silky dress. If this was a nightmare, it was the most realistic dream I'd ever had.

As we entered the hotel, I looked around at the magnificence of the lobby. A large chandelier hung down over the center, creating a feeling of wealth and elegance. Underneath, three overstuffed sectional couches formed a large circle. Two bored-looking teenagers sprawled across the cushions, waiting for their parents to finish checking in. Soft piano music played over the speakers, and a few people milled about. As I entered, wedding gown heaved up, I ignored all the stares and hoofed my way over to the reception desk.

"Lila Thurston, checking in for the bridal suite," I announced, my head lifted proudly.

Eyes wide, the receptionist took a deep breath. "We weren't expecting you for several hours, Mrs. McKenzie."

"I am *not* Mrs. McKenzie," I huffed, my confidence leaking out of me like a deflating balloon, "as I stated. And our plans changed! Is the room ready or not?" My words, although not as loud as my initial declaration, were sharper than intended.

The clerk's eyes softened as realization dawned on her. Tucking back a loose strand of hair, she said gently, "Let me call and check." She picked up the phone, turned her back, and quietly made a call before turning back to me. "It will be about fifteen minutes."

I didn't mean to take things out on this young woman, who seemed nice enough. Softening my tone to match hers, I replied, "Thank you. In the meantime, do you have a clothing shop?"

She nodded, pointed us in the direction of the souvenir shop. "Come back in a few minutes, and I'll have your keys ready for you."

I grabbed Callie by the arm. "Come on. I need different clothes. And so do you."

"We could go up to our rooms and change clothes?" Callie suggested. The realization hit me that this was also the hotel many of our guests were staying in. And while Callie's suggestion made the most sense, I did not want to be shopping for replacement clothes in the hotel boutique shop if anyone else arrived here while they were upstairs changing.

"Nonsense! This will be fun. And you can take back some souvenir shirts, on me!" I insisted. Philippe was still holding the heavy box of champagne. "Why don't you two and the box of champagne wait over there?" I pointed the two guys in the direction of the couches. "Callie and I can handle this."

Fifteen minutes later, Callie and I emerged with a variety

of Washington, DC branded T-shirts, flip-flops, and shorts for the four of us.

"Did you find everything you needed?" Julien asked.

"We were only able to find bright, Hawaiian-style, floral swim trunks for you two, but that will work for tonight." Callie explained.

"Bonus points for already being in swim trunks if we decide to use the pool," I chirped enthusiastically.

"Pool?" Philippe asked nervously.

I shrugged my shoulders and giggled. "Who knows what's in store for us?" I had no intention of leaving the suite tonight.

As she'd promised, the lovely woman at the front desk had keys ready. I quickly signed the paperwork, and she passed them over the counter to me, wishing us a pleasant evening. The four of us and our giant box of champagne made our way into the elevator and up to the penthouse.

As we exited the elevator, I turned right and walked a few steps to the door. I scanned the card to open the interior door, and gasped as I looked into the room.

Julien whistled. "Wow. This is gorgeous."

I'd never seen such a large and beautifully decorated hotel room. Could this even truly be classified as a hotel room? It was at least double the size of my apartment. Throwing the bag of clothes on the couch, I hiked up my dress and ran into the bedroom.

"You have to see this!" I hollered back over my shoulder. The room was massive, with a king-sized bed in the center of the room. Rose petals were strewn across the floor and over the bedspread. A heart-shaped hot tub gurgled under the large window. Two champagne flutes were perched on a small table next to the hot tub and candles lined its edge. Next to the flutes sat a bucket of ice on a stand with chilled champagne.

"What a waste of a beautiful room," I mumbled.

"I guess the receptionist didn't fill the maids in on the new situation?" Julien observed, entering the bedroom, which was clearly prepared for a very romantic evening with a bride and groom.

"I need to get out of this dress," I announced. My hands trembled, and for a minute, I was certain I would lose it completely. "Can you help me?" I asked Callie.

She nodded and stayed as the boys exited the room. "Julien, can you order us some food?" I called out. "I'm feeling a little woozy. Get whatever you want. It's on the McKenzie's."

I turned my back to Callie, and she gently unzipped the dress. I let the dress slip down to pool around my ankles and stood there for a moment before Callie reached for my hand and helped me step out of it.

"Do you want to talk about it?" she asked gently.

"Not yet. Right now, I just want to be in comfortable clothes, drink some booze, and get some food in me." I guess I wasn't the type to lose my appetite in moments of grief and stress.

She gave me a quick hug and exited, the door clicking shut softly behind her.

I stared at the pile of silk on the floor for a moment before kicking it out of my way. So much for being a princess. This was no fairy-tale ending. I wanted to take out my rage on the dress. Could there be some shears somewhere in this room? Maybe shredding the fabric would help the searing pain in my heart. I wanted to cry. I wanted to scream. I wanted to throw myself on the ground, kick my feet and pound my fists into the floor in an epic temper tantrum. I should track him down and make him pay. And yet I also wanted him to show up and explain it was all a misunderstanding. Maybe he'd been in a fender bender or stuck in traffic. He'd have a good explanation and we could all move on happily. But I knew that was not the case.

The most pressing question kept repeating in my head. *Why?* Why had he done this to me—to us? If he'd changed his mind, why couldn't he have told me? My eyes filled with tears, and a few slid down my cheeks. Wiping my face with my hands, I moved into the bathroom and stood in front of the mirror, staring at my reflection. I wanted the answers to these questions, but I did not want to call him again. I couldn't talk to him right now. Maybe ever.

How would my life go from here? Did I even know who I was without Matty? All my plans had been intertwined with his. How had I not seen impending trouble? Certainly there had been warning signs I must have missed? I racked my brain for any stored memories of conversations we'd had, comments he'd made, or actions he'd taken that might have indicated this was coming. I found nothing.

I squeezed my hands into fists, brought them up to my face, squinched my eyes shut while clenching my jaw, and screamed silently. Not surprisingly, I didn't feel any better. But I didn't want to alarm the others with real screams. Leaning on the counter once more, I studied myself in the mirror again. I looked feral. Some of my hair had escaped the elegant up-do, and raccoon rings of dark mascara circled my eyes. Sighing, I disentangled the many pins from my hair, brushed it out, and pulled it into a low ponytail before walking back into the bedroom.

The bag from the gift shop sat on the bed where Callie had left it. I rifled through it, pulling out the clothes I'd bought for myself downstairs and ripping off the tags. A few minutes later, I emerged from the bedroom in an oversized T-shirt with icons of all the key sites in Washington, DC, a pair of Hawaiian shorts, and hot pink flamingo flip-flops. I found Callie stowing a couple of bottles of champagne in the fridge and the guys on the couch, watching an American football game.

"Well look at you!" Julien exclaimed. "That is quite the fashion statement."

Philippe turned quickly my way, then glanced down at the floor, his cheeks flushed.

"Don't knock it," I said. "You'll be wearing a similar get-up in a second." I tossed the bag to the boys so they could change their clothes and went back into the bedroom to grab the cold bottle of champagne from the ice bucket.

Ten minutes later, everyone was out of their wedding clothes and in their new festive fashion choices. I took one look at Julien and Philippe, who resembled disgruntled tourists, and burst into laughter. Julien gave a good fashion model twirl, and turned to Philippe, whose face flushed deeply again with all eyes on him. But after a shove from Julien, he also twirled, one hand in the air.

I couldn't stop the giggles. I ran into the kitchen and poured four glasses of champagne, distributing it to everyone.

"To ridiculousness!" I shouted, holding up my glass. Everyone took a drink.

"To *love!*" I said sarcastically. That stopped the laughter immediately. Hands frozen in midair, the three stood awkwardly, clearly unsure of what to do next. I downed my glass of champagne and poured another one. Callie giggled nervously and clinked her glass with mine before also downing her drink. Philippe turned and walked over to the window, suddenly very intent on finding sights visible from this room.

"Let's put on some tunes!" I suggested, grabbing the remote and navigating to the music channels. Hard rock seemed appropriate. Cranking the volume, I grabbed Callie's hand and forced her to dance with me. I'd never seen the fake smile she had plastered on her face, but I appreciated the fact that she was playing along. Julien stood motionless, and Philippe continued to stare out at the city. "No party poopers allowed!" I approached the window, grabbed Philippe's hand, and dragged him over to join us in our mini mosh pit. OK, mosh pit might be a stretch. No one was slamming their bodies around. In fact, I was the only one even moving at the moment.

A look of relief crossed Philippe's face when a knock sounded. He opened the suite door and greeted the room service attendant. Or attendants, rather. It took two carts and multiple people to deliver all the food.

"*Mon Dieu*, are we expecting more guests?" Philippe asked as he watched them unload tray after tray onto the dining room table. Yes, this suite even included a dining room.

"I wasn't sure what you'd be in the mood for," Julien said sheepishly to me as we watched the procession.

My tummy rumbled as good smells filled the air. There was steak, lobster tail, some kind of pasta dish, a cheeseburger and fries, chicken fingers, macaroni and cheese, a hot dog, and multiple desserts, including key lime pie, cherry pie, and some kind of chocolate heaven.

"Philippe, let me recommend the hot dog, the macaroni and cheese, oh, and this." I scooped a pile of barbecued pork onto his plate. "This is real American food." He took the plate and sniffed it, and I could tell he wasn't sure if he was going to enjoy it. We all watched as he took a tentative bite of the mac and cheese. "Mmm," he said, clearly surprised.

"While the French may be the masters of cuisine, we have some really good, heart-stopping, vein-clogging, deliciously bad foods," I said in between bites of a club sandwich on a croissant. "Although this croissant is garbage compared to a *real* croissant!"

We all tried everything, sharing both the plates and our

opinions of the food while continuing to consume champagne, laughing about silly things and avoiding any discussion even remotely related to relationships, love, weddings, and Matt. For the moment, we were in a safe little bubble, despite being in a honeymoon suite.

JULIEN AND PHILIPPE finally left to go back to their rooms. I snuggled up next to Callie on the couch and rested my head on her shoulder. She wrapped her arm around me and we sat in silence.

"I wish I could stick around longer and take care of you the way you took care of me after Vic dumped me," Callie said.

"Me too," I slurred. At least I wasn't overseas and away from my support system, like we had been when Callie and I met. I knew my mom and friends would make sure I survived, but Callie and I had a special bond. We might not have been friends as long as my friends here, but in many ways, it was a deeper relationship than most of my others.

Eyes closed, but not quite ready to sleep, I murmured, "I just don't understand, Cal. This was the most hurtful thing he could have done. Why didn't he call me, tell me, end it Thursday night at the rehearsal dinner? Why would he humiliate me like this?"

She squeezed me tightly in a protective hug. "I agree, it was certainly a cowardly action. But I assure you, everyone sees that. This is on him."

I knew that, but it didn't take away the pain.

"Is Celine right?" I asked, fighting back sleep.

"Celine?" Callie asked with a dismayed tone.

"Celine Dion. Duh." I hiccupped.

"Oh, that Celine!" Callie giggled. "Is she right about what?"

"Will my heart go on?" I asked, sitting up.

Callie giggled. "That, my friend, is up to you."

4

Mid-November 2001

THE PLANE TOUCHED down hard on the tarmac, jolting me out of my sleep. Groaning, I rubbed my eyes, trying to focus, but my head swam from all the wine I'd drunk during the flight as my inner voice chastised me for poor life choices. Admittedly, I *had* tried to drink my plane ticket's worth of red wine while we were in the air. Bad idea. My stomach churned and a hammering sensation vibrated through my head. Choking back the bile, I pleaded with my body not to vomit before we landed.

Despite all the self-inflicted misery, I smiled. I was back in Paris, France. Angling my head so I could see out of the window, I noted the bleary sky. Cold, rainy weather paired perfectly with hot chocolate or hot coffee and a *pain au chocolat* or croissant with butter and jam. Or both. My tummy rumbled at the thought of delicious pastries. I'd missed the breakfast service, and desperately needed food to soak up some of the wine sloshing in my belly. Hopefully food would help quell the burn of the acid in my stomach.

As the plane settled in at the gate, I frantically searched for a pen to fill out the entry paperwork. Of course, it always took longer than it should—the process of landing, getting to the gate, waiting for the jetway to be ready and the doors to open, and actually getting off the plane. I shifted nervously, waiting for the slow line of people—moving barely faster than a sloth's pace—to disembark at Charles de Gaulle. Once we made it out of the jetway, I broke free from the crowd, picking up my pace as I hiked to the passport control area.

I swear, they bring in the planes from America at the absolute farthest point from the rest of the airport, I thought. The long white halls were empty, no signs, no decorations, no people, and temporary high walls put in place to direct traffic and keep people from wandering off in the wrong direction. It was so unlike American airports, where you generally exited into a bustling hall with people, shops, and restaurants. The only sounds were those of tired travelers huffing alongside me, looking for directions to the passport control. I kept my eyes open for a bathroom, desperately wanting to brush my teeth and reapply deodorant, while also hoping my detour would not make the passport line too long to escape into the wild.

The universal sign for toilets popped up in front of me, and sighing in relief, I exited right. Alone in the bathroom, I set my backpack on the counter and dug through to find my toiletry kit. I looked rough. My hair was a mess, my makeup was smudged, and dark circles had formed under my eyes. The bright fluorescent lights in combination with my dark hair made my face appear ghostly pale. Reminded again of my empty stomach by a sharp hunger pain, I quickly brushed my hair and teeth, applied a new coat of deodorant, grabbed my bags, and hustled to the exit.

With my passport in hand, I inched forward in the line through passport control. *Please let me get one of the controllers who just stamps my passport and passes me through,* I prayed. I approached the booth and tried to smile, but the security officer was unmoved.

"Can you please remove your sunglasses, Madame?" he asked. Madame? Had I reached that age? He was cute and I hoped my flirting skills had not withered away. *Can he smell the red wine that surely oozes from my pores at this point?*

Reluctantly, I pushed the sunglasses up on my head, squinting as the light blasted painfully into my eyes. I tried again to smile. He frowned back and flipped through my passport. I swayed a bit and placed my hands on the counter to steady myself.

"Are you alright, Madame?" The *madame* again. No, I was not ready to be a *madame*.

"Yes Sir. I may have had just a little too much good wine on the plane."

He chuckled, a break in his severe demeanor. "And what brings you to France?"

"Do you want the long or the short version?" I asked.

He looked perplexed. I looked behind me at the long line and realized I needed to just get through this. No Chatty Charlies today.

"I'm here to visit friends." I reached my hand up to press on my temple, which was pulsing hard from the wine-induced headache.

"OK, how long are you staying?" He glanced up at me again, awaiting my reply.

"Until my heart heals," I sighed, dramatically.

Bushy eyebrows raised, he stopped midair with his stamp and very seriously said, "You realize you can only stay for ninety days? How long do you expect this healing to take?"

Don't be a smart aleck, Lila, just get yourself through customs! "I'm here for two weeks," I replied.

"Ok, very good. And where will you be?"

"My friends have an apartment in Paris."

He looked at me long and hard for a moment. I wonder if he was trying to decide whether I was a threat. He must have decided that I was okay, because he stamped my passport, passed it back, and said, "Good luck with the heart surgery."

What? Why did he think.... Oh... Lost in translation. If only I could have a surgery to heal my heart!

That would be a nice and easy solution to the pain, unlike the many hours I'd spent trying to move past my feelings in the month since my failed wedding. I'd spent that first Sunday and Monday with Callie, Julien, and Philippe, playing tour guide for them, although we didn't get to see much and I was not much of a guide. We mostly bumped around from bar to bar, getting drinks and watching American football. Which, surprisingly, they all seemed okay with.

"I'm here to experience American culture," Philippe had announced when I apologized for the millionth time that I didn't feel quite up to museums and true tourism. "What is more American than this?" Although coming from his mouth, the word *this* sounded like *theessss,* making me chuckle.

I had gone back to my job at WaterCorps the following week, because, well, what else would I do? I thought working would distract me. Helping people get access to clean water around the world, especially women who had to walk miles in some countries to access water every day, truly filled my soul. My boss, Tom, completely befuddled as to why I was there, urged me to take some time off and basically sent me home the first day. He even added two extra weeks of vacation time "off the books," which I convinced him to allow me to take in November, so I could plan a better trip.

"I don't care when you take the time off, but take it. And some of it needs to be now. You'll be of no use to us here until you've had some time to deal with this. We have important legislation on all these clean water initiatives coming up that we need to lobby on, and I need you at your best!" I tried to argue, but it was futile. "*Not* a suggestion!" he'd practically yelled at me before turning and marching off.

So I'd spent a week at my parents' house, grateful for the chance to decompress away from my apartment, which remained littered with memories of Matt. I'd canceled the honeymoon and gotten some money back and a flight credit. My parents helped me cover the rest, and I'd booked a two-week trip to Paris for November.

The following week, I'd returned to work, reassuring Tom I could handle it and that I'd take two weeks in November. The entire staff was stretched thin, so he gladly accepted my return.

Throwing myself into work, I'd made little time for anything else in the meantime.

Now, a month later, I couldn't be happier to have escaped. I finally collected my bags and walked through the official customs area, happiness spreading over me as the sliding doors opened, welcoming me into the hustle and bustle of the main terminal. Ah, Paris. The sight of military men, big guns slung over their soldiers and escorted by patrol dogs was something I never quite got used to, even though I knew I was doing nothing wrong. I certainly did appreciate young men in uniform though. I scanned the crowd, picking out Callie from the crowd. Much to my surprise, she was flanked by Julien and Philippe. I ran to meet them, greeting them as if it had been years, not just a few weeks, since I'd seen them last.

"Well this is a surprise! You gave up your Saturday morning just to come meet little ole me?" I shoved my sunglasses briefly up on my head, batted my eyes to make them laugh and then quickly pushed the sunglasses back down on my nose.

Callie dropped Julien's hand and threw her arms around

me in a big hug. She ran her hands down my hair and patted my back, squeezing me hard. When she released me, I leaned in for the French greeting—kisses on both cheeks, first from Julien, then from Philippe. He smelled good and the slight stubble of his unshaven face rubbed delightfully against my cheek. I might have lingered slightly longer than normal in his embrace.

Stepping back, Philippe grabbed the larger of my two bags. Our hands touched briefly as he reached for the handle, and he smiled up at me warmly. His hazel eyes reminded me of springtime branches, and an unexpected sensation tingled through my hand and up my arm. Julien removed my other bag from my shoulder, pulling me out of the moment. What moment was I having, exactly? This was Philippe after all. My friend.

"We're so glad you came to be with us, Lila," Philippe said sincerely.

"Thank you, Philippe. It's good to see you too." I studied him for a moment. His brown hair fell softly over his forehead. I liked the way he shoved his glasses higher on the bridge of his nose. He had kind of a Clark Kent vibe, and I imagined what it would be like to pull the glasses off his face and run my fingers through his hair.

Lila Rose! Come back to Earth!

The four of us started walking toward the train station in the airport.

"Do you always wear sunglasses at 8 a.m.—inside the building?" Callie joked.

"Let's just say I imbibed on the plane ride."

"I don't blame you a bit, honey," she said. "Hair of the dog?"

"Blech, I can't even think about alcohol right now!"

"How about some fresh *pain au chocolate* or croissants and coffee?" Julien asked, trailing slightly behind us with Philippe.

I looked over my shoulder and gave him a big grin. "Now you are speaking my language!"

Julien pulled out a small brown bag I hadn't seen earlier. I recognized it immediately as a bakery bag, and my mouth watered. "Well, we've got the food, but we didn't want the coffee to get cold," he said. He looked around and pointed to a small stand up ahead and to the right. "We can grab coffee there."

Julien and Philippe set the bags down with Callie and I and went to get in line for four espressos to go.

Once they were out of earshot, I turned to Lila. "How on earth did you get both Julien *and* Philippe to come with you? You must have left your apartment at..."

"Seven in the morning!" Callie finished. "Well, Julien was already up since he went running early, and I'm not exactly quiet, and since we woke Philippe up, he decided to just come with us."

"Wait, is Philippe staying at your place too?" Panic set in, and my heart rate increased at the idea of Philippe and I being forced into sharing the living room, especially in light of my new reaction to his presence. "Is there enough room for me?" I stammered.

"Yes! He'll only be there tonight and tomorrow night. He gets the keys to his new place Monday." Callie placed her hand on my arm reassuringly. "Don't worry, we have it all figured out!"

An uncomfortable sensation buzzed through my belly as I thought about having to share a small space with anyone else, especially a guy. Even if the guy was Philippe, who had, admittedly, seen me at my worst. But even though I hadn't been to Callie and Julien's apartment yet, I'd been in enough Parisian apartments to imagine the space, and there wouldn't be a lot of it.

I chewed on my bottom lip as the men came back, each of them with two cups in hand. Philippe handed me a tiny shot of espresso, and we made our way to the train platform. Even though Callie insisted the situation was *not* an issue, knowing Philippe was also staying at her apartment was anxiety inducing for me. Reminding myself that Callie wouldn't put me in a bad spot and I trusted her enough to be sensitive to my needs wasn't enough to stop the whirring sensation in my head. Of course, that could also be from all the red wine. Without even trying to be covert about it, I stared at Philippe, taking note of his mannerisms as he walked and laughed at whatever Julien was saying, volleying back his own quips. As if seeing him for the first time, I noticed that he was kind of cute. Yes, I was definitely still drunk.

The train rumbled in, and we boarded. It was a regional train, with both an upstairs and downstairs, so I led the crew topside. We found four seats that faced each other with a table in between, and I sat next to the window facing Callie. Philippe slid in next to me, his thigh pressed against mine, creating a warmth throughout my body that once again took me by surprise. I stared out the window, willing myself to calm down and stop being so weird.

Julien pulled out the bag of goodies again and I eagerly snatched up a *croissant aux amandes,* leaving the *pain au chocolat* for Callie. I had only been introduced to the almond croissant shortly before leaving Paris, and I found the almond paste on the inside of the croissant to be one of the most delightful things I'd ever experienced.

Turning ever so slightly, I stole a glance at Philippe. A little dusting of powdered sugar sat on his upper lip from the *croissant aux amandes* he was eating, and I desperately wanted to wipe it off.

Thankfully, Callie interrupted my thoughts before they got

any weirder than simply wiping off the powdered sugar. "Okay, what shall we do today?"

"I hope a nap is included somewhere on the agenda?" I moaned dramatically.

"The best way to get on Paris time is to push through," Callie said. Then, seeing what was probably a cross between a devastated and disgusted look on my face, she added, "We'll keep it light and have an early night."

Relief flooded through me.

Philippe said, "I'm going to be packing up the rest of my stuff today."

I turned fully toward him. "So you're moving to Paris then?"

He shrugged. "Yep. They basically forced me." He raised his chin in the direction of Callie and Julien and chuckled. Julien gave him a universal signal, wiping the top of his lip with his finger, and Philippe quickly grabbed a napkin, wiping off the sugar.

I glanced over at Callie and raised my eyebrows.

"There was not a whole lot of forcing happening," Callie said. "When he saw how much fun Julien and I were having here, he decided to leave Strasbourg and come this way too! I just didn't plan on him living with us for two weeks!"

"What can I say? It's hard to find a reasonably priced place on your own when you don't have a job yet!" he said.

I nodded in agreement, having been in a similar situation two years prior, although thankfully my parents had paid for a nice hotel room until I found my flat.

"Well, you'll have all that sorted soon. He'll be working for FIDH, the International Federation for Human Rights, starting a week from now," Callie said, proudly.

I turned to Philippe, a bit of excitement surging through me. I'd found a kindred spirit!

I suddenly remembered talking with him at length about human rights when we'd met on New Year's Eve in 1999, when Callie, our friend Emilie, Matt, and I had thrown a party and Emilie had invited Julien, who had brought Philippe and another friend of his, Fred. But at the time, I'd thought I was in love with the perfect man and hadn't really paid much attention to any of the guys. And then, while we'd spent time together when they'd been in DC for my failed wedding, we hadn't really talked about anything important. Mentally shoving away the unpleasant resurgence of memories of Matt, I turned my gaze back to Philippe.

"Yes, I am really thrilled about this opportunity," Philippe said, staring down at the table. He seemed embarrassed. Shy. It was an attractive quality.

"Lila works for a nonprofit in Washington, DC that serves women globally and more importantly, brings potable water to communities that don't have it. Before that, she spent some time volunteering in Africa building a school!" Callie said, sounding equally as proud of me for my accomplishments as she did of Philippe. She loved telling people about me.

"I remember you saying that when we met on New Year's," Philippe said. He perked up and this time actually made eye contact with me. It was my turn to blush. His eyes lit up as he continued. "I'm going to be working for a relatively new department to protect people in countries who are vulnerable to torture."

"Wow. That's intense. And you look so excited about it!" I studied him, realizing that there was far more depth to this guy than I'd realized. I appreciated this piece of him that seemed genuinely interested in doing good for others.

Philippe laughed. "I'm excited about the opportunity to help others, not the actual torture." I smiled. Torture, with a French accent, sounded so much less painful.

"Is it too much for me to ask if you've heard from Matt?" Philippe asked.

I heard a thump under the table and Philippe yelped.

"That's an inappropriate question!" Callie chided, looking over at me to gauge my reaction.

"It's okay," I replied. I could only make eye contact with Callie, but I answered Philippe's question. "I haven't heard from him. But I blocked his phone number and I've been at my parent's house, so if he tried to stop by my apartment..." I shrugged. Callie looked sad, Julien busied himself with something invisible on his shirt, and Philippe's expression indicated he regretted asking. "His mother called me once to inform me he would stop by and get some of his things, and how sorry she was, but she didn't offer any answers, and I didn't ask."

No one said anything after that. My head and heart heavy, I leaned against the window and closed my eyes.

AFTER LUGGING my luggage up four flights of stairs (okay, I exaggerate, I watched Julien and Philippe lug my luggage up the stairs, but in my defense, my backpack was pretty heavy), we reached the apartment. I oohed and ahhhed as we entered. "Wow, this is a big step up from the closet you lived in before, Callie!" I teased.

She laughed. "No kidding! I'm so glad not to have my shower right next to my kitchenette. We actually have three separate rooms! We're like real adults now!"

While the boys went into the kitchen to make drinks for everyone, Callie gave me a quick tour. And it was quick because, while this place was massive compared to the places we'd lived before, by American standards it was still pretty tiny. The apartment consisted of the main living room area that you walked into, which was filled to the brim with a large pullout couch and two chairs, a television and stereo, and a massive bookshelf. This would surprise no one, as Callie loved her books. A double window provided plenty of light.

"Well, hello you!" I leaned down to run my hand across the back of the shiny black cat sprawled across the papasan chair. She arched her spine to meet my fingers, purring loudly.

"This is Queen Socks," Callie said, bending down to scratch the cat's head. Well, that was appropriate considering she was a black cat with four white paws. "Queen because Julien and I started falling in love at the Queen."

"She's super sweet," I said. The cat licked my hand in approval. "You and Julien are quite the old married couple, aren't you? A real apartment, and a *cat*?" A sudden sadness enveloped me as I observed the life Callie had built in Paris without me. I'd been so self-absorbed the last few months, first with planning the wedding, then with getting over it, that I wasn't even sure I realized she'd gotten a cat.

Callie grabbed my arm and steered me toward the kitchen, off to the side of the living room. It was galley style and fairly small. Somehow all the major appliances fit, but they were mini versions of what we had in the States. Philippe and Julien took up most of the space, so I just popped my head in to briefly take note of it. Apparently, the cupboards offered enough room to store all the cooking gear and food, because her counters were empty and clean. We crossed back across the living room into the bedroom, stopping to pet Queen Sox's head on the way.

"Ooh, this is lovely." The queen-sized bed was covered with a fluffy black-and-white duvet and the pillowcases were blood red. I loved the contrast of the red on black and white. Bedside tables sat on each side, each with a lamp. I could tell which side was Callie's because a dangerously high stack of books precariously balanced on her nightstand. The room contained another bookshelf, also packed to the gills, and a wardrobe closet that spanned one entire wall. I nodded in appreciation. Most apartments in Paris didn't have actual closets. Instead, they had large vanity wardrobes or built-ins that include hanging space, cupboards, and drawers. I explored her bookshelves and examined all the neatly organized nooks and crannies. You pretty much had to be a minimalist to survive in a Parisian apartment. Callie might have kept her kitchen minimal, but she certainly kept a ton of books. Across from the wall with the sprawling wardrobe, a big window overlooked the courtyard.

"This place is perfect, Callie. I love it." And yet, as I spoke the words, a small knot formed in my stomach. As we returned to the living room, I wondered where I would sleep. Certainly they wouldn't put both Philippe and me on the couch?

"You can leave your bags in here if you'd like," Callie instructed, pointing to a small space in her bedroom. "And here's the bathroom, if you'd like to take a shower or freshen up?"

I nodded vigorously. "Yes, I'd love to get the airplane germs off me!"

"Great. I'll help the guys prepare lunch. You've got plenty of time."

I pulled the necessities from my bags and made my way to the bathroom.

Their bathroom was not tiny, but there wasn't a lot of space either. The full-sized bathtub had a hook for the shower head so I could stand up and just let the hot water pour down on me. Sighing, I scrubbed off the airplane funk, letting my muscles relax in the hot water, and feeling a million miles away from my home and problems.

Should I have come to Paris? I had spent the last month running away from my feelings, stuffing everything down, and avoiding my emotions by keeping so busy at work that I'd had no time to feel any of it. I was now staying with the happiest couple on the planet, and my heart would now have the space to feel again—and I'd definitely see affection between other people, especially given who I was staying with. How would I hide from love in the City of Love?

Leaning into the stream of hot water, I closed my eyes and breathed in deeply. *You're with people who care about you. Embrace it. And you're a long way away from home.* I had two weeks to face my demons, sort out my emotions, and reemerge back into my life. And if having some fun fantasies about Philippe, who was an impossible suitor, helped—then so be it. I, unlike Callie, would never move to France. But the fantasies could be fun. Maybe.

5

We enjoyed an incredible midafternoon meal of roasted chicken, potatoes, salad, bread and cheese, of course, and sealed the deal with a delightful kiss of *tarte tatin*, something similar to apple pie. But better, naturally.

Julien and Philippe decided to go out for the evening, so Callie and I had the place to ourselves. Even though fatigue from jetlag nearly zombified me, we both agreed a walk and fresh air would be best. And going to bed at 6 p.m. would just mean I'd be awake at 3 a.m., which would be unpleasant.

"Where should we go?" Callie asked.

"I'm shocked you'd even give me the option!"

"You're right," she said, grinning. "Let's go."

It was warm for a November evening in Paris, which only enhanced the jaunt to one of our favorite places—to see Callie's best girl, the Eiffel Tower.

The tower, lit up in all her glory, reminded me so much of the reverse situation Callie and I had faced two years prior, when she was healing from a broken heart. How ironic that we'd be back here now, together, but dealing with my broken heart. After standing in complete silence for several minutes, both of us lost in our own thoughts, I finally asked the question I'd been pondering.

"How did you survive the heartbreak, Callie? There are days it feels massive, so I've smashed it away and run from it. But it's still in there," I whispered.

"I survived because of you. And Emilie. And maybe a little bit of good ole Southern stubbornness." Callie winked.

I turned to face Callie, and half-smiled. "You are pretty stubborn."

Callie put her hand on my arm. "You'll survive this because you're strong, smart, young, and ambitious. And while this may feel like the worst pain you've encountered yet, eventually all those stupid clichés like, 'Whatever doesn't kill me makes me stronger,' and, 'All things happen for a reason,' and, 'I would have never found you if I hadn't gone through this,' etc., will suddenly start sounding less stupid. Even if you can't believe it now." She wrapped her arm around my shoulder and pulled me in for a squeeze. "And not to be really ridiculous about it, but I would have never found Julien if it hadn't been for Vic breaking up with me. Or *you*, for that matter."

I sniffled. Callie reached into her coat pocket and handed me a tissue from a packet she was carrying. I hadn't allowed myself to shed many tears up to this point. Now I was afraid I might never stop the flow if I opened the lock. "It's not even the fact that he ended our relationship that bothers me the most, Cal." I stared out at the tower, thinking about the wedding day. "It's how he humiliated me. Not showing up, never even calling to say he's sorry."

"Ouch," Callie whispered. "I'm so disappointed in Matt."

"Just goes to show you never truly know someone, do you?"

"Maybe he's just really embarrassed about his actions or is afraid of reaching out to you?"

I shot her a withering look, not ready for anything more than complete support and sympathy from one of my best friends. Screw Matt.

Recognizing the error of her ways, Callie quickly added, "You're right, he's an absolute jackass! Is it driving you crazy that you haven't heard from him?"

I turned back to face the Eiffel Tower. "I mean, I blocked his number. But he could have tried to call my parent's house." I sighed. "The truth is, I've reanalyzed everything from the very beginning: all our interactions, especially from the last few months, everything he said and did. Monday-morning quarterbacking, I don't think he ever wanted to get married. He'd never directly said, 'I don't want to marry you,' but he'd said other things that should have clued me in to his position." I paused for a moment, watching tourists take their pictures with the tower behind them. A young child with a Nutella crêpe ran by with chocolate all over his face. I continued. "He never even got down on one knee."

Callie shook her head back and forth but didn't say anything.

"I forced the issue. And the closer the wedding got, the more distant he seemed. Clearly we were not meant for each other if I didn't know him well enough to recognize these things and if he didn't feel comfortable just telling me the truth. We just weren't forever material."

"Like me and Vic," Callie said softly.

"Yeah," I agreed. "It's really hard to believe it's only been two years since the last time we stood here together, you rehashing the nightmare of your relationship with Vic, me, so chipper in my own solid relationship, encouraging you to think about the future and open your heart to the potential of a fling or love, or whatever might come your way. I had no idea what you were going through."

Callie turned toward me, wrapping an arm around my shoulder and squeezing me close. "But you listened. You were my rock. You cared for me, loved me, and provided me with an outlet whenever I needed a shoulder or an ear. And I'm here for you too, Lila. You didn't deserve to be treated that way, and it breaks my heart that this happened to you."

I nodded my head in agreement, sniffling.

"These next few weeks and months may feel like hell on earth. But it will get easier. You have to give yourself the time to go through it."

"Blech," I replied. "Sitting in my own emotions sounds like Dante's Inferno."

Callie laughed. "It may feel like that some days. But you can't go around it. You have to go through it."

I giggled.

"What?" Callie asked.

"That reminds me of that nursery rhyme—bear hunt. Do you remember that one?"

She turned to me. "We're going on a bear hunt..." and so on and so forth, "...you have to go THROUGH it."

I shook my head, laughing at my dear, sweet, silly friend. I'd absolutely made the right choice coming here. Because if anyone could help me go *through* it, it was Callie.

***

THE FRESH EVENING air and a visit to the Eiffel Tower reinvigorated me. Back at Callie's, we sat on the couch, sipped some wine, and worked on devouring a fresh baguette and a wheel of brie, as we had done so many times when we'd both lived in Paris. There was no French bread in the US that came close to the real deal, and I intended to get my fair share on this trip. Queen sat perched in the open window, raising her nose to catch a whiff of the smell of our neighbor's dinner.

"Whatcha thinking about?" Callie asked. "I'm so sorry that Philippe asked you about Matt."

I had been staring out the window, lost in my thoughts. I shook my head back and forth, waving it off. "I'm sure everyone was dying to ask it." I smiled. "Did *you* ever go back and reflect on all the evidence to see if you saw the signs?"

"What do you mean?"

"With Vic, I mean. Do you ever look back and think about some things that in hindsight you can clearly say—oh yes, I should have seen this coming?" I crossed my legs and shoved another big chunk of the glorious cheese in my mouth.

"Yes, afterward I replayed every conversation, every moment, every possible time that I might have missed anything. And," she leaned forward and pulled off another morsel of bread from the baguette, "in hindsight, it actually seemed so clear."

"Like what?" I demanded, turning on the couch to face her.

"Well," Callie began, "for example, I rarely received communication from him when I was back home. And Vic went out a lot. On his own. He said he was just playing video games with his friends or doing guy stuff, but I have my doubts whether that was all he was doing. And the biggest issue was I never felt fully seen by Vic, if that makes sense?"

I tilted my head to the side. "How so?"

"He never had any interest in discussing the things I found the most important. As long as our relationship was centered on going out and having a good time, we were perfect. But the moment I wanted to discuss deep topics, he shut down. Then there was the whole discussion of when and how I would come back."

"I don't think you ever told me about that." I leaned in.

"I was too embarrassed to say anything. Because looking back on it, it's so obvious." Callie stood up and went to the kitchen, grabbed the wine bottle, and came back to top off both our glasses. "When I left here after my year abroad, he asked me to stay. But I wanted to finish my last year of school at home. He was disappointed, and we nearly broke up at that point."

"Really?" I leaned back and pulled my knees up to my chin, contemplating whether to grab more cheese. The bread won, and I grabbed two pieces and leaned back on the couch. I decided my truest love might be French baked goods. Forget the men!

"Yes." Callie chewed on her lower lip before continuing. "I had to convince him that it could work. That should have been the biggest red flag, right?"

I nodded in agreement.

"He hated the idea of long distance. I put in all the effort over the next year. I was the one who planned our visits to see each other. I wrote letters; I did all the things. But I didn't let that bother me because he said the right things when I needed him to, so I just ignored it and pressed forward, believing everything would be perfect when I returned to France. I feel so silly for having just ignored all those things, ya know?"

I nodded my head slowly in agreement. I did know. I'd been the one to make all the plans and special efforts in my relationship with Matt as well. I'd believed it was because he was easy going and just went along with everything.

"I pushed the relationship forward, and I think if I'd stopped making that effort, it would have ended sooner," Callie said, shrugging.

"Hm." Those words resonated deeply. "I'm not sure either of us could have realized that at the time, or done anything differently," I said softly.

Callie nodded. "I think you're right. We've grown because of these situations, and to be honest, people tried to warn me, and I wouldn't hear any of it."

I dropped my knees and turned in her direction. "Do tell."

"One of his friends hinted at me that he might be seeing other girls. He didn't come out and say it, but he said something about Vic having a lot of female friends. I shoved it aside, because I was so convinced he was in love with me."

"Ouch," I said, giving Callie a sympathetic pat on her leg. I had been hurt badly by Matt's abandonment. But at least he hadn't been cheating on me. At least, not with another girl. Maybe with the video games that consumed his life.

"Vic loved me, at least at some point. I believe that. But I think he got so deep into his own concerns about how complicated our lives would always be that he made a unilateral decision that it couldn't work." Callie turned to look at me, her eyes darkened by thinking about that painful time in her life.

I nodded my head, reflecting on how unfair it was for both of us that the men we loved had not been bold enough or were too selfish to end things, and instead hurt us terribly in the process.

"I would say I wish he'd just ended it before I returned to France, but, as we've already established, if he'd done that, I would never have met you and I would never have met Julien." Callie's eyes teared up. As if on cue, Queen hopped up in Callie's lap and settled in.

We both giggled. "Seriously though, the thought of not having what I have now," she motioned with her hand at the things in the apartment, "is far worse than any pain he put me through."

I pulled my knees up to my chin again and wrapped my arms around my legs, trying to fight the tears. But instead of slowing down, they came harder, faster. Soon I was sobbing. It was hard to imagine a day in which I wouldn't feel this much pain.

Callie placed her arm around me, holding me tight, and allowed me to just cry. "Lila, it will get better. It will get easier. It won't always hurt like this."

I leaned into her.

"But don't try to get there tonight. Feel the wave of emotions. Give yourself time to process it."

When I was adequately soothed, I stood up and walked over to the bathroom to grab some tissues. On the way back, a photo on the bookshelf caught my eye. It was the four of us— me, Matt, Callie, and Julien—from that New Year's Eve party in 1999. I picked it up, and then returned it to the shelf.

"Oh Lila, I'm sorry, I haven't removed any of the photos of Matt!"

"It's okay," I said.

"It's not!" Callie stood up, dumping an irritated-looking Queen on the floor, and grabbed the frame. "Remember that episode of *Friends*? The one that they do a cleansing ceremony after, uh, I think one of Monica's breakups? And they burn her ex's stuff?"

My eyes sparkled with anticipation, and I shoved myself up off the couch. "Yes! Do you want to burn that picture?"

Callie smiled wickedly and handed me the picture before heading into the kitchen. She brought back a metal bowl and a lighter. "It's time to say goodbye to Matt!" She placed the picture in the bowl and was about to light it when she said, "Oh wait. I have an idea." She rifled through her CDs and put one in. She skipped to the right song and hit play.

I burst out laughing as "Earl Has to Die" by the Dixie Chicks pumped into the apartment.

Callie and I sang loudly as we lit the picture on fire.

"My neighbors are going to kill me!" Callie screamed over the music.

"As long as we don't set off a smoke alarm, who cares?"

"Then again, there's some pretty hot guys at the nearby fire station. Maybe they'd respond, like in the episode, and one of them could swoop you away!"

We laughed almost maniacally as we watched the fire destroy the reminder of Matt.

———

THANKFULLY, there were no fire alarms, but that also meant no hot firemen coming to our rescue. For the sake of the neighbors, we turned down the music as soon as the song was over and sat back on the couch.

"Movie?" Callie asked.

"Yes, something funny please. Preferably not a rom-com." I had many thoughts right now, but I was all talked out.

"Let's see what Julien has. I'm sure there's something that will do the trick."

I watched her shuffle through his extensive DVD stack. She turned around, laughing. "I wouldn't have expected to find this in his collection." She held up *Clueless*, and we both laughed.

"Nope. Rom-com."

She rummaged a bit more. "Ooh, how about *The Ninth Gate?*"

"I haven't seen that one yet!"

"Ok, I'll set this up. Go get snacks!" Callie ordered. I saluted her and headed to the kitchen. I found a pretzel nut mix, some peanut puffs, and I grabbed another bottle of wine. Returning to the living room, I saw Callie pulling out some blankets. We cozied in on the couch.

I wasn't even a little bit surprised when Julien and Philippe entered just as the opening credits were rolling.

Callie stood up and pulled Julien in for a tender welcome home kiss, and in an effort to escape the moment, I went to the kitchen and grabbed some beers for the guys.

"Movie night?" I asked, handing them over.

"What are we watching?" Philippe asked.

"*The Ninth Gate* with Johnny Depp."

"I haven't seen that yet! It looks good. Do you generally like horror movies? Or what do you prefer?"

It had been a long time since a guy had asked me about my preferences, and I had to think about it for a minute. Matt hated horror movies, and I hadn't watched a horror or thriller in years.

"Yes, actually, I love horror movies." What else did I like that I'd forgotten about in the last few years?

"Me too! And something really cool about this movie. It was filmed here in France in nearby towns." Philippe said.

"Nice! Point out the local places, if you recognize them," I said.

Philippe nodded, reaching into the bowl for another handful of nut mix. I turned to watch the TV and was soon lost in the enthralling plot of the movie, which sure beat crying.

6

I'd fallen asleep a couple of times during the movie, and when I woke, I saw Callie laying out a pallet of sorts on the floor for Philippe.

"I feel terrible that he has to sleep on the floor," I said. But I wasn't going to lie, relief washed over me as I saw the solution I'd fretted over. There would be no awkward bed sharing.

"Don't. He's been here for two weeks. He can handle it for a couple nights. Besides, this pallet is nice and comfy." Callie winked at Philippe, went into the bedroom, and came back with a pillow, sheets, and blankets, handing them to me. "Will you be okay if we don't pull the bed out? The couch itself is super comfy!"

"I'm so tired I think I could sleep on the floor *without* a pallet. This will be fine."

"OK. Go get ready for bed, and everything will be ready for you when you get out."

I looked at Callie for a minute before following her orders. She definitely had a knack for caring for others. I kissed her on the cheek and went to the bathroom to brush my teeth. As she'd promised, when I emerged, the couch was made up for me. Dragging my weary legs the short distance across the living room, I hugged Callie, tumbled onto the couch, gave a limp wave to the guys, pulled my eye mask down, and immediately fell into a deep sleep.

THE SMELL of fresh coffee pulled me out of my blissful dream state. I shoved my mask away from my eyes and instantly regretted the decision not to remove my makeup last night as I wiped at the crusty leftover mascara. The pallet and all signs that anyone else may have slept in the living room with me had disappeared. Disappointed that Philippe was gone, I pulled myself off the couch, stretched, and wandered into the kitchen where I found Julien preparing fresh cups of coffee.

"Lila!" he exclaimed. "I'm sorry to wake you," he said, pulling me into a big hug. That was unusual for the French, I thought. Either Callie's ways had rubbed off on him, or he was overcompensating for my broken heart.

"What time is it?" I asked.

"It's just a bit after ten," Julien said.

Ten a.m.? "Wow I can't believe I slept in that late."

"I knew you needed your sleep. I was trying to be quiet."

"No worries. Where is Callie?" I asked.

"She's in the shower. She'll be out soon."

"And Philippe?"

"He had some things he needed to get done this morning."

I nodded and gratefully accepted a cup of coffee from Julien. While he prepared breakfast, I wandered back into the living room, inhaling the smells of onion and ham sizzling away.

Wandering over to the bookshelf, I saw that Callie still had the book I'd given her, *Mutant Message Down Under* by Marlo Morgan, back when she was navigating her own heartbreak. I pulled it from the shelf and began flipping through it, smiling at all the highlighted passages and the dog-eared pages. While I personally hated it when someone broke the integrity of a book by turning down the corners, my heart warmed at the obvious fact that she loved this book. The book detailed a woman's journey on what was called a walkabout with an indigenous tribe in Australia, and how her life had dramatically changed as she immersed herself in their lifestyle. Callie said it had changed her outlook on life as well. How fitting that it would be the book that jumped out at me today.

Maybe I needed to go on a walkabout. A soul-cleansing journey to get rid of these yucky feelings. To find myself again. However, that would entail endless days in the desert with no hot shower and little food or water, so Paris would have to serve. What a sacrifice! A piece of paper bookmarked one page, so I opened it.

A highlighted passage read: "I was beginning to see that more than blood passes through the human heart. I closed my eyes and said, 'Thank You' to the Power above." Sighing, I pulled the book to my chest as I let the words sink in.

Callie and I had discussed this book in depth, over a lot of red wine, in my studio apartment one rainy afternoon. In context, I knew this passage was referring to the great connections between people, regardless of their differences. Maybe even a little about understanding that life is bigger than just one person. I wasn't sure I was ready to be grateful for the things that had happened, nor could I willingly accept Callie's belief that everything happens for a reason. But I grabbed the new journal Callie had so thoughtfully given me the night before. She'd said, "Write down your thoughts now. Because one day, you'll want to see how far you've come."

I curled up on the couch, opened the journal, and allowed the words to pour onto the page. I realized I was not only mad at Matt, but at myself. I was especially perturbed for allowing myself to ignore my intuition, my gut feelings, and every instance where I'd wondered if Matt was truly the person I wanted to spend my life with, or just the person I'd become comfortable with.

WHEN I'D GOTTEN those feelings on paper, I didn't feel much better. My mom's words rang through my head. *We can't change or control what anyone else does. We can only control how we respond to the situation.*

So rather than end my journaling on a negative note, I envisioned what I wanted in the future.

I KNOW that I want to do something to really make a difference in the lives of people, and I am glad I can through my work. I want to get past this place of sadness and dream of the things I can do to help others, to find joy through helping to make the world better for other people, like the trips I've taken to Africa to build schools, and other community projects. This is important.

But I also want what Callie and Julien have. A partnership. A friendship. A solid love.

I need time to heal and am not ready to find the next guy but seeing them together gives me hope.

I give myself permission to put ME first for a while, and not think about others until I can heal this gaping hole in my heart... this sadness in my soul. And to recognize that I am worthy of someone who loves and cherishes me and puts me first. I believe it will happen one day.

I will not waste this time in Paris. I will use it to reconnect with me. To figure out what I like again.
Love will be there later.

THE ACT of writing these words on paper soothed me. I closed the journal and tucked it away in my bag.

I HAD JUST FINISHED CLOSING the bag's flap when Callie emerged from the bathroom.

"Good morning!" She crossed the room and gave me a big hug. "So, what do you want to do today?"

"I think I'd like to get out. See some sights. The Louvre is always a good option." It was also a safe choice because I had no memories of Matt there. Art was not his thing.

"I haven't been there since the last time you and I went, so I think that's a great idea," Callie said.

Julien popped his head around the corner and asked, "Would it be okay if I invited Philippe?"

"Sure, that would be great," I said, thankful to not feel like a third wheel. As much as I loved seeing Callie and Julien together, a tiny knife drove into my heart each time they did something cute and mushy.

As we arrived at the Louvre, I spotted Philippe waiting at the entrance. I took a moment to take in the scenery. Paris is so breathtakingly beautiful. This place in particular provided immense visual pleasure. My eyes scanned the glass pyramid in the center of the courtyard, a very modern symbol, surrounded on three sides by the massive and ancient museum. Small fountains and other miniature glass pyramids, which offered light to the bowels of the hallways below, surrounded the large pyramid. The fourth side of the courtyard opened toward the Jardin de Tuileries and faced down the Champs-Élysées.

To enter, we had to go to the pyramid and descend to the bottom level via an escalator and buy our tickets at one of the desks. The line was long but moved quickly. Since we only had a few hours, we'd made use of the time in line to create a plan to see the items we most wanted to see. We chose a path that would take us to the hall with the Mona Lisa. As we climbed the white marble staircase, we stopped in front of the Winged Victory.

I eyed the white marble statue standing on the rocks in front of us.

"Why exactly is this so famous? She has no head and no arms. What makes her so special?" I asked.

Philippe stepped up next to me. "It's more because of her history than anything. Although, it is a beautiful piece of work." As he spoke, he studied the sculpture with admiration. His voice was soft, as though with reverence for the sculpture. "The Winged Victory was discovered in the late 1800s in Samothrace, Greece. They believe it dates all the way back to 190 BC. She's been here since 1883, about twenty years after they discovered her. But interestingly, she didn't originally have her wings. They found those and painstakingly added them a few years later. That's when she really started getting attention." He turned back toward me and gave me a little smile as he shoved his glasses up.

"Wow. How do you know so much about her?" I asked.

Philippe turned his gaze downward, suppressing the tiniest smile. "My mother is an art history teacher. She dragged us through the Louvre on more than one occasion, and while her stories bored me to death as a kid, some of it stuck."

I laughed. This was an interesting piece of information about him. "I can relate! My mother insisted I see every museum in DC by the time I was out of elementary school, and then several times over after that!"

He chuckled as we continued up the staircase. Callie and Julien had moved ahead of us at a faster pace and were already on the next floor, but Philippe and I took our time examining the frescoes on the wall. Philippe commented on several pieces along the way, which I enjoyed tremendously. It was nice having my own personal tour guide.

Standing in the extensive halls lined with incredible paintings, in the presence of another person with the same appreciation for art and history, I had to suppress a smile. This. This was what I'd been missing. It didn't necessarily have to be Philippe—I certainly wasn't trying to throw myself into a relationship with someone on the other side of an ocean. But I knew this was something I wanted.

I found myself glad that the halls of the Louvre encompassed something like eleventy-billion miles, because I didn't want this afternoon to end.

7

"You sure you'll be okay here for a while on your own?" Callie asked.

"I got dumped at the altar, Cal, I'm not dying," I replied, perhaps a little over dramatically.

"I just hate to leave you alone when we have such a short amount of time together," Callie said, embracing me in a big hug.

"Don't you worry about me," I insisted. "Just focus on showing off how amazing you'll be at this job. I know this is important. And we can celebrate tonight!" Callie's big interview for a position at the American Embassy was today. I was nervous on her behalf.

"Thank you! How do I look?" she asked, twirling and showing off her adorable A-line dress. Black and chic, it stopped respectably at her knees, not exposing too much leg, but also not extending too far down her calves. She wore black tights and black boots that came up to just under her knee, and a bright red scarf added a pop of color around her neckline.

"Like a million bucks. Seriously, you look gorgeous. You're

the perfect blend of professional meets classy. If they don't pick you, at least based on your fashion choices, they are crazy!" I gushed.

Callie gave me a deep curtsy. "Thank you!" She blew me a kiss. We both giggled. "OK, there's food in the kitchen. Help yourself to anything you want." She looked around the apartment. "I showed you how to work the stereo remote and we don't have cable, but you can..."

I cut her off. "I'll be okay, I promise! You've got a great bookshelf full of things I haven't read yet, and besides, I am looking forward to a hot shower and some time to decompress. Now go!"

I hugged her, gave her a kiss on the cheek, and playfully shoved her out the door. I watched her walk down the hallway, closed and locked the door behind her, and leaned against it, releasing all the air from my lungs. As an introvert, I relished alone time. I simultaneously wanted to process everything that had happened in the last month and wanted to just lose myself in a good book and let someone else's drama take center stage.

But first, I needed to take care of something. Our conversation the night I'd arrived had sparked a need deep inside for closure. I sat down at the little table desk in the far corner of the living room and turned on the computer monitor. Navigating to the web browser, I signed into my Yahoo account. Ignoring the many unread messages, I composed a new email.

Matt,

I don't understand why you did what you did.

It would have been nicer if you'd told me in person, or at least had had the guts to end it before I stood there in my wedding dress in front of all our friends and family.

I'm releasing myself from the choices you made.

Have a good life.

Lila

Hands shaking, I hit send and blew out a huge breath. It didn't really matter to me if he ever read it or not, I just needed that closure for myself. Queen rubbed on my legs, bringing me back into the present.

After giving her a quick scratch under the chin, I wandered the short distance into the kitchen, put the kettle on to boil, and smiled as I noticed Julien's work phone number scrawled on a piece of paper and taped to the fridge. In case something came up, obviously. Just like Callie. I tried to imagine a scenario in which I would resort to calling Julien at work. Coming up with nothing beyond me being locked out of the apartment, in which case the number on the fridge would do me no good, I snuggled onto the couch, hot tea in one hand and a book I'd grabbed from Callie's shelf in the other.

Queen climbed onto me and kneaded on my lap, purring loudly as I stroked her black fur. *Maybe I should get a cat when I go home?* Would I become a lonely cat lady? What if I never met anyone else and got married? My parents wanted grandchildren *so* badly. Did I want kids? *Not today, that's for sure.*

The thoughts would not stop. After restarting the book several times, I set it down, removed the cat from my lap, and decided to take a hot shower.

The heat worked out the knots in my shoulders. Gratitude surged through me that I could spend this time with a friend who knew exactly what I was going through. I did not want to spend my time in Paris crying or feeling sorry for myself.

Drying off, I wrapped the towel around my head and

reached over to grab clothes... that weren't there. "Oh shoot!" The realization dawned on me that I'd left them sitting on my bag in the bedroom. Grateful to be alone in the apartment, I hung my towel on the door and wandered into Callie's room in my birthday suit.

A sudden crash made me jump. Philippe stood in the entryway to the kitchen, mouth hanging wide open, shattered teacup on the floor.

Simultaneously, we both screamed.

"Noooo. Why would you DO that?" he yelled, as I scrambled to hide behind the door and slam it shut.

"Are you freaking kidding me?" I screamed through the door, shaking as I threw on a tie-dyed Phish T-shirt from their concert a few years ago, and my favorite tan corduroys. "Why are you here?" I yelled as I swung the door back open, praying he hadn't seen anything. Why *was* he here? He was supposed to be settling into his new place today.

"Why were you naked?" he yelled back, throwing his arms in the air. "Do all Americans just wander around other people's apartments in the nude?"

"Are you seriously blaming me for this?" We stood there in a standoff, my arms crossed across my chest, my cheeks burning in embarrassment at the thought of him seeing everything. "Seriously, why are you here?" I asked, my voice high and squeaky.

"Callie told me you were alone, and I decided to come by to offer you some lunch." He held up a bag with a baguette sandwich in it. The hot air escaped from my lungs, and the anger shifted to guilt. He was here to do something nice for me, and I'd berated him. Slowly, I reached for the bag and gave him a small smile.

"Thank you," I squeaked out, but it came out sounding more like a question than a statement.

Philippe shook his head, and returned abruptly to the kitchen, probably to get what he needed to clean up the teacup mess. Still a little sheepish over my response, I joined him in the kitchen to see if I could help. He jumped backward, putting more space between us.

"Really hope this wasn't one of Callie's favorites, butter fingers," I said as I picked up the broken pieces of the teacup.

"Butter *what?*" Philippe asked, not understanding the colloquialism.

"Never mind." I didn't feel like explaining it to him, and I probably couldn't find the vocabulary to do so anyway, not in a way that would make sense. His English was good enough for us to speak conversationally, and my French was decent, but some things were simply lost in translation.

He sighed, waiting for me to get out of the way, and once I did, he bent down to mop up the tea, returning to the kitchen several times to wring and rinse the towel. I stood in the living room, hands on hips, waiting for him to finish so he could just leave. I *really* wanted to be alone now.

"Thanks for bringing the sandwich," I said, perhaps a little more harshly than I should have.

His eyes flashed and he muttered, "You're welcome," as he grabbed his coat and rushed out the door.

Opening the bag, I pulled out the contents. Ham and cheese baguette and *pain au chocolat*. My favorites. And Callie's. And pretty much anyone who has ever had the pleasure of eating a *pain au chocolat*. Despite my irritation, the gesture was sweet. But I was pretty sure he now believed I was the worst person ever.

"Aaargh!" I flopped on the couch and screamed into one of the throw pillows. "Why does everything have to be so messed up right now?"

Queen jumped up and perched on my back before starting

to knead my head. Her gentle massage eventually put me to sleep.

THE FRONT DOOR CLOSED, startling me awake from my nap. My eyes fluttered open to see Julien standing in front of me, smiling.

"I heard you had an interesting afternoon," he said, chuckling as he lifted Queen from her napping position on the nape of my neck. The warmth of her body had been quite comforting.

Oh crap. Of course Philippe would have told him the details.

"Exactly what did you hear?" I asked, mortified.

"Nothing important. Only that you were caught quite off guard, and it's safe to say you gave Philippe the shock of his life." Julien laughed as he walked into the kitchen and opened a can of food for Queen, who now yowled loudly.

I hopped off the couch and followed him. "Yeah, well, he broke one of your cups!" I said defensively.

Julien just laughed again. "It's okay, we have nothing of any real value."

That didn't make me feel better.

"Where is Callie?"

"She called me to let me know she wasn't quite done with her interview. I think they took her to meet someone else, which I think is a really good sign."

I nodded my head eagerly. "Yes, that is definitely a good sign!" I was so happy that Callie had found this opportunity. We had spent many hours discussing her love of policy and international relations and how she wanted to get more involved. I knew she had always dreamed of having some type of job with the State Department. A tiny twinge of envy crawled up my spine that Callie was close to having pretty much everything she'd ever dreamed of.

"I am as nervous as she is, I think," Julien admitted, setting the bowl down for Queen, who was rubbing against his leg aggressively. "She's so smart. They would be stupid not to take her!" Pride oozed through his words. I wondered if Matt had ever bragged like that about me to any of his friends. It seemed unlikely.

Julien and Callie had met and fallen in love in just over four days, while I spent almost five years with Matt, and we didn't share nearly as strong of a bond as they had formed in such a short time.

"Do you want something to drink?" I asked Julien.

"What do you want? I'll take care of it," Julien insisted. "You're on vacation. So... vacate..." he furrowed his brows. "Would you say that?"

I giggled. "Nope. Vacate would mean get out!"

"Well, that's not what I meant! Relax. Can I get you a drink? Tea? Something harder than tea?"

"Tempting. What time is it?"

Julien checked his watch. "Four p.m."

"I will start with tea."

"Suit yourself," Julien said. He came back from the kitchen a couple of minutes later with a hot tea for me and a beer for him. I was glad to see he'd added milk.

He noticed me examining the drink and said, "Oh, I fixed it like Callie drinks it. Hope that's okay?"

"That's perfect." She and I both drank black tea with a splash of milk.

We sat in silence for a few minutes. Then Julien said, "Philippe is not a bad guy, Lila. He doesn't have a lot of experience with women, so he gets nervous and a little weird sometimes."

I laughed out loud. "Yes, I suppose seeing someone buck naked is grounds for nervousness."

"I can only imagine what his face looked like."

"It looked like this." I stood up and did my best imitation of his deer in the headlights look, complete with his hand still in the air, like he hadn't realized he was no longer holding the teacup.

Julien laughed heartily. "When we were kids, you know, boys, we liked to try and get into the shows with nudity, not like that's hard to do in France, and he would be so embarrassed." His smile disappeared. "I probably shouldn't be telling you this!"

I smiled down into my tea mug. "Payback for him telling you he saw me naked." I joked. Julien didn't seem appeased by that reply. "Don't worry, I won't say anything. I feel a little bad for yelling at him."

"He didn't tell me that part."

"Yeah. I wasn't very nice. Then I snatched the food he brought me and kicked him out."

Julien laughed again. "Well, that's good training for him, so he understands how volatile women can be, for when he finally meets his match."

"Touché!" I said, raising my teacup and clinking against his beer, trying to imagine what type of woman would catch Philippe's interest.

The door slammed open. "I made it to the next level!" Callie yelled, running into the living room.

"That's wonderful!" I exclaimed, shoving up off the couch to hug her. We jumped around excitedly. Julien pulled her into a long embrace and gave her kisses all over her face. I smiled at the two of them, hopeful that when I was ready, I would find the same kind of love. Today might have started rough, but tonight we would celebrate.

"What's the plan?" I asked.

"We're meeting Philippe at one of our favorite bars for happy hour," Julien said.

"Which bar?"

"This is a new one we discovered a few months back. You'll like it," Callie insisted. "It's a cool place."

AFTER WE FRESHENED UP, the three of us left the apartment and walked the short distance to the Latin Quarter. We wandered down a street I'd never walked before, and then down a flight of stairs and into a hole in the wall I never would have discovered on my own. The bar was dimly lit, fairly empty, and basically a dive. Just my style.

"Sit here," Callie commanded. "I'll get the first round."

She reappeared a few minutes later with some mystery blue, fruity drinks and a beer for Julien.

"To assholes," Callie stated, clinking her glass hard with mine.

"Why would we want to toast to them?" I asked.

"Cause if they hadn't been assholes, we never would have found the good ones!"

"I'll drink to that!" Julien stated, raising his drink high.

"Mmm, this is good!" I said. It went down way too easily, and we were soon ordering our next drink. And our next. By the time Philippe arrived, Callie and I had both had at least three drinks and were giggling like little kids. Prior to his arrival, Julien and I had filled Callie in on the events of the afternoon, and she nearly lost it when Philippe finally stood in front of our booth, looking sheepish.

"Seen anything interesting lately?" Callie snorted as she kissed him on both cheeks, which reddened instantly. He looked at me and I shrugged my shoulders. Julien handed him a beer and he sat down.

""What's happening?" I asked, as I saw the commotion near the bar. I hadn't realized how many people had filed in. The place was now packed.

"Oh, the best part about this place! Karaoke!"

"Oh *no*," I groaned. I was not a fan of karaoke. Like, at all.

"Oh yes!" Callie grinned at me.

"I'm happy to make fun of others, but I will not be singing," I declared.

"Give it a few more blue drinks!" Callie winked, raising her glass.

We snickered as we listened to song after song being karaoke'd by French guys who didn't really know the English words or how to pronounce them in the songs they were singing but tried to sing them anyway. We heard some highly entertaining renditions of Bon Jovi songs, but my favorite was probably the little punk rock dude who got up and sang "Pour Some Sugar on Me" like he believed with all his heart he was Joe Elliott of Def Leppard.

I tried not to spit my drink through my nose as the songs and singers got worse and worse.

After draining my latest glass, I stood, crawled out of the booth, and pushed through the crowded room to get to the karaoke machine. I had an idea, if I could manage to stay brave enough to do it. I yelled my song choice up at the DJ, who gave me a thumbs up.

I could see our table, but they had not seen me yet. They would soon enough. The alcohol fueled my courage, and I grabbed the microphone as the song started. "Strumming my pain with his fingers..." my voice cracked. Callie's head snapped up in my direction, a huge smile spreading across her face. She pushed out of the booth and made her way over to me.

As more people watched me perform, I closed my eyes. "Killing me softly..."

I might be killing them with my voice, I thought. Now sweating from the heat of the spotlight, I opened my eyes to see Callie standing in front of me, one hand up in the air, singing the song with me. "One time, one time." I forgot about everyone else and sang to Callie. Lauren Hill and the Fugees. We'd listened to this album over and over, crooning out this song.

"La la la la la la," we belted out. By this point, Callie had joined me on the stage, and we screamed the song into the microphone together when we weren't doubled over in laughter. We kept on with what had to be a horrendous performance and completely out of key, to a very robust round of cheers and a standing ovation.

"How'd I do?" I hollered at Callie, over the cheers of our fans in the bar.

"It was like a really terrible scene from *Bridget Jones's Diary*! It was awesome!" she yelled back.

I took a deep bow, and brought my head back up, making direct eye contact with Philippe as I did so. He stood up from the table and made his way to the bar, as if I didn't exist. My face suddenly flushed, and I quickly handed the mic back to the DJ, wondering what had just happened.

I dragged Callie to the bar closest to the stage. "Two shots of tequila please!" I yelled at the bartender. We knocked them back, ordered another round of the blue drink, and stumbled back to where Julien was waiting as Philippe reappeared.

"Wow, that was... something else," Philippe stated, trying to hold back a smile. He handed a beer to Julien and waited for me to sit down before he slid into the booth next to me. "I had no idea you were such a singer."

Julien guffawed. "They are quite the duo," he said, through snorts of laughter. "My favorite part was when you both *screamed* the lyrics, as if you wanted to kill us all hard, not softly."

I couldn't stop laughing as I imagined what it must have been like for the audience to experience that performance. Maybe I had imagined Philippe was ignoring me? Maybe he'd just needed to go to the bathroom. If there had been tension between us at the start of the evening, it seemed to have dissipated by now. *Thank you, alcohol!* I thought.

I didn't want the rest of my trip ruined by a sour moment, and I hoped we'd still be past it tomorrow. As I looked over at Philippe, he smiled, one that reached his eyes, as if silently acknowledging a truce.

8

"I can't believe I've been here five days and I still haven't seen Emilie!" I admitted to Callie.

Callie shot me one of her *don't be ridiculous* looks. "Um, I'd say it was not your fault that she was visiting her parents the first few days. It's okay," Callie reassured me.

The door phone buzzed, and Callie answered. "Come on up!" She pressed the button to release the door for Emilie to enter, and I raced into the hallway. Standing at the top of the spiral staircase, I hollered at Emilie to hurry up. She looked up at me and gave me the middle finger. I laughed and gave her the bird right back. Underneath her punk rock angst hid a sweet soul.

I met her in the middle of the stairwell, and we practically slammed together in a hug that lasted longer than I knew made her comfortable.

"I'm so sorry, my friend," she whispered into my ear. I stepped back and examined her.

"You look radiant!" I exclaimed.

Emilie's short pixie cut perfectly framed her beautiful face.

Her petite frame barely cleared five feet, but I knew her big personality more than made up for her tiny stature. Decked out in her punk rock outfit—a short black mini skirt, a form-fitting top, and Doc Marten boots—she somehow gave off a hardened look.

"A holiday in the South of France will do that," Emilie beamed.

"You got a new piercing!" I pointed to her eyebrow piercing.

"I did!" she giggled. She looked me up and down, taking in my flowing top and cargo pants. Touching the brightly colored scarf I'd rolled up and wrapped around my hair as a headband, she said softly, "You haven't changed a bit, my sweet, hippy Lila girl."

We entered the apartment and Callie immediately embraced Emilie. "It's been too long."

Callie handed each of us a glass of wine, and we sat down on the couch, munching on snacks as we shared stories of our adventures since we'd seen each other last. We had to open a second bottle of wine to get through the details of the wedding, and of course, being jilted at the altar. While the pain was still very fresh, it did feel refreshing to laugh about it.

"I can only imagine how I must have looked, running down the reception hall stairs with the bartender and all that champagne, dress hiked, yelling like a maniac." The imagery was funny. Once I stopped giggling, I looked at the two of them and a certain sadness reclaimed the moment. "I certainly never imagined being here with you two right now."

"I hate that the road that brought you here was paved with heartache," Callie said.

I nodded, looking down at my wine glass intently, struggling to hold back the tears. I sighed. "Despite my anger at Matt, despite knowing that it definitely would have been wrong to marry him, the heart doesn't just instantaneously heal, even when you choose a different path forward." I paused. "I think of how much fun we all had together."

Callie nodded. "I know what you mean, Lila. Not all memories are bad, and those can betray your heart when it's trying to recover."

"Our relationship wasn't all bad."

"I think this is a normal part of the process," Emilie said softly. "I've never loved anyone else enough to truly understand what you're going through." She looked over at Callie and added, "Or what you went through. I know that you're going to survive this. But we don't have a full month together to drink and party out your pain and suffering like we did with Callie. So, what will help you the most tonight?"

"This is exactly what I need. Just being with you guys," I said.

"Do you want to stay in or do you have any interest in going to the Frog tonight?" Callie asked. "I thought it might be fun to go see if Charlie's there."

"I'd love that!"

The Frog and the Princess, an English pub that I'd worked at for a short time when I'd lived here, was one of our favorite pubs. Thankfully, Matt hadn't spent too much time there, so there wouldn't be memories of him there. And it would be good to connect with some of our other friends.

"Do you mind if Philippe and Julien meet us there, or should it just be a girls' night?"

"The more, the merrier!" I said. And I meant it.

We gathered our belongings and made our way to the pub, which was about a twenty-five minute walk. The evening was not too cool, and I reveled in every opportunity to stare at the beautiful sites. Walking in Paris was never tiresome, and certainly provided a good distraction from my inner turmoil. I listened passively to Callie and Emilie chatting, enjoying the beauty all around me. Shops, restaurants, and other businesses occupied the lower levels of the buildings, with apartments occupying the upper floors. The buildings were old, built of stone, and had absolutely breathtaking architecture. Holly and berries, wreaths, and other signs of the upcoming holiday season adorned some of the windows. Restaurants and bars were already prepared for colder weather with the heat lamps out and lap blankets placed thoughtfully on the chairs at some of the nicer places. The terraces were covered by canopies with plastic sides that could be rolled down at any moment to protect the outdoor seating areas from rain and snow. Sitting outside a café and enjoying a coffee and a cigarette (a habit we'd all kicked in the last two years) while watching the world pass by had been one of our favorite pastimes when Callie, Emilie, and I had all lived here.

We arrived at the bar, and I peeled off my coat, eager for a cold beverage. "Let's grab that table," I suggested, pointing at the large table in the corner. It was still early in the evening, so we had our choice of spots. I claimed a chair, draped my coat off the back, and walked toward the bar, looking around to see if any of my friends were working. In a place like this, the staff changed over quickly as people came and went. A lanky figure with a whole lot of swagger appeared from the back and walked behind the bar. With short, spiky, dirty-blond hair, he was a dead ringer for a young Jude Law.

"Charlie's here!" I announced, and Callie and Emilie immediately got up to say hello.

His back was turned, so I coughed and said, "Excuse me, we're finding the service a little slow today."

He turned around, probably prepared to give me an earful about having just started his shift. But when he saw who it was, a huge smile spread across his face, giving me a great view of perfectly straight, white teeth. "Lila? Callie? Emilie? Are you all really here? It's been ages!" He came around the counter to give us all proper hugs.

Charlie was a dream with deep, creamy brown eyes that one could easily get lost in. Raised by a French mother and English father, he spoke both languages perfectly. We had spent many nights drinking at this bar until closing, talking about the world's problems and relationships, and Callie's adventures when she started trying to break into the dating world again, post Vic. He'd become a good adviser and a good listener.

"What are you doing here?" he asked again. "I mean, not that I'm not happy you're here, but wow! I thought you'd both returned to the US. Where's Matt?"

Callie and I exchanged a look.

"What?" Charlie asked, perplexed.

"Well, we probably don't have enough time to fill you in, so let me give you the CliffsNotes." Callie began.

"The what?" Charlie asked.

"Oh, the short version. The highlights," I said.

"Okay, so the last time we saw you was just after New Year's Eve in 1999. Callie had just met Julien, who she fell in love with, he went back to the US with her, spent some time there, and, well..."

Callie held up her ring finger to demonstrate the point. "We got married!"

"What? You're MARRIED? Thank God, after all that whining about hoping you would find another person to love you," Charlie teased as Callie turned beet red. "Well congratulations! First round on me!" He started pouring the draught beer. "And you, Lila? Did you and Matt get married?"

My face fell a bit, and Callie threw her arm around my shoulder.

"About that," Callie started. "They should have a month ago. But," she looked at me as if asking for permission to tell him what happened, and I nodded. "Matt didn't show up."

"*What?*" Charlie stopped dead in his tracks and focused completely on me, his eyes boring into my soul.

I nodded. "Yep. It's true."

Charlie's already wide eyes now looked dilated, the pupils were so big. "Okay, the second round is on me too!"

Callie and I laughed. "Yes, it's been quite an eventful couple of years. And I decided to run away from the States, back to Paris, to forget about it."

Charlie nodded his head, looking between the two of us. "Clearly we're helping you do exactly that! I have so many questions for you both. Hang tight." He walked over to take the order of two other ladies who were waiting at the far end of the bar. Looking back over his shoulder, he called out, "I'll come to your table in just a minute, girlies. And we can keep catching up."

We took the three beers he'd poured and got back to the table just as Julien and Philippe arrived. "Charlie will be here in a second to get your order," Callie told them, stretching up to kiss Julien quickly on the lips. Julien smiled at her as they took their seats.

I took a chair next to Emilie, facing Philippe.

He smiled shyly. "Looks like you've recovered well from the other night?" he asked.

I nodded and returned the smile. "I needed a full day but feel better today." Then I stood again. "Looks like Charlie is getting busy. I'll go grab two more beers. Blonds good for you two?"

I waited at the bar for Charlie to finish up with his new clients. Picking at my nails, I glanced over to our table just in time to make eye contact with Philippe, who shifted his eyes quickly when he saw I caught him. While he wasn't looking, I studied him. His brown hair was a little longer than it had been at the wedding, not too much, but a little shaggy. It always looked a little like he'd just rolled out of bed and not brushed it, but I kind of liked the messy look. I'd realized the other day, as we were sitting so close to each other during the scary movie, that his eyes had flecks of green. Tall and lanky, he stood at least a head and a half taller than me, but unlike Julien, he was not athletic in the least, just super skinny. He was interesting and got bonus points for his love and knowledge of art and history. Although he seemed serious most of the time, he'd shown glimpses of his playful side.

What are you doing, Lila? Because it feels like you're analyzing him as if you're interested in him as more than just a friend. He's not more than just a friend, and you're heading into dangerous territory, I chided myself.

Thankfully, Charlie interrupted my thoughts. He delivered two beers and gave me a half smile. "It's so good to see you, Lila. And I'm sorry about what happened. But honestly, I never liked Matt to begin with.".

"Oh, how did I not know that?" I said, more to myself than Charlie. Tilting my head and bracing for the answer to my next question, I asked, "Why didn't you ever say anything?"

"Because it's not right to intrude on someone's relationship. I don't know all sides, and you seemed happy."

"Yeah, I thought I was. Apparently, I didn't know all sides either." I fluttered my eyelids to hold back the tears that threatened.

"I'm sorry, Lila. I'd really love to catchup more, but..." he nodded his head toward the rest of the room, now full of patrons waiting for a beer.

"If it slows down, come say hello," I said, standing on the pipe that ran along the bottom of the bar to give me enough additional height to lean over the counter and give him a quick kiss on the cheek. I understood how crazy life as a bartender could be.

Charlie placed his hand over mine, and before dashing off he said, "You're an amazing woman, Lila. You're smart and gorgeous. Any man would be lucky to have you."

Sweet Charlie. I knew this was him being completely genuine, and I also knew he wasn't flirting, he just cared about me. There had never been anything more than friendship between us, as Charlie had been in a happily committed relationship for years. But I could also admit that I didn't mind being complimented by a guy like Charlie. And while I certainly wasn't ready to even imagine falling in love with someone else at this point, I didn't mind hearing him tell me I was beautiful.

I picked up the beers and glanced back at our table. Philippe was waving his arms vigorously and everyone laughed. Oh good grief, I hoped he wasn't telling everyone about our little post shower run-in the other day. My cheeks warmed at the thought.

As I approached our group and handed beers to both Philippe and Julien, Emilie scooched over so I could slide back into my chair beside her.

"Seems like you and the bartender have a cozy relationship," Philippe commented, as he traced the top of his beer glass with a finger.

Was I imagining things, or did he sound like he could be jealous at the thought? Turning in his direction, I tried to make eye contact, but he wouldn't take his focus away from the glass.

Callie, who seemed oblivious to the tension between me and Philippe, laughed. "Charlie's been a good friend of ours for ages. And he's got a girlfriend who looks like a supermodel. Lila could flirt all day if she chose, and it wouldn't matter."

Philippe just nodded, sipping his beer.

Oh my gosh. He *was* jealous. This new piece of information caused unexpected flutters in my tummy, growing and funneling into a tornado of mixed emotions. If he was jealous, that meant he had feelings. He *couldn't* have feelings. We were just friends.

We are just friends, I repeated to myself. *You're here to heal, not to have a fling.*

Not wanting to explore these thoughts any further, I turned my attention to Emilie. "Tell me everything!"

AFTER ONLY TWO DRINKS, it seemed like everyone was wilting. "What's next?" I asked. I was not ready to be done. Callie yawned. "Come on you guys, it's early. And it's Thursday. Are we really already this OLD?"

"I have a really early train tomorrow, or I'd gladly party more with you," Emilie said. In our catchup session, she'd told me about her new job in Strasbourg and that she was in the process of moving there.

"Okay, *you* get a pass," I told her.

I avoided eye contact with Philippe, afraid of getting any more weird vibes for him. Callie yawned.

"Pleeeeeaaase?" I pleaded. "Just for a little while. Just a few dances? We don't have to stay out too late."

Callie turned to Julien, who shrugged. "I can go out for a little while. You?"

"Alright. For a little while," Callie acquiesced.

I squealed. "You're my favorite, Julien!" I stood quickly, and scooched my chair away from the table before they could change their minds.

We walked Emilie as far as the Metro, from which we took

different trains, and headed to a club we'd frequented back in the day, Le Loco, in the Pigalle district.

The place was packed. Techno music exploded over the speakers. A rush of energy flowed through me. I was more of a Pink Floyd and Grateful Dead kind of girl than techno, but there was a time and place for everything. And Emilie and Callie had dragged me out and made me dance with them on quite a few occasions. Looking around at the largest dance floor, taking in the scene, smelling the fog machines and sweaty bodies moving wildly to the beat as the lights flashed around us, I smiled. This energy was exactly what the doctor ordered. I grabbed Callie's hand and pulled her onto the floor. A good sport, she danced several songs with me before going to find Julien. Reluctantly, I followed.

Callie yawned and I knew she was at the end of her rope. She leaned against Julien, whose arms were wrapped around her shoulders. But I was not ready to go.

Julien leaned forward and yelled above the pounding techno, "Do you want to stay much longer?"

"I can leave if you guys are ready. Mind if I just go dance one more song?" The irony was not lost on me that the last time all of us had talked about going to a club, Matt and I had left early while Julien and Callie were scrambling to stay out every possible moment.

Philippe leaned into Julien and said something I could not hear over the music. They discussed for a minute and I saw some head shaking. Then Julien leaned into me. "Callie's done, but Philippe said he's willing to stay with you and see you home, if you want to stay longer?"

I looked up at Philippe. "Are you sure?" I had not pegged him for a clubber and thought it would be a big sacrifice for him to stay here, especially without his friends. "Like are you really sure?"

He nodded his head. "It's okay!" he yelled.

Callie pulled me in. "I'm so sorry to bail on you. It's been a big week." I knew she was tired from her interviews and all the things she'd had to do for the process of securing a job at the Embassy.

I hugged her tight and kissed her on the cheek. Nodding toward Philippe, I said, "He'll take care of me."

Callie laughed. "Yep. Don't do anything crazy," she warned.

"Don't worry, I just want to dance a few more songs, and we'll be home not long after you guys."

Callie nodded and stretched up to kiss Philippe on both cheeks. I saw her mouth *Merci* to Philippe, whose expression indicated he wasn't necessarily thrilled to stay, but then he turned to me and gave me a huge smile, offering me his hand and nodding toward the dance floor. I screamed, "I like this song," and pulled him into the crowd. The beat was deep, pulsating through my body. Hardly paying attention to anyone around me, I swayed to the music. I wove my hands through my hair, eyes closed, moving faster as the pace of the song increased. I felt hands on my hips, and turned, expecting to see Philippe, and surprised that he would make such a bold move. Other than giving me the expected kisses on each cheek, and beyond the moment we'd had when I gripped his arm during the movie, he had not touched me at all.

It was not Philippe. I turned face-to-face with a guy who looked to be in his mid-forties, balding, and overweight, eww. He was trying to close the gap between our bodies. Although it was to be expected of drunken people in a nightclub, I didn't like the forwardness of someone putting their hands on me without my permission. I tried to remove his hands from my hips, and he gave me a very drunk grin, tightening his grip on me. He pulled me in closer, putting his lips on my neck, despite my efforts to shove him off. He was stronger than I was and I was unsuccessful in escaping.

Suddenly I was jerked back, and Philippe was in between us.

"Back off, man!" Philippe insisted.

"Oh yeah? What's it to you?" the man slurred.

"I'm her boyfriend," Philippe blurted.

I stood there, stunned. My boyfriend? Philippe shrugged. "Go with it!" he yelled, wrapping his arm around my shoulders.

"Didn't look like she was with you to me!" The drunk guy tried to shove Philippe out of the way, but Philippe was stronger, sturdier, and far less drunk. He didn't move and I hunkered behind him. When the guy tried to move past Philippe, he gave him a good shove, and as if in slow motion, the drunk guy went down. Stunned, I stood still, staring at the man as he reached for me. Philippe grabbed my hand and dragged me off the dance floor, maneuvering through the swaying bodies, making a path that I followed, hoping that the drunk guy was not following. Once we cleared the dance floor, we ran up the stairs and into the lobby area, looking over our shoulders for the other guy. Grabbing our coats from the coat check, Philippe and I ran out of the club, half expecting him to come racing out after us, but he never came. Philippe and I looked at each other, both of us panting, his eyes wild, and I started laughing. Not just a little giggle. I was bent over laughing so hard it almost hurt. I couldn't catch my breath.

Philippe started laughing too.

Then he stopped and looked me over. "Are you okay? Did he hurt you?"

I shook my head. I was fine. "What just happened? Who knew you were literally a bodyguard? The look on that poor guy's face as he went down to the ground. Slow mo!" I was still laughing so hard that I could barely speak the words.

"A confession." Philippe stated, seriously. "I was really worried he was going to fight back. And I didn't know what I would do."

That made me laugh even harder. I threw my arms around his neck and hugged him tight. "My hero! Or rather, *my boyfriend?*" His body suddenly became very rigid, and his arms hung limply by his side.

I dropped my arms and stepped back, embarrassed by his lack of response to my affection. Apparently, I'd taken one step too far.

"I, um, thought it would make him back off," he admitted, a bit curtly. He pushed his glasses up his nose in his signature move and turned, studying our environment. "I think the closest Metro is that way." He pointed to our left and we began walking toward the station in silence.

I'd been genuinely grateful for him saving me. I'd even had some more-than-friendly thoughts while watching him defend me (I'd never experienced that before!) and while he didn't have to announce himself as my boyfriend to stand up for me, I was surprised at the emotions it stirred. Even if it wasn't true. But his response to my attempt at a hug demonstrated he was only saying what he thought he needed to in the moment and had no interest in anything further. And that was probably the safest option anyway, considering I'd be returning to the States in a few days.

We continued the trip in silence, and I continued to chip away at the nail polish on my fingers, wishing a bottle of water would magically appear. My head spun a little and my mouth was dry.

Arriving back at the apartment, he blocked the door as he jammed his key in the lock. But he didn't turn it. Instead, he turned back to me and with a pained expression said, "Lila. I don't know why you're angry with me. I didn't like the way that guy was touching you. You looked uncomfortable. And you deserve better than some drunk dude feeling all over you in a nightclub."

Wait, what? He thought I was mad at *him?*

He turned around, opened the door, and practically shoved me into the apartment. Before I even had a chance to say anything to him, he exited, the door clicking shut behind him.

What the hell had just happened?

The door to Julien and Callie's room was closed, and I imagined they were sound asleep. I wanted to talk to Callie about what had transpired. It had been a weird evening.

I washed my face and pulled my soft jammies over my legs slowly, then pulled my bra off under my T-shirt and settled onto the couch. Not quite ready to sleep, I turned on the television and put in a DVD. I wanted to rewatch *The Sixth Sense* to see if I could catch all the clues this time. I turned the volume down so that I wouldn't wake the other two, and Queen jumped up into my lap. I found my thoughts wandering and realized I wasn't really paying attention to the movie at all. My mind drifted to thoughts of Philippe grabbing my hand and leading me off the dance floor. How protective he'd looked as he stood in between me and the other dude. How he'd been so concerned for my well-being. Goosebumps popped up all down my arms.

I *liked* Philippe.

No.

Philippe wasn't my type.

I wasn't ready to think about other guys.

The movie played on in front of me but all I saw was Philippe's hazel eyes and the way they lit up when he laughed.

THUMP, *thump, thump!*

"Errrrr," I moaned, sitting up on the couch and rubbing my eyes.

Another thump on the door startled me.

"Good morning!" Callie practically sang from the kitchen. "Can you open the door for me, please? It's probably Julien with the groceries I sent him after." Random strangers at apartment doors in Paris were not a thing since you had to have a code to get into the building and a key for the second interior door.

Still in my jammies, I pulled open the door. Philippe, not Julien, stood in front of me, and my breath caught at the sight of him. He shifted nervously, hands shoved in his pockets, his posture less imposing in the daylight, but he sported an expression of pure disdain. Uh oh.

"Bonjour, Lila. May I come in?" he asked softly.

"Uh, sure," I stammered, stepping aside to let him enter, really wishing I had a robe to pull on or had at least brushed my hair and teeth before he saw me. Confusion twisted my insides as he stepped past me and into the apartment. A waft of his cologne pleasantly tickled my nose.

Callie shot me a questioning glance from the kitchen, her eyebrows knitting in curiosity. I shrugged in response, just as confused by the unexpected visitor.

"I came to apologize for last night," Philippe started, his gaze flitting around before landing on me.

"Apologize?"

Callie's head snapped around the kitchen door; her task forgotten. "Hello Philippe!" She walked to him and kissed him on both cheeks, shooting me a *What's going on?* look. She seemed to hold her breath, her eyes darting between us, waiting for one of us to do or say something. When neither of us did, she disappeared back into the kitchen.

Philippe's face tightened, the muscles in his jaw working. "I was rude last night," he replied coolly.

Tick tock. Tick tock. Tick tock. Heavy, awkward silence hung over the room as time passed slowly.

"You saved me from a bad situation. Apology accepted. But really, it's no big deal. I'm sorry for putting you in that situation."

Philippe's eyes darkened, and he took a step closer. For a moment, he just looked at me, his gaze intense. Then he turned sharply on his heel and strode toward the door. "I hope you enjoy the rest of your day."

The door closed with a soft but definitive click, and I stood still, trying to catch my breath. Callie came out of the kitchen again and put her arm around my shoulders in silent support. "What in the world happened last night?" she asked, a mix of concern and curiosity on her face.

"Nothing important. He saved me from a drunk guy, escorted me home, basically shoved me in the apartment, and left without a word. It was strange."

"Hmm," Callie stared at the door, as if it might hold the answers. "I wonder if he has a crush on you? This is not his typical behavior."

My cheeks warmed at the idea. Philippe was cute, kind if not grumpy, and had many of the same interests as me. The possibility of a love affair with Philippe flickered through my mind, but the stark reality was clear—there was no scenario in which this could work out for either of us. Especially now, when it would be nothing more than a rebound for me. I was alone, and that was exactly how it needed to be. For now.

9

QUEEN HOPPED up into my face, purring, and demanding attention, pulling me out of my slumber. I smiled, scratched her chin, and placed her gently on the floor as I stood and stretched. Callie had left a note on the counter next to the teapot that read, "I've got some errands to run. Should be home in a few hours. Help yourself to whatever you need." A set of spare keys to the apartment lay next to the note, in case I wanted to go out.

I showered, ensured no one was in the apartment this time before I came out of the bathroom, and got dressed. I decided to take a walk down to the Seine and enjoy the beauty of the water and the city. My first stop was the charming area of Montmartre. As I strolled slowly along the cobbled lanes, each corner triggered a memory of time spent in Paris. Bittersweet nostalgia rolled through me as I replayed the Sunday afternoons Callie and Emilie and I had drunk tea or coffee in the quaint cafés, fended off aggressive artists with their easels who wanted to capture our portraits, and the hours we'd spent sitting on the stairs in front of Sacré-Cœur, the impressively large and beautiful basilica that overlooks the city, taking in the incredible view of the Parisian skyline.

A quaint café on the corner of the artist's square provided the perfect location for watching the rest of the world go by. Tour guides, their umbrellas high in the air, marched along with their gaggle of tourists following behind. Families with children in small strollers navigated the bumpy cobblestones. Waiters in white button-down dress shirts, black slacks, and black aprons darted back and forth between the restaurants and the covered seating areas in the center of the square. The bustling atmosphere was not enough to keep my thoughts from drifting to Philippe—his kindness, his shy smile, the way he stepped in to protect me at the club, and our mutual love of philanthropy and service to others.

My coffee cup was now long empty, and the café was beginning to fill with the lunch crowd. I walked down the hill from Sacré-Cœur and grabbed a bus to the Eiffel Tower. Couples openly expressed their love all around me, walking arm in arm, stopping to look at the beautiful imagery surrounding them, stealing kisses, and asking people to take their pictures with the magnificent tower behind them. I imagined all the engagement announcements and Christmas cards that would be mailed in the next year with the tower in the background. Why had I decided coming to the City of Love was the best place to heal my broken heart? What exactly about being in a place that was globally known as a destination for engagements, weddings, and lovers, made me think, *Paris is just the place to go when I'm grieving a broken heart?*

Of course, it wasn't the city I was here for, was it? It was Callie. And Emilie. I just needed to avoid the Eiffel Tower—while one of my favorite places, it was causing nothing but pain with all the visible love—and all would be fine.

Notre Dame seemed like a more reasonable solution. I sauntered along the sidewalk paralleling the Seine River, and realized after about twenty minutes that it was a much farther walk than I had thought. Consulting my handy dandy pocket map, I realized there was no real direct route, so I kept walking, taking in all the sights along the route.

After about forty minutes of beautiful bridges and architectural delights along the river, I finally reached the massive cathedral. My breath caught, as it did each time I saw the structure. I wandered slowly around the building, and then entered through the massive main doors. Cool and damp, the interior only offered shelter from the wind, not from the cool October temperatures. The stone structure climbed high to the arched ceilings. My eyes were drawn upward, and as if I was seeing it for the first time, I was struck with awe as I stared at the ribbed vaulting of the ceiling. From the center aisle, the intricate stained-glass windows became visible, each depicting either saints and angels or a story from the Bible. The rose windows cast colorful patterns of light on the stone floors.

Turning, I glanced up at the large organ, and imagined how powerful the sound must be, wishing I could experience a concert here. I lit a candle in one of the alcoves along the side, and then sat in a pew, closing my eyes and lowering my head. I wasn't a very religious person, and I didn't pray often. But today, my thoughts formed into prayers.

"Please God, help me through this time. I don't know how to go back to my life or how to get over this. I don't recognize myself anymore." Resting my back against the pew, I sat in silence for what seemed like hours, but a quick glance at my watch told me I'd only been sitting for about ten minutes. No answer came to my prayer, but as I exited the glorious building, I was met with bright sun and brisk air and peace filled me.

After wandering around for about another hour, I made my

way back to the apartment. I opened the door to find Julien sitting on the couch, drinking a beer.

"You're home early!"

He smiled. "It's Wednesday. I work half days on Wednesdays."

"How lovely." One of the best attributes of the French was their commitment to a balance of work and life. In fact, they had recently passed a law for a thirty-five hour work week. I wryly reflected that we seemed to be moving in the opposite direction in the United States.

"Callie told me that you and Philippe had some awkwardness. He is super shy, Lila, and sometimes that makes him seem aloof." Julien set his beer down on the table and stood up. "Can I get you a drink?"

"I'd love a glass of wine," I said, contemplating his words. "Philippe is fine. He's just a little confusing. One moment, we're laughing. Another, I feel like he hates me."

Julien laughed loudly. "Yes, that's Philippe."

We stood silently in the kitchen. As he poured my wine, he said. "He definitely does not hate you." Julien handed me the glass of wine, and we clinked glasses. "He really likes you, Lila."

My cheeks flushed at this information. "I like him too. He's smart and wants to save the world like I do. I'd like to get to know him better. But is that opening doors that could lead to disappointment and hurt?"

Julien set his glass down and leaned back against the counter. "Two years ago, I probably would have had a different answer for you. But after what happened with me and Callie, I'm inclined to tell every person to take every shot they can at love. Even when it seems risky or silly, or if the timing is bad. Because you just never know what can happen."

I scratched my head, trying to think this through. "I don't

know, Julien. It feels weird to me that I'm even talking about this so soon after what happened to me."

He opened the cupboard and pulled out a bowl. Then a bag of peanut-flavored snacks. Offering me the filled bowl, he asked, "Would you be opposed to me inviting him over for dinner tonight? It doesn't hurt to get to know each other better as friends, does it?"

Looking for a place to discard the peanut snacks (I did not like this snack, which looked like cheese puffs but tasted like peanuts), I chased the one I had put in my mouth down with a chug of wine. "If he's not opposed to spending time together after our last weird exchange, I am okay with it." I chuckled, thinking of how awkward that had been.

"I'm sure he'll be fine."

I nodded as tiny knots formed in my belly. I couldn't tell if they were due to excitement or fear.

Callie came in through the front door, threw her coat on the couch, and entered the kitchen. After kissing Julien and accepting the glass of wine Julien poured for her as he filled her in on the plans, she looked at me, eyebrows raised. "You're okay with this?"

"Sure!" I said, perhaps a little too enthusiastically. "It's better than watching you two fawn all over each other all evening," I joked.

THE EVENING ARRIVED, and I found myself nervously excited to see Philippe. I changed outfits twice and finally landed on a nicer blue blouse and black slacks instead of my hippy clothes. When the knock at the door came, I sat frozen on the couch as Callie went to greet him.

Philippe entered, looking slightly awkward yet determined.

Kissing Callie on the cheeks, he handed her a bottle of wine and a small bouquet of flowers. "I hope I'm not intruding," he said, his gaze finding mine.

"Pfff! It's all good!" I waved my hand in his direction, as if it was ridiculous to even ask the question. Considering he'd been camped out on the floor here a week earlier, his entry seemed overly formal.

We exchanged awkward kisses on the cheeks, and I moved to the kitchen to get a glass of wine for him, topping mine off in the process. As the evening progressed, the tension that once hung in the air dissipated, replaced by a newfound ease, probably thanks to the wine. Also, Julien did a great job of keeping the conversation light and asked questions that got both Philippe and I engaged—starting with the topic of humanitarian aid. I answered all their questions about the clean water initiatives happening globally, and Philippe shared the progress his agency was making in human rights.

If they were bored, they disguised it well. Callie beamed at me as she listened. "You're truly my hero, Lila. And you too, Philippe. Many of us want to do something to make the world a better place, but you two are taking daily steps to ensure life is better for people. Cheers to both of you." She lifted her wine glass, and we each clinked our glasses together. Philippe held my gaze for a moment before he took a sip of his wine and returned his focus to the meal in front of him.

"So, what do you have planned for tomorrow? You only have another full day left before you leave, right?" he asked me.

"Yes," I said, looking down at my plate. "In the time I have left, I want to make dinner for these two, in thanks for all their wonderful hospitality. I thought tomorrow I might go down to the one of the markets I've heard so much about, but never visited when I lived here, to find inspiration and fresh ingredients."

"I wish I could go with you, but the Embassy wants me to come in for finger printing and filling out background information for the first half of the day," Callie said, frowning. "I hate to have to leave you alone on your last day."

"I'm available tomorrow, if you'd like some company," Philippe offered, reddening as the words left his mouth.

"That would be really nice," I replied softly. I meant it. I looked forward to spending more time with him.

***

THE MORNING SUN cast a warm glow over the bustling Parisian streets. Philippe and I walked side by side in silence. The air, filled with the vibrant buzz of the bustling city, created a stark contrast to the tension that had hung between us just days before. Today, we were on a mission to gather ingredients for what I hoped would be an epic meal. I was not known for my cooking skills, however. I hoped Philippe might offer some inspiration.

We passed a cute bookstore on the way. "I'd love to stop in here!"

Philippe nodded, and held the door open for me.

I entered, taking in the beautiful sight of the books shelved from floor to ceiling. I breathed in the smell of the leather-bound books and sighed. The soft glow of fairy lights illuminated the aisles of the quaint Parisian bookstore, casting a warm, inviting aura over its endless shelves.

"I love vintage novels," I said, running my hand over the books.

Philippe grinned. "I must admit, I do too." He picked up a copy of *Les Misérables* and smelled it. Replacing the book, Philippe leaned against a bookshelf, his eyes never leaving mine, causing an unexpected warmth to course through me.

I tilted my head, a smile spreading across my face. "If life is a book, Paris is certainly the setting for a most enchanting story."

"Indeed," Philippe said, his eyes twinkling.

We shared a moment of mutual recognition—two friends, connecting over books, but before I fell too far into the moment, I replaced the book I'd been holding on the shelf and turned toward the exit. "The market?" I asked softly.

As he moved toward the exit, I thought he looked disappointed that the moment ended.

"I did some research," Philippe said, looking around as if to find something that corroborated his new knowledge.

Of course he had.

"*Le Marché des Enfants Rouges* is the oldest covered market in Paris. Some say it's where flavors and cultures collide."

"Sounds enchanting," I teased. "I might never want to leave."

He chuckled. As we entered the market, the array of colors and scents enveloped us. Stalls brimming with fresh fruits, vibrant vegetables, and aromatic flowers lined the pathways, each vendor showcasing their produce with evident pride. As we meandered through the aisles, the air was rich with the scents of fresh produce and the exuberant chatter of vendors and customers. We stopped at a stall displaying an array of colorful vegetables.

"Look at these tomatoes!" Philippe picked up a plump tomato, inspecting it. "They are really nice for this time of year. You see, the secret to a perfect meal is in the freshness of ingredients. Like this tomato—it's practically bursting with the promise of flavor."

"How poetic." I leaned in, pretending to scrutinize the fruit.

I grinned, feeling empowered by the magic of the moment. Glancing mischievously at Philippe, I leaned in closer. "You know, they say tomatoes are an aphrodisiac," I said in a playful tone, my eyes twinkling with humor.

Philippe, caught off guard by my comment, let out a surprised chuckle. "Is that so? I wonder who comes up with these things," he replied, his grin widening. As he spoke, his fingers, still holding the tomato, involuntarily tightened. In a comedic burst, the tomato exploded, sending a spray of red pulp and seeds onto both of us. For a moment, we stood in stunned silence, looking at each other, our faces and coats dotted with tomatoes.

Then, almost simultaneously, we burst into laughter. Philippe, attempting to wipe a streak of tomato off my cheek, only managed to spread it more. I dabbed at a bit of tomato on his nose.

"Oh, look at us," I gasped between fits of laughter. "We're a walking advertisement for tomato sauce!"

Philippe chuckled, his eyes shining with mirth. "I always wanted to be in a food fight. I just never imagined it would be in the middle of a Parisian market, with the most charming accomplice."

Some other market-goers stopped to watch the amusing spectacle, smiles on their faces. A vendor, an elderly woman with a kind face, handed us a handful of napkins, trying to suppress her own laughter *"Ah, l'amour et les tomates, toujours une combinaison imprévisible!"* she said, shaking her head with amusement.

I stopped suddenly, realizing the woman believed we were in love. *Tomatoes and love, an unpredictable combination indeed*, she'd said.

The gentleman with her did not look so amused and I knew it was time to move on. "We'll take this one and four more!" I announced, glancing over at Philippe and instantly bursting into giggles as he, almost the shade of the tomato at this point, tried to clean himself up.

I took the bag and the change from the man, wished him a good day, and we continued to walk through the market.

Philippe took the bag from me to carry and quipped, "Well, I guess we've officially 'squeezed' the most out of this market visit."

Ah, he's funny, and a gentleman, I thought as I nudged him playfully. An unexpected lightness settled in.

"Did you know," Philippe said as we stopped by a stall with an array of colorful spices, "that Parisians weren't always known for their love of spices? It was the influence of exotic trade routes."

"Look at you, Mr. Historian," I quipped. "What other secrets are you hiding?"

He raised an eyebrow playfully. "Oh, I have many secrets. But I'm more interested in yours. What else is there to know about Lila, the unexpected Parisian adventurer?"

I shrugged. "Just a girl who decided to turn a mishap into a journey. The usual stuff of rom-coms."

As we continued our banter, our bags gradually filled with the freshest ingredients. Philippe selected a bunch of fragrant basil, while I exclaimed over the plumpness of the pears.

"You really love pears, huh?" he observed.

"The perfect cold weather fruit," I said, smiling.

Our eyes met, and for a moment, there was a flicker of something deeper, a hint of an unexpected connection that, despite the alarm bells also ringing in my head, was growing between us. I turned my attention back to the fruit, selecting a variety of apples, pears, and oranges for the fruit and cheese platter for dessert.

Once our mission was completed, we walked quietly through the Parisian streets. Confusion coursed through me as I realized how much I'd enjoyed spending time with Philippe, the layers of his personality slowly shifting to reveal a depth I hadn't anticipated. In the heart of Paris, amid the hustle of the market and the rhythm of a city full of life, I realized I hadn't felt sad all day. My heart was slowly mending, aided by the most unexpected of people.

CALLIE HAD ALREADY RETURNED by the time Philippe and I shoved through the door, our arms full of fresh ingredients and wine.

"Let me help," she insisted, relieving me of several bags. "Mmm, this looks promising," she said, perusing the ingredients as she pulled them from the bags.

She waggled her eyebrows at me when Philippe's back was turned, making me giggle. I knew exactly what she was insinuating. The lightheartedness of our interactions made it clear that something had changed over the course of the day between me and Philippe.

As it turned out, Philippe really knew his way around the kitchen. Minuscule as it was, we managed to work around each other as we set to work prepping the vegetables.

"What are we having for dinner?" Callie asked, popping her head around the corner. "Also, can you grab the cold bottle of rosé from the fridge and hand me three glasses?" Three of us in the kitchen was a tight squeeze.

"Philippe's surprise. There are lots of vegetables and spices and some meat involved," I replied, leaning over to grab the bottle of chilled wine. Callie took the glasses and bottle into the living room, and I heard the pop of the cork. She returned a moment later, handing each of us a glass. Philippe wiped his hands on a towel before taking his and nodded at her appreciatively.

"To men who cook!" Callie toasted, and we clinked glasses.

"To voluptuous tomatoes!" I toasted back and Philippe roared in laughter.

"What did I miss?" Callie asked, and I told her the story. She shook her head back and forth, a huge grin on her face, then gave me a long look.

I shrugged my shoulders. "When in Paris..." I started.

"Crush tomatoes?" Callie finished.

"Yep, pretty sure that's how the saying goes!" Philippe stated and we all laughed.

In the tiny, warm, kitchen, the air was soon thick with the scents of the herbs and vegetables searing in a pan. Philippe, Callie, and I performed a culinary ballet, dancing around each other in the very crowded space. Philippe, who revealed himself as a maestro of the kitchen, skillfully orchestrated *les petits farcis niçois*, stuffing the seared tomatoes, zucchinis, and peppers we'd gotten at market with fragrant, herbed ground meat. My mouth watered in anticipation.

I chopped vegetables for the salad, while Callie appointed herself the DJ and wine steward. The upbeat notes of a classic French chanson filled the room, mingling with the clatter of utensils and the sizzle of cooking. Callie, unable to resist the rhythm, danced around her living room. The door opened and Julien entered, smiling as soon as he saw his playful bride. He sashayed in her direction, pulled her in for a kiss, and patted her on the bum.

"What is that amazing smell?" he asked, looking in disbelief at Callie.

"Philippe!" we both said.

Philippe took a brief pause from his culinary masterpiece, extending his hand to me. "Mademoiselle, may I have this dance?"

I laughed and accepted his hand. We joined Callie and Julien in the living room and began to move, awkwardly at first due to the confined space, but soon with more ease, laughing as we tried not to bump into the furniture or each other.

Callie watched us and smiled at Julien. I knew that look. She was scheming. I silently pleaded with her to not make this more than it was: friends having a lovely evening. Callie, a romantic to the highest degree, was likely planning out our entire future together. There was one flaw in her love story. I would not stay in France. Unlike her incredible love story with Julien, I would not be falling in love with Philippe before returning home.

The thought brought me down. No longer in the mood to dance, I returned to the kitchen, making some silly excuse about the salad needing my attention. As the song ended, Philippe returned to his cooking tasks, but the energy in the room had shifted from something vibrant and playful to something else. Philippe showed me how to perfectly season the salad, and when his hand briefly touched mine, I pulled back quickly.

Callie squeezed her way into the kitchen. "Where did you learn to cook like this, Philippe?" She took a sip of her wine and leaned against the kitchen counter.

Philippe added the final touches to the *petits farcis*. "My grandmother was my teacher. She made the most amazing meals. Always cooked from scratch."

I looked at Philippe, once again softening toward him, and turned back to Callie. "And you, Callie, what's your secret talent?"

Callie smirked, smacking Julien as he snorted. "I can open

and pour a bottle of wine faster than any of you without spilling a drop. It's an art form."

Laughter filled the room again, comfortable and genuine. The evening progressed with more music, occasional dancing, and continuous banter. As we sat down to eat around the small table Callie had pulled away from the wall and expanded so that all four of us could eat around it, Philippe raised his glass. "To kitchen dances," he toasted.

"To good wine, delivered expeditiously," Callie added, winking at Philippe.

"And to Paris," I concluded, my gaze meeting Philippe's, "where even an ordinary evening can turn into something magical."

Not to be left out, Julien chimed in, "To fate."

Our glasses clinked in unison, and I wondered if Julien was referring to himself and Callie or if he was hoping for something more to happen with Philippe and me.

"I'll clean up the kitchen," Philippe announced.

"I'll help," I volunteered.

"But you cooked!" Julien argued.

"You've housed me for weeks. Relax!"

We made a good team. I washed the dishes and Philippe dried them, returning them to their rightful places in the cupboards. Not too many words were exchanged, but it was not awkward between us. Once the kitchen was returned to its normal state, Philippe turned to me, gently placing his hand on my arm. I looked up at him expectantly.

"I'm glad we got to clear the air. I hope your last memories of Paris are good ones," he said.

My cheeks warmed. "It's been a lovely visit. Paris has been full of surprises."

Neither of us spoke, and I wondered if he too was silently

acknowledging something that might have been had our situation been different but would remain unexplored.

After he left, Callie helped me make the sofa bed, kissing me on the cheek before retiring to her room. Flopping back on the pillow, I adjusted the blankets around me and sighed. Philippe had stirred something in me, a flutter of possibility, a hope that I would be able to open my heart to love again.

10

Late November 2001

I'D HALF EXPECTED to see Matt waiting for me at baggage claim, proclaiming his love and begging me to take him back. How he would know when or where to meet me was of course a mystery of the romantic comedy genre, since I hadn't told anyone the flight or time of my return, just the day. So obviously, no one met me at the airport. I took a train into the city and a cab to my apartment, too tired to deal with dragging my luggage through public transportation.

The door to my apartment moaned as I pushed it open slowly, echoing my fears. What would I walk into? I hadn't been back to the apartment since the wedding, having stayed at my parents' house until I left for Paris. Although Matt and I had not lived together, he'd spent so much time here that his belongings had been everywhere. But instead of seeing his things strewn chaotically around, a hollow emptiness engulfed the room. The walls, now bare of any of his stupid posters, echoed back a silence that was almost tangible. A quick scan of the apartment confirmed my sinking feelings and suspicions:

Every trace of him had vanished. No pictures of us remained. Five years completely wiped from existence.

My heart stuttered, a mix of betrayal and disbelief weaving through me. He had come and gone, taking everything with him and leaving behind nothing but the ghost of our memories in the now lifeless space.

I found his key and a note on the table that simply said, "I'm sorry." Crumpling the paper, I tossed it in the garbage and opened the fridge. My mother must have anticipated my return, as there were key staples and a variety of Tupperware boxes with leftovers. She might have played a role in the mystery of the missing pictures. Bless that woman.

Popping a container of lasagna into the microwave, I glanced at the pile of mail on the breakfast nook and decided that was a tomorrow-problem. It would probably be a combo of junk mail, bills, and the worst offender: cards congratulating us on our marriage.

No thank you.

I ate a few bites of the lasagna, but despite it being quite possibly the best lasagna on the planet, every bite tasted like sawdust, so I returned the plate to the fridge. After a long, very hot shower, I climbed into bed, pulled the covers over my head, and cried myself to sleep.

***

MY BOSS DIDN'T EXPECT me back until Tuesday, so I had a few days to myself. Therefore, I launched Operation: Chocolate and Sweatpants. My grand plan? Stay in my pajamas all day. Ignoring phone calls and emails like a pro, I ordered pizza and settled into my role as the anti-heroine of my own life story. Only this situation definitely had more the vibe of Sandra

Bullock in *The Net* than any cutesy rom-com. Only without the cool computer skills. Or the plot.

Callie had sent me home with two bottles of wine and a giant bag of Lindt chocolates. I was on a mission to see how many of those little spheres of bliss I could pop into my mouth before I started to resemble one. Still not wanting any interaction with other humans, I decided a movie marathon was my best bet. The lineup was a cinematic roller coaster, oscillating between sappy rom-coms and tearjerkers.

Somewhere into about my third glass of wine, I reached my sap limit. If I saw one more perfectly timed kiss in the rain, I was going to hurl something at the screen. Ugh. Watching these movies with their impossibly perfect characters and whirlwind romances felt more like a slap in the face and a reminder of my failures than was helpful. I mean, come on, who actually ran through an airport for love these days? TSA would have a field day.

"You're not fooling anyone!" I shouted at the TV, flinging chocolate wrappers like confetti. "Love isn't all grand gestures and running through airports!"

Unless you're Callie and Julien, that is.

Aaarrrggggh, I screamed into a pillow.

Monologuing to my audience of no one (maybe I really should get a cat?) I stood on the sofa, looking out into the nonexistent crowd. "So, here's the highlight reel of my love life: Only dated one guy through college. Check. Convinced him to marry me. Check. Left at the altar. Check. Only seem interested in guys that are an impossible situation. Check. Will die alone, with a bottle of wine in my hand and melted chocolate on my hands and face. Cue dramatic exit, stage left."

Naturally, I ended the night with *Bridget Jones's Diary*, belting out "All by Myself" like I was auditioning for a reality singing show. Despite the heartache, singing off-key and absurdly loud was wildly liberating.

"Oh, Mr. Darcy. Do you exist?" Philippe had a bit of that Darcy-esque broodiness, minus the happy ending with me. Mr. Darcy would remain undefeated as the champion of book and movie boyfriends.

That night, I dreamed a bizarre mash-up of *Pride and Prejudice*, *Bridget Jones*, and my own romantic misadventures. It was like a *Choose Your Own Adventure* book gone horribly wrong. Obviously, it ended with me standing at the altar, alone, as everyone pointed and laughed. I awoke, tears streaming down my face, on the couch, with a slice of pepperoni stuck to my cheek.

Peeling the slimy slice of meat from my face, I got up and went to the bathroom. The vanity mirror reflected a woman covered with pizza sauce and hair sticking out in every direction, resembling a cartoon character after a food fight. I burst out laughing at the sight. It was either laugh or cry, and I had done enough crying.

"How does one even manage this?" As I scrubbed my face clean, I decided today would be different. No more wallowing in self-pity. I was going to be productive. Or at least, I was going to get dressed. Baby steps.

After slipping into a comfortable pair of well-worn corduroy pants and a soft, long-sleeved shirt, I pulled on my favorite hoodie. It was like a security blanket, but for adults. After getting coffee brewing, the mountain of mail was next on my agenda. Bills, junk mail, and, as predicted, those pesky congratulatory cards. I couldn't help but snort at the irony.

"Congratulations on your non-wedding," I said to the empty apartment, doing my best impression of a game show host. "You've won an all-expenses-paid trip to Splitsville! Population: you." I laughed at my own joke, then winced.

MIDMORNING, I finally hit play on the answering machine. There were no fewer than eight hundred messages. Or at least that's what it felt like. The tape was full. As I listened and deleted, I opened my computer and quickly sent my mom an email that I was home and I was okay but needed some space. I also emailed Callie to inform her of my safe arrival.

Then I opened the messages from my best friend Amy. "Hey, you alive? I'm worried about you."

I called her. "I'm alive. Barely. And currently in a committed relationship with my hoodie and coffee."

"I'm kidnapping you for lunch. Be ready in an hour. And don't you dare wear that hoodie." Amy hung up before I could argue. I wouldn't have won the argument anyway. Amy was like a bulldozer when it came to dragging me out of my funk. Plus, I had to admit, the idea of human interaction sounded surprisingly appealing. An hour later, and less one hoodie, Amy whisked me away to a cozy café, the kind that served fresh bagels and had inspirational quotes on the walls.

"You're exactly where you're meant to be," one of these quotes said in a cheerful font. Unspeakable words ran through my mind, relating to where they could shove that sentiment.

It was almost too happy, but the smell of fresh coffee was a balm to my soul.

"So," Amy began, sipping her latte. "Tell me everything. The good, the bad, the ugly..." her voice trailed off.

I sighed, hiding my face in the oversized mug before recounting the highs and lows of my recent emotional rollercoaster. I refrained from sharing any details that would lead Amy to believe that Philippe was anything more than an annoying presence, although she nearly sprayed her coffee all over me when I recounted the shower situation.

"And then it all ended rather dramatically when I woke up this morning with pizza on my face," I concluded, shaking my head.

Amy laughed so hard she snorted, which in turn made me laugh. It was ridiculous, absurd even, but in that moment, my mood lightened. Maybe it was the laughter, or maybe it was sharing my woes with someone who cared.

"Look, Lila," Amy said, once our laughter subsided. "Life's thrown you some curveballs, but you're still here, still standing. You're like the heroine in one of those rom-coms, except it's real. And way funnier. And who says they have to end with a happily ever after? That's just stupid." She shook her head back and forth.

"Yes. I'm ready to find myself again."

"You're an independent, amazing woman. And you deserve only the best things."

Amy hugged me as we stood and gathered our belongings. "Get back in the game, girl. But play it your way." She was right. It was stupid to think everything ended up happy. The world had more than enough examples to prove her right. But my heart still hoped.

Tuesday morning, I woke before my alarm, still feeling like a character in a tragicomedy. I took my time getting ready, applying makeup carefully and even curling my hair. If I had to face reality today, I at least wanted to fool everyone into believing I was not dying on the inside.

11

January 2002

Work became my boyfriend. I buried myself in what I considered an incredibly important mission of bringing clean water to the world and providing better opportunities for women, volunteering for every trip and opportunity that came my way: India, Africa, South America. Watching a middle-aged woman flush a toilet for the first time, or hearing the laugh of a teenage girl as she emerged from an indoor bathroom (instead of having to walk outside to use the toilet, sometimes in unsafe environments) provided me with an incredible amount of satisfaction. My colleagues and I were so busy improving the day-to-day lives of others that I had no time to think about dating.

Amy, busy with her own budding career as an event planner, continuously nagged me to get out on the town when we could coordinate our schedules, but it was a challenge with my work travel. Also, while Amy would always be my oldest friend, the events of the last two years had changed me, and she didn't understand me the same way anymore.

I was learning what it meant to be single as an adult, for the first time, and on those weeks that I had no trips, loneliness crept in. I missed Callie and Emilie dreadfully, and the six-hour time delay made even catching up with each other challenging. I needed a local friend group that understood me.

Allison, one of the gals in my office, and I struck up an unlikely friendship after she found me crying in the break room one day. I thought for sure I'd endure a mean girls-esque torture from that point on, but she surprised me by consoling me. Before I knew it, we were sharing stories of heartache, and I realized that under the surface we were more alike than different.

A petite blonde, Allison came from a very wealthy family and dressed the part. I couldn't tell you what brand name she wore because I bought most of my clothes at consignment stores or department stores, but it was obvious her choices were high-end. She sported Prada bags; I had a knock-off purse I'd bought in a market in Paris that was starting to shred along the edges. The two of us came from different worlds, and her work at WaterCorps seemed to be more of a sentencing from her parents to "do something good for the world" before she got access to her trust fund, but somehow, we got along quite well. She wasn't overly friendly in the office, but for some reason, she took a liking to me, and she was fun to drink with. As an added perk—she knew everyone, and in a world where connections with deep pockets was a must, Allison was a great person to have on my side.

That was how I came to spend Friday nights in bars in Georgetown with coworkers and staffers like me from other government and nongovernmental agencies. Allison dragged me out the first time or two, but after that, I was a willing participant. All of us single people hung out in our spare time, usually just talking about work, but having a good time all the same. It should have been a mecca for finding datable men who understood my world and me theirs. Yet thoughts of Philippe haunted me, and every time I met a guy, he was colored by the comparison. Not smart enough, not cute enough, didn't speak a foreign language, didn't cook, didn't make me laugh.

I was too embarrassed to share this with anyone. Not Amy, not Allison, and certainly not Callie. I had no idea why I was still holding on to thoughts of Philippe. Was it some kind of weird Jedi mind trick to avoid a relationship with anyone else? Philippe and I were just friends, we barely knew each other, and we certainly had never dated each other, nor would we ever. Regardless, I never said yes if anyone hinted at going out, and I never acted too interested in any of the men, unless they provided an outlet for funds or supported legislation that was important to me.

The rest of the time I was pretty much a loner. Unless Amy dragged me out somewhere, or my parents insisted I come over for Sunday dinner, I spent a lot of time alone in my apartment. I drank more wine than I should have, ate chocolate like it was my job, binge watched holiday romantic comedies, became obsessed with the *Gilmore Girls*, and lived in my sweatpants.

All of this was fine and good until the morning I struggled into a pair of pants like an animal trying to escape a trap. They had fit comfortably, once upon a time, but now they clung to me like spandex. Sighing, I realized it was time to stop the downward spiral. *Lord help me, I think I need to join a gym.*

I expressed my little problem to Amy, who told me that she worked out regularly at a gym not far from my apartment and convinced me to join her. Begrudgingly, I got up early, put on a T-shirt and loose sweatpants (thank goodness these were still loose!), and grabbed my Walkman.

Amy met me at my front door, jumping around like an excited Pomeranian. "You ready? I mean are you *ready?*" she asked, hands up like a boxer, punching me playfully.

"Geez, are we going to fight Rocky or walk on a treadmill?"

"Who said anything about walking?" she taunted.

"Amy, you promised!"

"I'm just kidding. You can walk; I'll be in the grown-up area." She stuck her tongue out playfully and dragged me in the direction of the gym.

My arms and legs were heavy as I trudged alongside her. I imagined I appeared more like someone turning themselves into the FBI for a heinous role in a criminal gang rather than making a positive change for my well-being. Amy had a kickboxing class to get to, so she left me to get registered. I approached the front desk slowly.

"Welcome to Smith's Gym," an adorable and altogether too-happy woman about my age greeted me.

I grunted in return.

"How can I help you today?" She gave me a big, toothy smile.

As if it wasn't obvious. "I guess I need a membership," I said quietly. She launched into motion, telling me about the benefits their establishment offered. After a tour of the facilities and the many contraptions I couldn't imagine ever torturing myself with, I unenthusiastically signed up for a membership.

Looking around, I decided to start with the lowest hanging fruit. The treadmill. That seemed innocuous enough. I poked around on the buttons until I finally set it to just a manual workout. There was no need to get all fancy with the options this morning. I hit play on my tape and started to walk. It was awful. I had no problems walking from one side of Paris to the other at my own pace, but being forced to walk in one spot, with nothing interesting to look at, could certainly be used as a modern form of torture.

The music took over my thoughts, and I lost myself in the lyrics. I even found myself increasing the speed a time or two.

As I got really motivated, I nudged up the incline. My heart responded accordingly. I was sweating! I had tried hard not to sweat on purpose over the years, preferring slow nature walks and sightseeing in foreign cities as my exercise of choice.

Then I made mistake number one. I looked at the timer. Don't look at the timer. I was marching along at what I thought was a reasonable pace. After what I was certain had been over thirty minutes, the timer rudely told me I'd only been walking for four minutes. Maybe that was the countdown? Nope. Those numbers were definitely going up. This was going to be harder than I thought. So I played a little game. *OK, you're at 0.3 miles. Let's see if you can hit 0.5 miles before the ten-minute mark.*

After what had to have been two hours, I finally made it to one mile. *You can do this, Lila. Ten more minutes.* A song that reminded me of our nights in Paris played, and I tried to imagine I was dancing. I moved my arms around to the techno beat, smiling sheepishly when the woman next to me gave me a side-eyed glance. Staring at the countdown clock did nothing to make it move any faster. When it finally hit the twenty-five-minute mark, I pumped my hands (well one of them at least, I didn't want to fall off this dang torture device) and decided the last five minutes could be a cool down. I bumped the incline settings down a notch. Or at least I thought I bumped it down. It increased one more level. I hit it down a couple more times, only to watch it go up instead of down.

What was happening here? I stared at the button to make sure I was reading it properly. Yes, nudging it down should slow me down. For good measure, I bumped it down one more time. And it increased again. Now I was at an 8.0 incline and I held on to the rails for dear life as my muscles screamed at me. Sweat oozed from all my pores and my heart pounded, banging on the wall of my chest. The clock said twenty-seven minutes and thirty-two seconds had passed. *You're almost there! You've got this!*

Two options presented themselves: Stop the machine and reset it. Be done for the day. Or, keep going to hit my goal. I wanted more than anything to achieve that thirty-minute mark, so I held on for dear life and kept climbing the mountain.

As I gripping the handles tighter, the Walkman slipped out of my grasp. It hit the belt of the treadmill and launched off the back of the treadmill, slamming into the mirror on the wall behind me. I glanced back over at the woman next to me, who rolled her eyes. She was clearly a serious gym goer, running on her treadmill in her perfect workout clothes. *One minute and thirty seconds to go.* I was committed. I could claim my mangled device when I was done but this was a victory I would not allow to slide through my fingers.

Sweat dripped into my eyes, but the fear of flying off the back of the treadmill forced me to keep both hands firmly on the handlebars. I used my shoulder to try to wipe the sweat off the best I could. My heart rate reached "being chased by a bear" level and the seconds seemed to take minutes to pass. Finally, the clock hit thirty minutes and I cheered, finally daring to move my hand enough to hit the Stop button. Relief washed through me as the incline decreased and I slowly came to a stop. I bent over, catching my breath before standing, saying a little prayer of gratitude that I'd not been shot off the back of the treadmill. Turning, I ran smack into a wall.

Except why would there be a wall at the end of the treadmill? This was no wall. This was a very hard body. Attached to one of the nicest faces I'd ever laid eyes on. He smiled down at me, and my eyes widened. Those might be the most perfect teeth I'd ever seen. His blue eyes shimmered, and I was mesmerized. He held up his hand, holding my Walkman.

"This belong to you?" he asked. *Cheddar biscuits and gravy.*

No, that wasn't it... What was it Callie always said? *Cheese and biscuits.* I was dumbstruck.

Tucking my hair nervously behind one ear, I grabbed my towel off the treadmill and tried to wipe some of the sweat away. "Yeah," I said slowly, convinced he should be talking to the Treadmill Goddess next to me. Guys that looked like this generally didn't pay much attention to me. I snuck a glance at her, and she gave us both the full up and down look-over before rolling her eyes and returning her focus to her run.

"You training for a big hike?" he asked.

Mortified, I realized he'd been watching me.

"I, um, had a little issue with the treadmill," I stammered.

He laughed. "Yeah, treadmill number three is notorious for these types of issues."

Great. Had all the regulars been watching me for their form of entertainment? *Look at the new girl. Let's see what happens today on treadmill three. My bet's on the treadmill!* I couldn't admit he was correct, so I went with it. I refused to admit I couldn't figure out how to work the machine. Nor would I spill my guts that I was just trying to reverse the damage of over a month of chocolate and wine indulgence. "Um yeah, a very steep hike."

"Oh yeah? Which one?"

Busted.

I tried to remember any summit name. Nothing came to me. I shrugged, which caused him to chuckle. I snatched the mangled Walkman from his hand. "Thanks for retrieving this," I said quietly, assessing the damage. The spring was broken. This Walkman was officially retired.

"I'm Sam," he said, extending his hand. It was hard not to stare at his perfectly sculped biceps and shoulders. I was a big fan of good shoulders. I kept my eyes on his hands, not wanting to ogle what I was certain was an ogle-worthy physique. *Down, girl.*

I wiped my hand quickly on the towel and reached out to take his. "Lila," I said. His large hand engulfed mine, and he held it for a moment. All the blood rushed straight to my head, and I wobbled.

"You okay?" He steadied me.

Compose yourself, woman!

"Lila. I've never seen you here before." He propped himself up against the arm of the treadmill, watching me as I wiped down the machine. I tried to pretend like his presence wasn't amping up my entire body.

And you may never see me here again. "I'm new to the gym."

"Well, I hope I'll see you here again?"

Dammit. Now I definitely had to come back. I shrugged, avoiding eye contact because, well, this interaction was terrifying to me. "Thanks for rescuing my Walkman."

He glanced at the mangled device. "I'm not sure I rescued it."

We stood there in silence as I shifted my weight from one foot to the other, desperately trying to think of something clever to say. Nothing came.

"So, see you tomorrow?" Sam finally asked.

I nodded, simultaneously disappointed that our conversation was coming to an end and relieved. Apparently I was committed to working out now. But he was worth getting up at zero dark thirty to see again. *Philippe who?*

Gathering my belongings, I headed for the exit, hoping I'd be able to walk tomorrow. That mountain climbing treadmill workout had been no joke. My thighs burned, and yet I smiled, proud of myself. I'd done it. Thirty minutes on the treadmill, in a much more aggressive workout than I'd ever intended. I wished I could share this moment with Amy, but her class was a full hour. I had already warned her I probably wouldn't be there when she finished.

Peeking back over my shoulder, my excitement dropped a bit as I saw Sam talking to Treadmill Goddess. She looked far more like his type. Perfectly fit, with sculpted arms and abs, and she'd actually put on makeup before coming to sweat it all off. Maybe he was just being nice to me. My heart sank, but I lifted my chin and reveled in the glory that I had not succumbed to the murderous treadmill, and for today, that was good enough.

12

Rolling out of bed the next morning, I surprised myself by realizing I was excited about going to the gym. "Who are you?" I asked myself in the mirror. I'd stopped by Target and picked up some better workout clothes, since this was apparently going to be a thing, and I approved of what I saw.

When I entered the reception area, my heart immediately raced at the sight of Sam. I'd never really gone for blond guys before, but he had a sort of Ken look to him with thick, perfectly coiffed hair. I swear his pearly white teeth glinted, like they do in toothpaste commercials. Leaned against the counter on those bulging arms (I had the urge to feel his biceps) Sam smiled as he talked to the (admittedly cute) receptionist, who was literally fawning over him. She placed her hand on his arm affectionately (hey, that was supposed to be my move!) and I wondered if they had a more interesting history than just gym acquaintances.

He turned toward me. "Lila!"

I tried to pick my jaw up off the floor and pretend like I

hadn't just been ogling him. I glanced behind me. What were the odds there was another Lila? Nope, just me.

He strode toward me and thrust something in my direction. I looked down.

"I took the liberty of getting this for you."

"What is it?" I asked, turning the gadget over in my hands.

"It's an MP3 player! Welcome to 2002!"

"Oh." I'd heard of those. It was a way to store all your music on one tiny little device. All I wanted was my mixed tape, but this was a thoughtful gesture. "Thank you. I didn't bring my headphones, so I'll have to try it out later."

"I got you covered!" He whipped out what looked like tiny little plastic hearing aids on a wire. "Earbuds! The latest and greatest. You just shove these guys in your ears, and off you go!"

"Hm, now that's something." Technology was changing so fast. Computers, mobile phones. *Earbuds?* What was next? Video calling? Certainly not. I couldn't even call France without paying $100 for a twenty-minute conversation. It would be eons before we could video chat.

I shifted uneasily, marveling at the little device in my hand. "How do you get music on it?" The question made me feel stupid.

"You load it through software on your computer. It's not hard. But I took the liberty of filling it with '90s pop and rock."

I flushed, completely taken aback by this unexpected gesture. "Th... that..." I stammered, "that was a good guess, but I guess it makes sense, being we just left the '90s and, well, it was an excellent decade for music."

"I saw the label on your mixed tape." He winked. Did people our age really wink at each other? I guess Sam did.

A blend of emotions passed through me. This was a really sweet gesture. But we weren't in a rom-com. He had been flirting with Front Desk Girl when I arrived. Sure, our meeting was cute, but it wasn't a meet-cute, right? I was probably just fresh meat and he'd probably slept his way through half the gym.

"Well, enjoy your training," he said as he started to walk off. "And avoid treadmill three today!" He gave a big grin.

Front Desk Girl beamed at him as he passed. But when I passed through her line of sight, she scowled. I seriously thought about sticking my tongue out at her, but we weren't five anymore. Although she was probably closer to five than I was. Confidence surged through me. Regular old, hair-in-a-ponytail, no-makeup Lila, had attracted the attention of the hunk.

Thirty minutes, a lot of sweat, but thankfully no mountain death climbs later, I hopped off the treadmill and removed the little earbuds. Admittedly, the sound quality was great, and wow was it great to skip over a song I didn't feel like listening to without trying to guess how far to fast forward. Sam's music choices were pretty on target with my style, with a few exceptions on some heavier punk rock I didn't love. That was more Emilie's domain, but not something I'd ever gotten into.

"Lila!" Sam marched with a purpose in my direction, and I quickly wiped the sweat off my face, turning to wipe down the treadmill in the hope he'd assume the red blotches were a result of an invigorating workout, not his presence.

"I survived with no incident," I reported.

He chuckled. "Any chance you have time to grab a coffee this morning? There's this great place just around the corner."

I cut him off. "Beans and Bagels? It's my favorite!"

"Yes, that's the one."

I glanced at my watch. I'd be cutting it close, but I'd need coffee today. "Sure, I can spare a few minutes." It would mean my shower would have to be very fast, but I was okay with that for the opportunity to talk to him outside of the gym.

Surreptitiously I sniffed myself, hoping I didn't smell. But you'd probably have to actually work up a sweat to smell bad, right? We grabbed our things, and I avoided eye contact with Front Desk Girl, although I could feel her eyes boring holes in me. "What do you think about the MP3 player?" Sam asked, holding the door open for me.

"It's amazing! I love that I can skip a song easily and the sound is great."

"Oh, no. You skipped some songs?" Sam's face fell.

Immediately embarrassed that I'd made him feel bad, I stammered, "I, uh, it was only one. Not a huge punk fan."

"Whew." He wiped his brow. "That was a risky choice, I admit. Not my favorite either."

Despite my effort to hurry over to the coffee shop to beat the morning crowd, a long line met us at the door. We made small talk while we waited, covering the major things. Siblings, family life, work stuff. He seemed surprised when he learned my line of work.

"I think that's really admirable," he admitted, after I passionately explained why I worked for WaterCorps. His eyes weren't necessarily glazed over by my diatribe, but he had a slight smile pasted on his lips that I recognized from my many dealings with politicians, usually indicating they weren't exactly paying attention anymore.

Slightly embarrassed that I might have bored him into a catatonic state, I turned the focus of the conversation back to him. Blowing on my coffee, I asked, "What about you? What do you do?"

"Something along the lines of consulting and lobbying."

I knew it! That could be good or bad, depending on where he stood on the issues I cared about. But we were having a pleasant moment, so I just nodded my head.

"Thank you for the coffee, but I really have to get to work."

A short first encounter would save me from answering uncomfortable questions about my past.

"Will you be back at the gym tomorrow?" he asked.

Oh shoot. I had planned on taking tomorrow off from the treacherous treadmill. Two days deserved a day off, right? "Maybe?" I squeaked out, non-committedly.

"I hope so. I'll look for you!"

I never imagined the gym, of all places, would be the center of my next attempt at a relationship, but life was full of surprises.

A FEW HOURS LATER, after catching up with all urgent issues and surviving one very long staff meeting of dull weekly updates, I logged into my personal email account. The goal: update Callie on my latest news.

She'd already written to me.

> Subject line: Connecting you two via email!
>
> Hi Lila!
>
> Philippe is coming to DC for a meeting in a couple weeks! I wanted him to have your email address so he could have a friendly face to show him around while he's there. Now you're both connected!
>
> I assume you're okay with that, since it's Philippe, not some random stranger, like that dude I let stay with me in Paris that one time!
>
> Love you to bits.
>
> Bisous,
>
> Callie

Oh my gosh. How was this my life? I meet a seemingly nice guy, am not thinking about Philippe regularly anymore, and boom. He's coming here. That didn't matter, right?

You're just friends, Lila. You can be a friend to him and still be interested in Sam. Right, and I owed this particular friend for the time he'd spent with me in Paris. Certainly my social calendar had some space for an evening or two showing Philippe around. Maybe it was the "exercise high" people talk about, or the excitement of having had coffee with Sam, but I noticed my heart pitter-pattered a little as I typed up what I thought was a fun reply.

Re: Connecting you two via email

Oh Callie,

I had completely forgotten about that rando… wasn't it like the younger brother of your sister's boyfriend or something? All I remember is he stayed in your tiny place for like four days and ate all your food! You're always taking care of people.

Just kidding, Philippe! Great to be connected and I look forward to seeing you again. Let me know when you're flying in. If I can get there, I'll come meet you at the airport!

Bisous,

Lila

Re:Re: Connecting you two via email!

Hi Lila and Callie,

Thanks for arranging this Callie. You take such good care of me!

The Paris Predicament

Lila, that's a really nice offer to come get me at the airport. It's not necessary, but of course, I'm always happy to see you, as long as your clothes are on! :P :0 :)

See my itinerary below (I arrive Saturday) and I'm also looking forward to seeing you.

Bisous,

Philippe

Re:Re:Re: Connecting you two via email!

I just spit out my tea!!

Callie

Re:Re:Re:Re: Connecting you two via email!

Philippe!!!

Lila

Re:Re:Re:Re:R:e Connecting you two via email!

I'm just teasing, Lila. See my itinerary below and see you soon.

Xo,

Philippe

Giggling like a little girl, emboldened yet shaking a little with excitement, I replied quickly.

> Re:Re:Re:Re: Connecting you two via email!

> Ha! Well, it's really cold right now, so I probably won't be naked.

> Xo,

> Lila

I hit send, shaking from nervousness. Also a little nervous that if we didn't stop using the word naked, we might trigger the system into scanning for inappropriate content, I waited anxiously to see if he would take the bait. This game was fun, and certainly easier hiding behind the protection of the computer, but I worried about taking it too far.

The reply came instantly. I also noticed he'd removed Callie from the email.

> Re:Re:Re:Re:Re: Connecting you two via email!

> I'd gladly be naked with you.;-)

> Your fake boyfriend (at least when you need to be defended in night clubs).

> Philippe

What the...? What had just happened?

I nearly choked, and warmth spread all through me as I read and reread that email. Yes, that was what the words said. And it was English, so I knew I hadn't mistranslated something.

Standing up, I paced in circles around my desk, trying to figure out how and if I should respond to that.

I liked flirty Philippe. His words triggered feelings in me that had been hibernating for a long time.

Fanning myself, I sat back down at my desk. *Friends, Lila, you're friends.* I didn't reply. Let's let him wonder.

I scrolled back to find his flight details and wrote the information on my desk calendar: Friday, January 18. Philippe arrives! Air France: 4:40 p.m. And for some strange reason, I doodled a heart next to it.

My thoughts ping-ponged back and forth between Sam and Philippe again. My face couldn't stop smiling, despite feeling a blend of confusion and nervous anticipation.

13

After a night of bizarre dreams featuring both Sam and Philippe, I awoke, tired and angry at myself for thinking of Philippe when something might be brewing with Sam. Then again, should I be counting on anything coming from a guy who flirted openly with every female in the gym? Maybe it was just a game to him. The alarm blared at me, and I finally slammed my hand down on the off button after snoozing it several times. I'd promised Sam I'd see him again this morning, and I was a girl of my word.

Pushing Philippe far from my thoughts, I zombie marched to the gym, wondering if Sam would be waiting for me again. I pulled open the door, scanned the joint, and was disappointed when I didn't see him anywhere. Dragging myself to the treadmill, I shuffled along like an old man at a ridiculously slow pace, gradually increasing the speed, and finally reaching a more respectable pace for a twenty-four-year-old around the twenty-minute mark. I completed thirty minutes, achieving an elevated heart rate and a little bit of sweat. I was turning into a proper gym rat now. Too bad Amy wasn't here to see it, but her class wouldn't start for another hour, and all evidence of a real workout would be gone by then. Hopping off the treadmill, I scanned the room, but there was still no sign of Sam.

Figures, I thought. I actually get up to meet him, and he doesn't show. This was a recurring theme in my life. *Ouch, Lila, go easy on yourself!*

Swigging down some water and feeling like a proper athlete with a sweat towel around my neck, I made my way to the exit, chucking the towel in the bin along the way. As I walked into the lobby, the door flew open and Sam entered, sweaty and red. Man, this guy was hot. I tried to damper the enormous smile spreading across my face at the sight of him but was unsuccessful.

"Lila! I'm glad I didn't miss you! I overslept," he said, apologetically.

"I almost did the same," I admitted.

"I ran here, so I guess I got my cardio for the day!" His eyes twinkled, the blue of his eyes shining intensely.

"I think I'm going to need a rest day tomorrow," I admitted, hoping he didn't think less of me for wanting a break after only three days.

"Good!"

"Good?"

"Yes, good! Then I won't feel so bad about keeping you out late tonight."

What did I miss? How was he going to keep me out late?

Acknowledging the confusion on my face, Sam continued. "Lila, I'd love to take you out tonight. Will you have dinner with me?"

I shifted nervously. Chatting over coffee was easy. But a date? A real date? Just the two of us for an entire evening? I hadn't been on a date with a new person since I was nineteen years old. My palms moistened and I wiped them on my shirt.

"Well?" Sam asked, looking at me with such anticipation, I giggled.

"Okay, what did you have in mind?"

"Do you like Indian food?" Sam asked.

I freaking loved Indian food. But what I didn't love was the idea of spicy food making my nose run on a first date. And the other potential impacts of spicy food. *Ew.* Despite the gross thought of a runny nose, I nodded. It might be our only date anyway. I might as well enjoy the food. And at least he hadn't suggested wings, which I still had yet to figure out how to eat without getting buffalo sauce all over my face and hands. I'd just have to be careful to choose milder options tonight.

"That sounds wonderful," I said.

"Great. Can you meet me at seven o'clock?"

"Yes, that's perfect."

He gave me the name of the restaurant and general location, and I practically skipped all the way home, giddy with excitement, and a tiny bit nervous to be officially entering the dating world again. Still, I practically sang aloud and had to refrain from announcing to everyone I crossed paths with that I was going on a date with Sam, last name unknown.

As soon as I got to work, I emailed Callie.

Subject line: Guess who's going on a date?

Callie!

I have a date tonight! His name is Sam. We met in the gym. We're going for Indian food. I hope everything is going well with the job and you're not too overwhelmed. How is Julien?

Xo,

Lila

Nanoseconds later, my email pinged.

The Paris Predicament

Re: Guess who's going on a date?

Lila? Is this really you? A DATE? The GYM? Indian food and you do not have a good track record. Have you been body snatched by an alien? And you're such a slut. Naked with Philippe one moment, and on a date with someone else the next.

Xo,

Callie

PS - Just kidding! I'm so excited for you! Can't wait to hear all about it. Julien's great. The job is great. I'm in my element!

Re:Re: Guess who's going on a date?

Ha! Mentioning the gym must have really thrown you! Yes, I joined a gym. And I actually went three days in a row. Largely motivated by seeing Sam. He's funny and gorgeous. Tall, fit, light brown hair. These stunning blue eyes. He bought me an MP3 player.

And I'm just going to ignore your Philippe comments. :-)

Kisses

Lila

Re:Re:Re: Guess who's going on a date?

A what? An MP3? Is this some new dating thing? Does that mean you're betrothed or something?

And I think you and Philippe would be perfect together!

Kisses back to you!

Callie

Re:Re:Re:Re: Guess who's going on a date?

No betrothals here. :-) I'm still reeling from the last time I tried to do that. An MP3 player is the latest craze in music. Tiny little device that holds all your music. It's so cool! And light!

Gotta get back to work but I'll fill you in tomorrow!

XO, Lila

Re:Re:Re:Re:Re: Guess who's going on a date?

You better! Love you, sister!

Kisses,

Callie

THE DAY PASSED QUICKLY and I hardly had time to daydream or worry about the big date. We were busy preparing new testimony for Congress about the importance of globally funding clean water initiatives. I worked later than normal and ran out just before 6 p.m. Once at home, I wiped down quickly, reapplied lipstick and mascara, brushed my long hair, and threw on a fairly conservative but cute black top. Was this enough? Did I look date appropriate? Should I have put on more makeup? What in the world were the rules of dating in this new century?

With a MapQuest printout in hand, I made my way via Metro to the right neighborhood and followed the printed directions. Although I was not always the most punctual person, tonight I arrived at 7 p.m. on the dot.

"Wow, a woman who is on time!" Sam noted.

Sam wore khakis and a long-sleeved polo shirt that hugged

his arm muscles. He held a black pea coat over his arm. He looked smooth; debonair. A far cry from the grunge look Matt sported. I liked it.

"My father's ex-military," I shared, trying not to stare too hard. "If you're not ten minutes early, you're late!" I mimicked the words my dad had said to me my entire life.

"I guess you're late then," Sam teased, tapping his watch.

We sat down and Sam ordered both of us a drink and an appetizer. I'd never had a man order for me like that, without even asking my preference. What if I hated the wine he chose? Ok, that was probably a bad example. I'd never met a wine I hated. But more importantly, what if he ordered super spicy food and I turned into a human faucet? I did not want to gross him out. Also, the feminist inside of me wasn't sure whether to be pissed off, while the domesticated side of me fought hard for me to enjoy having a man take care of me. Should I feel like less of a feminist because I was enjoying not having to make the decisions and allowing him to command the evening? This was an internal battle I'd never faced with Matt, who rarely made any decision at all for both of us.

The conversation flowed easily, thankfully. Since it was a first date and we knew relatively nothing about each other, it could go in one of three directions. First, awkward silence, in which neither party could keep the conversation going, second, one person dominating the conversation and showing little interest in the other party. Luckily, we fell into the third category: easy conversation. We talked a lot about work, and I was relieved to hear him discuss his involvement in some projects that were in fact, for the betterment of humanity.

The appetizer arrived and as it turned out, his choice was spot on. I especially appreciated the fact that he did not order super spicy dishes, so for now at least, the potential horror of my runny nose was a moot point. The food was delicious. I tried to refrain from making the orgasmic noises that tried to escape from my mouth, since Matt had told me that it was annoying when I moaned over my food. So when Sam let out a loud *mmmmmmmmmm* when he tasted the chicken tikka masala, I relaxed.

"What are you thinking about?" Sam asked, after we'd been silent for a few minutes.

"Honestly, I'm trying to remind myself of how impolite it would be to lick this plate clean."

He laughed heartily. "I know! It's so good. This is my favorite restaurant!"

"I also realized how nice it is to be able to talk about my passions without being hushed or told how uninteresting my work is."

"Ouch. Who was the jackass that said those things?"

"Okay, I guess this is when we're going to have this conversation." I hesitated, worried about telling him my backstory. But it was bound to come out eventually, and sooner was probably better than later. He needed to understand what he was getting into.

"I was supposed to get married a few months ago."

"And obviously you didn't, right?" he winked.

"No. I didn't. It's not a happy story, Sam. In hindsight, I think I knew we weren't right for each other. But when he didn't show up on the wedding day, it became pretty obvious he'd had that realization first." I shrugged my shoulders, hoping to pull off a nonchalant delivery of the news that I'd been left at the altar.

Sam's jaw dropped. It took him a moment to recover. *Here we go*, I thought. I imagined his next move would be a run for the door. An escape from the pathetic woman whose fiancé had left her without a word.

Instead, he wiped his mouth with a napkin and reached

out, grabbing for my hand. Looking directly into my eyes, he said, "I can't imagine what kind of idiot would run from you."

Stunned, it was my turn to be at a loss for words. We sat in silence for a moment, his hand still on mine. Finally, I said, "I sure know how to set the mood on a first date, don't I?"

His brow creased and he removed his hand. He picked up his fork and moved his food around on his plate. As time ticked by, I wondered if I'd just killed any hope of this potential relationship.

Finally, he looked up at me. "I like you, Lila, and I hope this is the first of many more dates to come. Just one question. Are you still in love with him?" His tone was matter-of-fact and his eyes dropped back to his food as he waited for my response.

"I am not in love with him," I stated. And I meant it. "But if we're being honest, I also should say this is the first date I've been on in years, and I'm not ready to go running headfirst into anything."

He looked back up at me and nodded his head. "Thank you. That's all I need to know on that topic." He continued eating. I did the same.

After a few minutes of silence, I started to feel nervous that my proclamation had scared him. Or maybe he just really wanted to eat his food. Either way, I was grateful when the waiter stopped by to check in on us.

"I think we'll have another drink," Sam told him.

Relief shot through me. He wasn't ready to pay and get the heck out of here.

As if we'd never had that awkward interlude, Sam dove right back into sharing stories of his life. We talked about college, friends, travel. Like me, Sam had traveled quite a bit. His father's work took him all over the place. I told him about my trip to Africa, when I'd helped rebuild a school. He told me about his trip to Africa to go on a safari. I wondered if the two of us could really be compatible when our worlds and experiences were so different.

But I didn't need to map out our entire future tonight. Sam was good company. He wasn't rude, could carry on a good conversation, and most importantly, did not trash any of the causes I found important. He was easy on the eyes (have I mentioned his bulging neck and shoulders recently?) and made me laugh. But despite the plumpness of his gorgeous lips, I didn't find myself envisioning what it would feel like to kiss them. Rather, our chemistry had "good friends" vibes. Was I preventing myself from getting attached so I wouldn't get hurt again? Reflecting on that evening cooking with Philippe, I had definitely imagined kissing him, but Philippe might have a strange pull over me because I knew a future with him would be impossible. Was I putting roadblocks in my own way with Sam because this could have potential?

"So do you want to go with me to the gala next week?" Sam asked. This brought me back to reality.

Oh crap. What gala? What was I committing to? I guess it didn't matter. Sam wanted a second date, and I wanted to explore this, despite my fears. "Yes. What night again?"

"Were you paying attention to me at all the last twenty minutes?" Sam asked in a playful tone.

"Of course I was!" *Not*, I didn't add. "I just…"

"I'm just teasing. It's next Thursday night."

Being that my social calendar was completely empty, and I wasn't traveling next week, I knew there was no reason not to go.

"Yes, I'd love to go with you." *Oh my gosh, I have no clothes, nothing at all appropriate for a gala!*

"So why do you look so, well, *not* excited?" he asked.

"I don't have anything to wear," I admitted, sheepishly. I didn't normally get invited to galas.

"Certainly you have something fancy, right?" Sam asked.

"Uhh, the fanciest dress I own is my wedding dress. Which happens to be crumpled up in a bag waiting to be donated, and is probably inappropriate attire for this event?" I asked, trying to lighten the mood, and then instantly worried that reminding him of the almost-wedding would plunge us back into brooding silence.

Sam chuckled, shaking his head. "Definitely not. You seriously don't have any formal dresses?"

I sighed, pushing my hair behind my ear. "Sam, I don't *do* fancy. In college, I always borrowed dresses for formal events. And so far, my boss hasn't sent me to any galas or anything requiring evening wear. These days, my idea of dressing up is not wearing my oldest jeans or faded-out corduroy pants."

Sam's eyes lit up at my description. "Probably not the best choice for an event of this nature."

"Also, it's not really in my budget right now."

"How about we find something that's very 'you' but also gala-appropriate? And it would be my treat," he added, before I could object again.

We? What did he mean by *we'd* find something? And he'd buy the dress? Was that weird?

"You barely know me; why would you buy me a dress?"

"I'd like to get to know you better, and I think you'd be a great date for this event. Plus, it would be really good for you to meet the people there. You could find some great partners."

Scrunching up my nose, I prepared a rebuttal. "I just find it weird to let you buy me expensive gifts."

Sam laughed. "It's not a big deal, Lila. I have plenty of money. But," he added quickly as my expression soured, "if it makes you that uncomfortable, we can consider it a loan."

Thinking about his offer, the promise of meeting key

donors and potential legislative partners beat out any objections I had.

So weird or not, that's how date number two got planned as a shopping trip.

We finished dinner and Sam escorted me home. The entire walk, I tried to listen to him and engage in the conversation, but I was plotting how I would end the evening. Afraid of botching a first kiss, and terrified of doing or saying something that might set the wrong expectations for how the evening would end, I yawned when we reached my apartment and gave him a peck on the cheek. "Thanks for a lovely evening, Sam."

He didn't even try to hide his disappointment about not being invited in. But I was not in a hurry to move forward too quickly, even if that meant leaving him unsatisfied. I placed my hand lightly on his arm. "I'd invite you up, but my place is a wreck, I've got an early day tomorrow, and well, I need to save all my energy for dress shopping this weekend."

He laughed. "A woman who doesn't like to shop. There's no end to the surprises with you."

He pulled me into a hug and placed a light kiss on my lips, which sent vibrations through my body, and I realized that, even though I didn't feel a thrill, I would like to go back for more. However, the fear of getting carried away intervened, and I stepped back.

"So, this weekend then?"

I stepped toward my apartment building door and nodded yes. Maybe there weren't butterflies in my tummy, but cautious optimism about the potential relationship flowed through me.

14

On Saturday morning, Sam waited for me at the front of my building, just as we'd arranged. As I exited, he smiled. That smile should have knocked me off my feet, but it didn't stir anything. *Why aren't you stirred?* Should I be concerned that maybe the hottest man on the planet was here to take me shopping for dresses, and I wasn't fawning all over him? Either my self-defense mechanisms were of the highest quality, or there just wasn't any chemistry between us. I really hoped it was option A.

"You ready?" He looked fabulous in a pair of loose jeans and a navy-blue sweater, which ironically, was a very similar shade to the sweater I sported with my khaki cargo pants.

I raised an eyebrow. "Do we really have to go shopping? Haven't they invented a service to just deliver dresses to you in your size yet? That's what I need."

"To my knowledge, no, but new things are always rolling out, but it probably wouldn't get to you by Thursday even if it did exist. And, if you want to go to the gala, then yes, we have to."

I sighed. "Okay, if you insist." Even if nothing further came of this relationship beyond friendship with Sam, I had to admit that the gala would be the perfect opportunity to be introduced to the type of people who could really make a difference to my organization. Part of my job included securing donations, which was certainly easier if you had personal connections to people with deep pockets. Which I did not. But Sam did. I had assumed that was part of the reason he invited me.

"Come on, beautiful, let's go find the perfect 'Lila' dress," Sam said, eyes twinkling.

My cheeks warmed at being called beautiful. "And what exactly screams 'me' at a fancy gala?"

"Something unique, stunning, and utterly unforgettable," he shot back with a grin that made my heart do a weird little flip. Ok, now we were getting somewhere.

A flip was a good sign! Maybe I wasn't completely immune to his charms after all. I rolled my eyes, despite the ooey gooey feeling spreading through my chest. "Fine, but nothing itchy or that requires a corset."

"Deal," Sam agreed, his smile broadening. "Let's find a dress that lets you eat, dance, and breathe."

The prospect of dress shopping did nothing to excite me—I hated shopping. The endless choices, the fitting rooms, the mirrors. Oh sweet Delilah, the judgmental mirrors. Three days at the gym had not been enough to work off the chocolate and wine frenzy, and I worried that I wouldn't find anything flattering.

But as we stepped into the boutique, Sam's enthusiasm was infectious. He grabbed a sequined monstrosity off the rack. "How about this?" he asked, holding it up. It was so sparkly it could blind someone.

"Only if we're crashing a '70s disco party afterward," I joked.

"Noted for future date ideas," Sam said with a wink, and I laughed, surprised at the ease of our interactions.

Hours slipped by as we sifted through dress after dress. We talked as we shopped. Sam filled me in more on his upbringing and family life. He didn't spill all the details, but it sounded like his dad was very successful and traveled a lot. I empathized, since my father had traveled a lot too while on active duty.

Our conversation was largely through dressing room doors as I tried on one dress after another. One was too tight, another too frilly, and one was... well, let's just say it looked better on the hanger. With each wrong choice, Sam's playful commentary made me forget my hatred for shopping a little more. It was like we were in our little world, and I found myself enjoying... shopping? Even if I was skeptical that we'd find something that I loved.

Shop number four. I was exhausted, and I wondered when Sam would reach his breaking point. But somehow, he continued to keep up his good spirits while mine began to dampen. "This one?" He presented a dress so frilly it could have served as a fancy lampshade.

I burst out laughing. "Perfect, if we're crashing a royal tea party in Wonderland."

He tweaked my nose playfully with his finger. "Keep an open mind, Lila."

Then came a neon-green nightmare that made me squint. "For when I'm undercover as a highlighter?"

Sam chuckled, holding it against himself. "Or not so undercover. You're right. This outfit is more my color."

"Seriously? *That's* your color?" I shook my head in amazement as I imagined him wearing anything that obnoxiously bright.

He shrugged his shoulders. "There's so much more for you to learn about me," he teased.

I thought about that as I sifted through the racks, looking for anything that stood out. I wondered how many layers he had, and what more I would find.

Sam interrupted my thoughts. "What about this one?" he suggested, holding out a simple black dress with a flowing skirt.

Skeptical but curious, I took it to the dressing room. It was perfect—comfortable yet elegant, and I could definitely eat a meal without worrying about the seams bursting.

When I stepped out to show Sam, his reaction was priceless. His usual confidence was replaced with genuine awe. "Wow, Lila. You're... breathtaking."

His words sent another warm glow through me. Twirling in the mirror, I saw not just a woman in a dress, but someone vibrant and alive. "I actually love it. And I can move in it!" *And I looked amazing*. I kept that thought to myself.

"That's the one, then. You'll be the star of the gala," Sam said, and something in his tone made me believe him.

I twirled again, the dress flowing around me. "I feel like a different person in this."

"I see the same gorgeous woman," Sam said softly.

As the salesclerk announced the astronomical price, I turned to Sam. "That's too much. I can't ask you to pay for this. Even if it is a loan. Let's keep looking."

"Absolutely not. And don't you worry about it. It's worth it. You're worth it. I insist, and I don't want you to pay me back."

There it was. I felt the start of a swoon. Was I that simple? Was the act of someone spoiling me and complimenting me enough to make me fall? Or was it more than just those magical words? His treatment of me today was unlike anything I'd ever experienced, and I wanted more. But were my feelings truly for Sam or for the circumstances?

Does it matter? He wants to take you to this gala, and you have to have a dress. It doesn't mean you're betrothed. You can pay him back.

As we left the boutique, dress in tow, Sam reached for my hand. I caught his eye and a wave of excitement fluttered up and through my body. Shopping, which I'd always loathed, had turned into an adventure. And Sam... there was a silliness to him I hadn't expected, a side of him that made me laugh and feel light. I wondered if maybe, just maybe, there was more to us than I'd thought.

"Thursday night is going to be great. You'll see. We're going to have fun. I'm going to introduce you to some influential people. And when those donations start rolling in, you'll realize just how worth it this awful day was."

I squeezed his hand back, smiling. "As long as I don't have to wear high heels, I'm ready for anything."

Sam grinned. "Deal. No high heels."

"And Sam?"

"Yes?"

"It wasn't an awful day. You made it entertaining. Thank you."

He reached toward me and tucked a loose strand of hair behind my ear. "I enjoyed every minute of it."

Now. Kiss me now. I finally felt the pull, the urge, the desire. But Sam turned and walked toward the car. I'd just experienced my very own version of *Pretty Woman*, without, you know, being a prostitute. Happiness flowed through me.

I booted up my computer with the intention of emailing Callie and filling her in on all the details. But when I opened my email, the first message was from Philippe.

Subject: See you Friday?

Hi Lila!

I'm looking forward to seeing you in a few days! My flight details, again, just in case. Air France, arriving at 4:40 p.m., Friday, Reagan National. Clothing - optional. ;-)

Xo,

Philippe

GUILT SPREAD THROUGH ME. He was flirting. What did he expect might happen between us? Was he just kidding or was he expecting some weird fling? Should I nip any flirting with Philippe in the bud? I didn't want to lead him on.

Was I cheating on Sam if I hung out with Philippe? Were Sam and I even to the stage where one of us could even cheat on the other? We'd been on two dates, one of which didn't even really count because it was shopping (but he had just bought me a really expensive dress!). But we'd barely kissed (that light peck the first night did *not* count) and I was quite certain he didn't consider me his girlfriend. But we had another date Thursday and he'd certainly asked enough questions to indicate that it could lead somewhere. I was so new to all of this! I needed Callie's advice, stat. But she was 5,000 miles away and unlikely to respond quickly.

I called Amy before I worked myself into a state of hyperventilation.

"Wait, what? Slow down. Who is Sam? He bought you a *dress?* And you never mentioned you have *feelings* for Philippe?" She chuckled.

I filled in the missing details. Ending with, "And it's a *loan.*"

"This is so unlike you, and so, very, very *fun!*"

"Amy, not helpful! What should I do?"

"Well first, I recommend replying to Philippe, so he's not stressed about showing up to DC alone."

Surprised that Amy would place the feelings of a stranger as the top priority, I realized she was right. While this wasn't his first trip to the US (thank you, non-wedding) it could be really overwhelming visiting a foreign country. Yes, he lived in Paris and was used to big city life. Yes, he spoke enough English to get by. But all those things could be true and he could still be nervous about the trip.

As Amy and I chatted on the phone, I paced my living room, careful not to get the long cord wrapped around a piece of furniture.

"Or maybe the little devil's not nervous at all and he is just trying to scheme a way into your pants."

I stopped pacing. There she was. That was the Amy I knew and loved.

"Not helpful, Ames." I thought for a moment. But what if she was right? "I don't think that's the case. I feel like maybe he's just being funny. Or maybe hiding behind email gives him courage. Or maybe..."

"Maybe he's actually into you and is using comic relief to feel the waters?"

Damn, she was insightful.

"But what do I do?" I begged for advice.

"Enjoy the ride, Lila! I don't believe you're ready to jump into anything committed at this point. Neither guy has proposed marriage, so keep your options open, and see what happens. Don't close the door on anything right now."

Could I do that?

"First, I'm not sure Philippe is trying to do anything except give a whirl at being a funny, flirty guy." Even though I thought

Amy was right and I actually thought it sounded fun, I wasn't sure if I could even pull off trying to date two guys. If that was even what was happening. Philippe might have been drunk when he replied to my email and was now desperately wishing there was some way to retract his statement.

"Well, there you have it! Don't try to assume anything is happening and have fun. You deserve it."

She was right, obviously. But I also didn't want to lead anyone on or hurt anyone.

As if she could read my thoughts, Amy said, "You're not leading anyone on at this point, Lila, because Philippe is basically a nonstarter, and Sam has never said he's looking for a girlfriend. Just a date to a gala for which he probably doesn't want to show up alone."

Ouch. I hoped that wasn't true, but considering his flirty nature at the gym, and the way he talked about his father, it was entirely possible that I could be someone people would approve of. Or maybe he liked me and just wanted to help me make connections. "But he bought me a dress!" I whined.

"It's a dress, not an engagement ring, Lila. Don't be Callie."

"What's that mean?" I shot back.

"I'm not insulting Callie. I just mean, I seem to recall a conversation you and I had that you were surprised she wanted to move so quickly into marriage, and that wasn't your style."

Point taken. I loved Callie deeply, but Amy was right. I was in no hurry to find myself on the road to marriage again. I'd never really been single as an adult, and this was a chance for me to explore my options. With no guilt, no preconceived notions, and certainly not because I owed anything to anyone but myself.

"I'm proud of you, Lila. This is a big leap from the girl who was drinking wine like water and on a mission to eat everything chocolate within a fifty-mile radius."

"Hey now!" My tone was light. She was right. I was getting back on my feet and there was no need for me to put a label on anyone or anything.

I hung up the phone and sent a quick reply to Philippe.

Re: See you Friday?

Hi Philippe!

I'll see you then!

Bisous,

Lila

15

IT WAS GALA DAY! Which meant Philippe would arrive tomorrow. Which event was I more excited about? Unzipping the garment bag hanging in my closet, I delicately fingered the material of the dress. The thought of wearing the soft, elegant fabric excited me. Surprising.

But first, I had a full day of work. No gym this morning. Too many preparations to be made for my introduction to high society. High energy rock music set the mood as I dressed.

It was going to be a good day!

"Ready to make us some money, Lila?" my boss cheerfully called out as I entered the office. He waggled his eyebrows in my direction.

I giggled. "I'll see what I can do."

He insisted I leave work early so I had plenty of time to get ready. He jammed a stack of notecards in my hand at the elevator door. "Cue cards, just in case you aren't sure what to say, or how to ask. And the key people you should try to talk to, with a few notes. Read these over." He patted me on the shoulder. "And Lila, this crowd can be slimy."

The fatherly protection was a new side of Tom Clark, the "nothing but business" man I'd worked for over a year. He resembled a mama bird, waiting for her chick to take first flight. I smiled. "I'm all over this."

"Hiring you was the best decision I've ever made."

Stunned, I nodded. "Thank you for these." I held the cards out in front of me. "I'll be prepared. This mission means a lot to me, too."

He nodded and turned away, leaving me standing in front of the elevator. As I flipped through the cards, his thoroughness impressed me. He had hobbies, names of children, last major donation made, and other key details about the biggest potential donors expected to attend the party. I studied the cards on my Metro ride home, and hoped I'd be able to retain the key details.

Amy waited for me at the entry to my building. I knew I would need help with my hair and makeup. I pulled out my barely used set of rollers and the two of us got to work.

"Man, you have a lot of hair!"

"I probably should cut it one of these days."

"Don't you dare!" Amy insisted. "Many women would kill to have long, thick, silky black hair like this."

Once all the rollers were in, I sat on a chair at the small round table in the breakfast nook for Amy to play makeup artist. "Not too much!" I insisted. "I don't want to look like a clown or a hooker."

Amy paused her application of eye shadow. "Thanks for the overwhelming vote of confidence."

"I trust you, I just wanted to reaffirm we agree."

"Got it. No hooker makeup. Just a slight transformation of a hipster gal to a modern, elegant woman. Piece of cake!"

Once finished, she handed me the mirror. "Wow, I look... *different*." I admired my face from a number of angles. "Amy, this is really nice." She'd given me a soft, smoky eye and chosen a very natural shade of light pink gloss for my lips. "I should wear makeup more often!"

Amy nodded. "You look incredible! Now, hair up or down? Let me see your dress."

Amy followed me to the closet and oohed and whistled when I pulled it out. "Definitely an up-do, so we can show off your gorgeous neckline." She touched the spaghetti straps and admired the moderately plunging V-neck. Then she flipped the price tag. "Holy monkey balls, Lila. This dress was $800!"

"I know," I said sheepishly. And I dreaded the idea of paying it back, but this dress was incredible.

"Who is this guy?"

"Come to think of it, I still don't even know his last name. How weird is that? I'm wearing a dress he bought for me—correction, bought on loan for me—and he's just 'Sam no last name.' He's in consulting and lobbying and apparently makes decent money. Not that that's the most important thing, obviously, but it would be nice to be spoiled for a change and not the one footing all the bills."

Amy nodded emphatically. "Well, if he said it would be a loan, maybe he just really wants the opportunity to take you on a fancy date? I don't know what it's like to be so wealthy you can just bestow gifts on people, but do you think he has expectations based on the gifts?"

I pursed my lips. "I don't think so. I mean, no more than any other person assumes that dating will lead to that. So far, he's been the perfect gentleman," I said. But now I worried about whether Amy was right. Would he assume I owed him? I should have thought all of this through.

Sensing my concern, Amy reached out and cupped my chin. "Hey. Don't stress about it. You're a strong woman. Don't drink too much, try not to flirt too hard, and don't go home with him."

I nodded. Sam had given me no indication that I would "owe him" for the dress, but maybe I was just naive.

"Chair please," Amy ordered.

Thirty hair tuggings and a ton of extra-hold hairspraying later, Amy completed her masterpiece. "Ta da!"

"Wow." She'd done it. She'd completely transformed me. My hair was pulled up in a twist with tendrils framing my face. "I look even better than I did on my wedding day."

"You've got to impress to get those big donors! And yes, you're beautiful, Lila."

I admired myself once more before having Amy assist me with pulling the dress over my hair.

"Here are the shoes you requested," she said, handing me a pair. I smiled at her. It was convenient to have the same size foot so I didn't have to buy a new pair of shoes.

"These are perfect." They had a slight wedge, so they weren't flats, but they weren't a heel either. And they were sexy.

"Also, I figured you might need this." She pulled a lovely wrap out of her bag.

"You thought of everything! I certainly didn't and I would have been freezing all evening."

Throwing the wrap over my shoulders, I grabbed my clutch purse and made sure I had my ID, keys, some cash, and my lip gloss. Amy and I exited the building together as Sam pulled up in a limo. A limo? Seriously?

Amy whistled. "You're in for a Cinderella night, my friend. Just don't lose one of my shoes! And you've already had one dramatic departure from a building, so maybe let's avoid that tonight?" She winked, hugged me, and we both laughed at her offbeat joke about my wedding day.

Amy waved at Sam, who was emerging from the limo.

Wow. Frozen in place, I could barely breathe at the sight of him in his tuxedo. His hair was slicked back, and the cut of the suit hugged his body closely. Flames shot across my cheeks and my heart somersaulted a time or two. Who said there was no chemistry?

"You look amazing," Sam stated, eyeing me up and down. "This is, wow."

My cheeks warmed at his compliments, and I curtsied, which made him laugh. I smiled, batting my eyelashes slightly, enjoying the admiration. "Thank you. Amy is responsible for this." I briefly introduced Amy to Sam, and Sam assisted me into the car.

"You don't look so bad yourself," I said. And that was an understatement. The "James Bond effect" of a tuxedo caused flutters throughout my body. Was I starting to feel things for him?

Deciding to heed Amy's advice and let the evening play out, I sat back and accepted a glass of champagne from him. I sipped slowly, not wanting the alcohol to impair my ability to speak coherently to potential important connections and avoid making bad decisions.

We arrived at the hotel and entered the ballroom, which was filling quickly with men and women dressed in their finest. Some of Washington, DC's richest people were in attendance this evening. I looked around and did my Who's Who count of people in the room. There were senators and House members, their spouses, some DC socialites, and even a few celebrities.

I looked over and nudged Sam. "Is that Christine Galloway?" A gorgeous blonde woman with her hair pulled up wore a short, red cocktail dress that fit so well, it looked airbrushed on. Her bold red lip matched her outfit perfectly.

She displayed an enviable sense of self-confidence, standing among a group of male admirers.

He nodded his head. "Yes, apparently she is very much into the social justice scene. And she was really pleased with the legislation that Senator Brown has been pushing forward for more access to mental health resources for children. She's really been in his ear about gun control too, especially after the events in Colorado."

I nodded my head. We'd all been completely devastated after the shootings at Columbine High School. "Good for her!" It was sad that it took Hollywood's finest to cajole our elected officials into doing the right thing, but hopefully she'd make progress.

"Would you like a drink?" Sam asked, leading me toward the bar area. His hand, gently placed on the small of my back, filled me with a sense of security. I'd always loved that move when I saw it in movies.

"I would love a glass of champagne." I could continue to sip without getting too buzzed. I needed the boost of courage in this room of one percenters. We walked to the bar and as I sipped my champagne, I blinked in surprise as Christine waved in our direction and began walking our way. I glanced behind us, assuming she was waving at someone else, but she sauntered right up to us.

She halted in front of Sam. "Hello, Sam," she said, leaning forward to give him a kiss on the cheek. She lingered longer than I deemed appropriate and left a lipstick stain on his cheek. "I wondered if I'd see you here. I assumed your daddy would be here but wasn't sure about you."

Daddy? Who exactly was Sam?

"Christine." Sam acknowledged her. "I'd like to introduce you to my *date*, Lila." His tense emphasis on the word 'date' made it clear there was some sort of history I'd have to ask about later.

"How lovely to meet you, Lila," Christine drawled, giving me a head to toe once over, making me feel like I was back in high school, my worthiness being assessed by the cool kids.

"Lila works for WaterCorps and would love to connect with people interested in supporting their mission of clean water for everyone and initiatives for women in destitute situations. I think you two would hit it off!"

"Is that right?" Christine asked.

I nodded. "We've got some really exciting programs in the works that will really make a difference to these communities globally."

Christine nodded. "That's great. I'm focusing more on domestic issues right now, but I wish you the best of luck. See you around, Sam?" she asked, before turning and making her way toward another group.

"Well that didn't go too well," I muttered. "And what's the story there?"

"She and I once had a very short fling. Nothing serious." He paused, grabbed my hands, and looked straight into my eyes. "Don't worry about her. She's not the person you need in your pocket right now anyway." And with that, he grabbed my hand and escorted me to a group of gentlemen I recognized from the Hill.

Despite the rocky start, the evening couldn't have been better. Sam was the perfect gentleman. He introduced me to some of DC's most influential donors, several key senators and House representatives, and I filled my clutch with business cards and promises for follow up conversations. I also finally learned Sam's last name, Harrison, and why he could afford a limo and the gorgeous dress I was wearing. The Harrisons were one of the most affluent families in Washington, DC. Samuel

Harrison, Sam's father, had inherited his money from *his* father, an oil tycoon out of Texas. With bigger aspirations, Samuel had moved to DC after college and established a tech company. It was rumored that he had his money in the pockets of several key politicians. So when Sam told me he was a lobbyist, I now understood what that meant. My stomach churned a bit at the idea of them essentially buying votes for their benefit, but over the course of the evening, he seemed legitimately interested in supporting environmental initiatives and WaterCorps.

Eventually, we crossed paths with his father. Samuel's lingering gaze on my cleavage made me squirm. Sam was the spitting image of his father, who carried himself like a giant. And he was. It was clear he owned half of the room.

"Dad, this is Lila Thurston."

"Thurston, huh? Who's your father?"

Was this what rich people did? I guess so. Trying to ignore the sweat gathering on my palms as I endured this interrogation, I lifted my chin and stated confidently, "Nick Thurston. Retired Colonel, USMC, and current defense contractor."

"I don't believe I've ever crossed paths with him, but *Semper Fi*. Now, if you'll excuse me, I need to catch Senator Brown before he leaves." And he rushed off.

My cheeks flamed. "Did I just fail a test?" I asked Sam.

His eyes followed his father, a look blended with disappointment and concern. He turned back to me and forced a smile. "No, no. You're fine. That's just my dad. Work always comes first."

"Why didn't you tell me who you are?" I asked.

"What do you mean?" he asked. "I've told you a lot about me."

"But you never told me you're famous."

"Famous?" He laughed out loud. "I would hardly call

myself famous. My dad just happens to have a lot of money and spends a lot to sway things in his direction, so naturally people know our name. It's annoying so I try to lay low. I certainly don't want my family name to be the first topic of discussion, especially with women that I'm interested in."

"Fair enough," I replied. I imagined many women had tried to date him solely because of his family name, and the fact that I apparently had no idea who he was may have been very appealing.

But a niggling concern tickled my brain. Was I good enough for his family? Would they accept me? I'd never dated someone rich and famous, but I'd learned from watching lots of TV and reading Danielle Steel books that generally super wealthy parents weren't thrilled when their child chose a match that wasn't of the same pedigree.

As if he could read my thoughts, he wrapped an arm around my shoulders and said sincerely, "You are the perfect date for me."

I lifted my head up toward him and smiled. "You've been an exceptional date this evening, Sam Harrison. You've made tonight a success for me. Tom's going to be thrilled with the connections I've made tonight!"

"Good," Sam whispered, and kissed me softly.

It was a quick kiss so as not to arouse any sensationalism, but it left my lips burning. I'd worry about Sam's family if it ever got to that point. For now, this moment was absolutely perfect. And while Amy was right, I didn't have to make any decisions right now, my lips certainly wanted to explore this relationship further.

Before I got too lost in my steamy imagination, I refocused myself. There was still work to be done. "Sam, I'm going to go over and talk to Congressman Richards for a minute. He's been supportive of WaterCorps in the past, and I'd like to get his opinion on some things that we're doing."

Sam nodded at me. He leaned in and kissed me softly on the cheek. "Don't be gone too long," he whispered, his lips grazing my ear. "I'll miss you."

Chills shot up and down my spine and I already looked forward to returning to him.

My conversation with Congressman Richards went well. I don't know if it was the borrowed credibility of being here with Sam, or a new confidence that the evening had given me, but he accepted an invitation to a more formal meeting. Pleased with my efforts, I made my way across the room to where Sam was standing at the bar. He'd been watching me and moved in my direction.

"Wanna dance?" The formal part of the evening turned into fun as couples made their way to the floor.

"I do!" I agreed. And my Prince Charming, at least for the evening, whisked me into his embrace.

16

Sam certainly knew how to dance, but now that I knew more about his upbringing, that wasn't surprising. Sam led me around the floor gracefully, and occasionally he threw in a silly dance move, causing me to laugh. By 11 p.m., the crowd was dwindling, so Sam called for the limo. I shivered a bit as we waited for the car, pulling my wrap tighter around my shoulders and then Sam did the thing we all love in our romance movies. He took off his tuxedo jacket and wrapped it gently around my shoulders. I looked up at him and smiled. The quiet of the night enveloped us, and while we waited in silence, it was comfortable.

"I had an amazing time tonight," Sam said, his voice low, filled with a warmth that made me tuck into the crook of his arm a little tighter. My heart was still dancing to a rhythm set by the evening's excitement, and Sam squeezed me, warming me a little more.

He hesitated for a moment, then added, "I... I really want to see where this could go, Lila. With us."

His words, sincere and hopeful, sparked a flurry of

emotions within me. This was what every girl wanted, right? The hot young millionaire who, for some reason decided I was the girl he wanted? Thoughts bounced around in my head, jumping from a fear of jumping into anything serious too soon to wondering what life would be like dating a guy like Sam. And finally, my thoughts landed on Philippe.

I hated to admit it, but I'd actually liked the idea that Amy planted of dating around. After such a long relationship with Matt, I wasn't certain if I even wanted to be in a serious relationship. But I didn't know if I knew how to just date casually. And if I was dating someone regularly, I didn't think I could have more than one beau. Part of me wanted to dive into the possibility of "us" to explore the depth of what I was beginning to feel for Sam. But the little devil on my shoulder wondered if Philippe and I might want to explore something, let's say, fun and uncommitted, while he was in town. That didn't seem very Philippe, and honestly, it wasn't very *me* either, but I had just gotten left at the altar, and I was open to exploring new things. But was it worth potentially disrupting what I had just started with Sam?

The angel on one shoulder yelled at me for even thinking about playing with two different guys' hearts. The devil on the other shoulder, who looked surprisingly like Amy, reminded me that I could in fact explore options without having to commit to anyone.

"Lila?" Sam asked, and I realized I'd never responded.

Lifting my eyes to meet his expectant gaze, I murmured, "I had a wonderful time tonight too. You're the perfect date."

"But?" he asked.

The limo pulled up as I thought about what to say next. "No 'but,'" I replied. "I'd like to see you again too. And we'll see what happens."

Sam's gaze, so full of questions and hope, met mine, and

without thinking, I leaned in, our lips meeting in a kiss that was gentle yet full of unspoken promises. His lips were soft and warm, and his tongue moved softly, luring me in for more. My knees went weak, and I sunk into Sam. The kiss was not urgent in nature, but gentle, and his movements matched mine perfectly. As far as kisses went, this one ranked very high. I'd like to do that more.

Pulling back, I caught the look in Sam's eyes—surprise, happiness, a hint of something deeper. It was a look that made me question everything, including my anticipation of Philippe's visit. Could what I felt for Sam eclipse the crush I had on Philippe? The thought was both thrilling and terrifying. Because my will to date around was starting to falter after that kiss.

He opened the door to the limo. "After you," he said.

I climbed in, thankful for the warmth. Sidling up right next to me, he placed his hand on my thigh and moved in for another kiss. I was grateful for the privacy window in the limo as our hands explored each other and our kisses deepened. The soft kisses became more urgent. The car pulled to a stop, and I realized we'd already made it back to my apartment.

Sam released me from his grasp, opened the door and stepped out. He reached his hand in to help me out, and I slowly climbed from the limousine. The cool night washed away the heat from our passionate exchange, bringing me back to reality, and as I stood on the sidewalk, my hand in his, a whirlwind of unexpected emotions encircled me. Confusion, fear, happiness, lust. I longed to invite him in and spend the night together. I missed intimacy. But I also knew I wasn't ready to move forward that fast.

"Sam, tonight was wonderful," I began, my voice steady despite the tumult inside me. I saw a flicker of hope in his eyes. "I just need to take things slow."

Sam nodded. Understanding, albeit mixed with disappointment, flashed across his features. "I get it, Lila. I'm not asking for any promises. Just a chance to figure out... whatever it is between us."

I smiled, touched by his patience and sincerity. "I'd like that, Sam. I'm looking forward to more time with you. But for now, it's been a long night, and I'm tired." I dropped his hand and stepped toward my building. Looking back over my shoulder at Sam, I added, "Thank you, for everything."

Sam reached for my hand, pulling me back to him. "I can move slowly for you, Lila, you're worth it. But I can't wait to see you again. Are you free tomorrow?"

My heart raced again. I almost said yes, when I remembered Philippe. "Actually, I'm not. My friend is coming in from France, and I promised to show him around."

His eyes darkened and he dropped my hands. "Him?"

"Yes, Philippe. He's my best friend's husband's best friend. Wow, that's a mouthful! You should meet him this weekend!" Why was I saying so many words and so fast and why for the love of Pete had I just invited him to meet Philippe?

Sam nodded. "I'll call you Saturday." He leaned in and placed one more deliciously soft kiss on my lips before ducking back into the limo.

The limo pulled away, leaving me standing alone, the night suddenly quiet around me. The excitement of the night, the make out session and warmth of Sam's kisses, the anticipation of Philippe's visit—and now the anxiety of them both being in the same place at the same time—all swirled together in my mind. A mix of emotions and possibilities.

Well, this had suddenly gotten complicated. While I basked in the afterglow of my evening with Sam, anxiety coursed through me about Philippe's arrival tomorrow. Sam had shown me a side of him I hadn't expected, one that was silly, kind, and genuinely interested in me.

My thoughts whirred too loudly for me to even think about sleeping, so I sat down at my desk and logged onto my email.

Subject: Confused

Hi Callie,

The gala went so well tonight. Sam was the perfect gentleman and he's a fun date. He showed up in a limo! Get this—he's the son of a millionaire! What the heck? He introduced me to so many people, we danced, and he's so much fun!

And... he kissed me.

He's a great kisser, but I'm really confused right now. He wants to see me again, and I want to see him too. But I'm not sure if I'm ready to jump into a relationship right now. And while the kissing was, well, pretty much perfection, I didn't feel what I thought I would when we kissed.

Should I have all the butterflies after just one date? Was that the way it was for you and Julien? Did it take some time before you warmed up to him physically? I mean, things moved pretty fast for you... he flew home to the States with you after just four days after all! But did you know the first time you kissed him? I just feel like I should've felt more.

Maybe I'm just tired. I was working all evening, and that took a lot of energy, meeting these important people. Maybe I'm just scared?

Sorry for all the questions! I'm just dipping my foot back in the dating pool and finding it to be more confusing than I thought it would be. Not because I have any remaining feelings for Matt. That's in my past. But I wonder how I'm supposed to feel. Matt and I were together for so long, and we didn't really "date"—we just kind of fell into a serious relationship after the first time we went out.

I don't know what I'm supposed to feel right now, or if I'm supposed to just keep going out with Sam until it turns into something more?

Any advice is welcome.

Love you.

Lila

I AVOIDED any mention of the role Philippe played in my confusion. Callie was my closest friend, but I did not want her to worry about me hurting Philippe, or worse, be disappointed if she thought we might actually get together. No need to muddy all those waters now.

One thing was clear. Sam had expressed an intention to continue dating. While we did not say anything about dating or not dating anyone else, it certainly felt like he was interested in something more than just being casual. Which meant I needed to close the door on flirting with Philippe and make it clear that we were just friends, in case our emails had given him any other impression. It wasn't fair to anyone involved to do anything else.

Was I overthinking all of this? Was it possible to just get out of my head and have some fun for a change?

I turned off the computer and slipped out of the gorgeous dress, hanging it back in my closet. After removing all my makeup and hairpins, I finally crawled into bed. The events of the night replayed in my mind. Sam had been fun, and I could definitely imagine continuing to date him. However, as sleep finally claimed me, my last thought was not of Sam, but of Philippe in the marketplace, with tomatoes squished all over him.

17

Thankfully my boss had given me Friday off, so I slept in, skipping the gym.

There was something magical about taking time off when everyone else is working. I tried to relax, but as the clock ticked down for my departure to the airport to meet Philippe, I couldn't sit still. I cleaned my bathroom, straightened my living room, and even made my bed, maybe for the first time other than when I changed the sheets. If Philippe came over to see my place, I didn't want him to think I was a total mess.

And why are you worried about what Philippe thinks if you're just friends? Shouldn't you be thinking about straightening up for when Sam sees the place?

After the apartment was satisfactorily straightened, I logged into my computer.

A message from Callie waited.

Re: Confused

Lila!

Who cares how things are going for me (great, by the way!)—you went on a DATE!!!!!! I'm so excited and happy for you.

The first few guys I met after Vic did not excite me. (Remember Luca??) I don't know if it was the romance of being in Paris on New Year's Eve when I met Julien, or if it was just something I knew deep down, but from the moment I laid my eyes on him, there was something different. Maybe it was the alcohol, maybe it was the excitement of a new year, a new century, but when his lips touched mine, the explosions that happened inside me paralleled the fireworks display on the Eiffel Tower. I never wanted my lips to touch anyone else's after that moment. But don't give up hope! My parents have been married, happily, for almost thirty years, and my mom told me it took her two or three dates before she started to fall for my dad. If you like Sam, explore it. And if you don't feel more after a couple of dates, then you can reassess.

I love you and hope you have fun with Philippe. He's excited to see you!

XO,

Callie

NATURALLY, Callie was right. Physically, there were no issues at all. Emotionally, we were building something that might turn into something real. We had no problems communicating and had plenty of common interests. There was no need to put a label on it or overanalyze my feelings this early.

For now, I needed to get ready to meet Philippe. I changed

my outfit three times, finally settling on my favorite cream corduroys and a light-blue V-neck sweater. Hair up, hair down? Hair partly up and partly down? A low ponytail won out. I applied minimal mascara and some lip gloss. I left my apartment and locked the door, my hands shaking so much that I dropped my keys three times before successfully turning the key.

If my mind was settled on Sam, why was I this worked up about seeing Philippe?

I arrived at the airport with plenty of time in case his flight was early. The stress of flying alone into a foreign country could be overwhelming, especially since it was still just months after 9/11. I wanted to be there to meet him as soon as he got to baggage claim.

Thankfully he'd have already cleared customs in New York, so the wait shouldn't be too bad. While I waited, I went to the bathroom twice, reapplied my lip gloss, checked the board at least seven times to make sure I had the right baggage claim, and sipped on water to quell the anxiety gnawing at my stomach. The loud beeping of the baggage claim belt made me jump, and I watched as bags started to appear. But still no Philippe.

As more passengers grabbed their bags from the belt, the anxiety that I had somehow missed him increased. Finally, I saw him. He smiled. Wiping my sweaty palms on my corduroys, I tried to dampen a smile that must have shown every single one of my teeth.

Flip flop. Why was it that the harder I tried to suppress these feelings, the more my body responded to him?

He reached me and leaned in for the awkward exchange of kisses. No matter how many times I performed this ritual, it always felt weird.

Mmm, he smells good. Stop it! "How was your flight?" I asked, trying to behave normally.

He let out a sigh. "It was packed and noisy. I was able to nap a little bit on the flight to New York, but this last flight had a family with a bunch of small children, and they were very excited to be on the plane." Philippe laughed as he ran his fingers through his tousled hair.

Resisting the urge to reach out and run my fingers through his hair, which looked so soft, I turned and led him to the baggage claim. While we waited for his luggage to appear, I filled him in on the plans for the evening. His face fell a little when he found out we'd be dropping his bags at his hotel and going out to meet my colleagues. "You'll love them. They are a fun bunch!"

"I'm just a bit tired," he admitted.

"Listen, the cure for jetlag is to push through! It may already be 11 p.m. *chez toi*, however, it's only 5 p.m. here. We haven't even reached the dinner hour! You'll get on this time zone faster if you stay up until at least 10 p.m." I just kept talking.

He nodded, his expression conveying that he didn't fully believe me, but wasn't going to argue.

We gathered his bag and took the Metro from the airport. I asked him all the typical questions. Did he sleep? What movie did he watch? How was the food?

I tried to concentrate on his answers, but truthfully, the buzzing in my ears was so loud I could barely hear the words he spoke. Soon the trains were crowded with rush hour traffic, so we couldn't hear that well anyway.

Philippe's hotel was near Dupont Circle, which made it convenient to get from the airport via the Metro.

We climbed out of the Metro and walked the short

distance. As we entered the hotel, we were blasted by the warm air blower, designed to keep the cold air out of the hotel lobby. "Oof," he grunted, dragging his suitcase into the lobby while pulling his jacket off. I had a flashback to the last time we'd entered a hotel together. Hard to believe that was only four months ago.

I waited patiently on one of the couches in the lobby while he checked in and then quickly went up to his room to deposit his bags. He returned about fifteen minutes later, hair wet and clean clothes on. He looked a little more awake. It was truly unfair that guys could shower and change so fast.

Also, he looked hot.

Shut up, Lila. You're just friends. Tomorrow you're introducing him to the guy you've just started dating. But the truth was he looked really good in his black jeans, blue shirt, black-and-white Adidas sneakers, and the *pièce de résistance*, his wet hair. My imagination drifted to what a shower with Philippe would be like.

Lila!

I self-consciously tucked my hair behind my ears. Something seemed different about him. He seemed more confident, more at ease.

"Sorry for making you wait so long," he apologized breathlessly.

"Ha! You have no idea how long that would have taken some of my friends! That was lightning fast."

He gave me a half smile that seemed to sear my insides. *Stop this, Lila! It's Philippe!*

I smiled shyly and told him where we were going. "There's no Metro to Georgetown, and the fastest way will be by cab," I explained, as I hailed a taxi.

"I don't have any cash yet."

"Don't worry about it, Philippe, this is on me. And we'll look for an ATM while we're out."

"Well, thanks. This has all been really nice of you to do." He gave me a look that made my heart clench again.

Desperately trying to play it cool, I shrugged my shoulders. "I owe you for the time you spent with me in Paris." I stated, a little flatly.

Disappointment registered on his face, and I realized he might think I was only hanging out with him from a sense of obligation. Before I could say anything else, he waved his hand, indicating I didn't owe him anything.

"My colleagues and I like to hang out in Georgetown because so many staffers from the Hill—that's what we call the place all of our elected officials work—come here. It's always good to have friends in the right places when you work for the types of companies we do, right?"

He nodded in agreement, fully immersed in the sites we were passing by.

Traffic was heavy, typical for a Friday night, and it took a little longer to get to Georgetown than it usually did. Entering our favorite spot, I saw my colleagues crammed around a table and was relieved that there were two open seats. Allison saw me first and waved us over. Perhaps it was my imagination, but I thought I saw her give Philippe a lengthy stare, checking him out from head to toe. Why did that bother me?

Before going to the table, Philippe went to the restroom, and I went to the bar to order our drinks. It was packed, and sometimes table service could be a little sketchy. Squeezing my way between the barstools, I ordered a dirty martini and a beer for Philippe. A guy in a suit stood next to me and I avoided eye contact, not wanting to spark up any conversations.

"So you like it dirty, huh?" he asked, raising his glass to mine as I picked up the drinks, clinking them together lightly.

"Excuse me?" What a random thing to say to a stranger.

"Er, your martini. I heard you order it extra dirty."

"So you thought that was an invitation?" I replied, with no hint of kindness or suggestion.

"Well, you're here on your own, you're not bad looking, and you're ordering the type of drink that says you might be looking for some fun tonight." His words slurred a tiny bit and he practically fell into me.

"Woah," I said, steadying him before backing up. "That would be a no," I replied. "And I'm not alone. I mean, I won't be in a minute." I turned toward the bathrooms, praying Philippe would be back soon.

"Well I can keep you company 'til he gets here," he said, leaning in again. The overpowering smell of his cheap cologne nearly made my eyes water.

Why did guys think girls were just waiting for them to swoop in and hit on us? I was definitely not dressed in a manner that screamed *I'm looking to pick you up tonight*. I'd just been minding my own business, waiting for my friend.

"I'm good." I replied, turning back to face the bar and setting the drinks down while I waited.

"Oh come on," he said, leaning in, stumbling again. I put my hands up in front of me, in case he fell into me.

"Hey babe. You doing okay?"

I recognized his voice and all my insides flipped completely around at the word *babe*. That was certainly not a physical response appropriate for a friend. Philippe rapidly placed himself between me and the other guy. Before I even had time to react, he leaned in and kissed me softly on the lips. *Mmm*. Minty. Wait, what had just happened? Why was Philippe kissing me?

I stood there, a bit stunned, as he turned to the other guy. "I'm here for my girl," he said.

"Yeah, well, I..."

We didn't wait to hear what else the guy had to say. I grabbed my drink, Philippe took the beer, and we turned to walk to the table with my friends.

"What was that?" I hissed. Why was I so angry at him? I didn't understand the mélange of feelings in me, but anger at Philippe for kissing me was easier than admitting I wanted more from where that came from.

Philippe's smile disappeared. "It looked like he was about to get handsy, and I don't know, I just thought pretending to be your boyfriend would help."

"I was handling myself just fine, thank you." The sharp tone was unpleasant even to my ears.

Philippe looked hurt. "Sorry," he mumbled, looking down. "It just seemed like 'no' would not stop that guy and I was worried he was going to knock you over."

"I'm sorry. I didn't mean to respond like that." I placed my hand on his arm. Sincerely, I said, "Thank you for rescuing me."

He smiled but it didn't reach his eyes, and I wondered if he was regretting kissing me, just tired from his trip, or nervous about spending an evening with strangers.

"This place is cool," he yelled over the music.

I nodded. "I come here almost every Friday night to meet up with my colleagues and friends. Pretty much everything on the menu is good, but I highly recommend the burgers," I said, trying to lighten the mood a little bit.

He spoke, but all I could see was his lips as I remembered how soft they'd felt on mine. How had I not noticed them before?

Allison stood as we approached and after introductions, insisted he sit at the chair next to her. She'd spent a semester in France and was just dying to connect with him. Philippe glanced at me, and I gave him a brief smile and nod, taking the other chair at the opposite end of the table.

I tried to focus on the discussion at my end, but my attention kept getting hijacked by the dynamics unfolding between Philippe and Allison. Every so often, she would casually place her hand on his arm, leaning in close, and laugh uproariously as if he had just told the world's most hilarious joke. The sight stirred an unsettling feeling in my stomach, an odd mix of annoyance and jealousy.

"Don't you agree, Lila?" The question snapped me back to my immediate surroundings.

I glanced sheepishly at the guy to my right, who clearly expected a response. Racking my brain for his name—he was a staffer for one of the more influential senators, and I should know this—but I came up empty. "Sure, that sounds right," I said, taking a sip of my drink and eating one of the fries from a shared basket on the table in front of me. Catching the eye of one of the girls from my office, Kate, I realized her expression displayed a mix of amusement and confusion. I wasn't sure what I just agreed to, but she found it entertaining.

"I'm heading to the ladies' room," she announced, looking pointedly at me. Seizing the opportunity to escape, I followed.

"What's going on with you, Lila? You seem miles away."

"To be honest, I'm not sure. Maybe it's just the exhaustion from a long week," I confessed, though I knew it was more than just fatigue clouding my focus.

Kate eyed me knowingly, then delicately probed, "This wouldn't have anything to do with Allison practically draping herself over Philippe, would it?" She raised an eyebrow in question.

"No! Absolutely not!" I responded, perhaps too quickly, my voice tinged with defensiveness.

"Okay," Kate replied, raising her hands up, suggesting she

wasn't entirely convinced. "But it's understandable if that bothers you. He is quite charming, and you've been laying low for a while now."

"Philippe and I are just friends," I insisted, though a part of me questioned whether I was trying to convince Kate or myself.

Kate looked at me thoughtfully, then countered, "That's not the impression I get."

"What do you mean? What kind of impression do you have?"

She leaned in, lowering her voice. "Well, I've noticed him stealing glances at you, too."

I waved my hand, dismissing her observation outright. "If anything, they might have been looks for help. He's had a long trip, his English isn't perfect, and trust me, it's exhausting to be thrust into a group of people talking quickly in their native tongue. And Allison can be, well... Allison." Yet, even as I spoke, doubt crept in. Was Kate observing something I was too stubborn to acknowledge? No, that path led to complications I wasn't ready to navigate, especially not with Philippe.

Kate's next words mirrored advice I'd once offered to Callie, echoing back at me with an ironic twist. "He's only here for a short time. Why not enjoy it? A few magical days with no strings attached could be just what you need."

She made a compelling argument, but my resolve held firm. Philippe and I had a history, albeit a platonic one, and if there was ever a window for something more, it had seemingly closed from his end. Even though he'd just kissed me. That was just for show to get me away from the drunk guy, right? And there was Sam. I wasn't going to wreck everything based on a whimsical suggestion. Based on the way I was physically responding to Philippe's presence, touch, and kiss, I suspected that if I allowed anything to happen between us, I'd hurt one or both of us. It was easier to just keep it platonic.

Returning to the table, the sight of Allison inching ever closer to him as they laughed about something made it more challenging to stick to my decision. I was admittedly jealous of Philippe's apparent ease in Allison's company, but I had made up my mind. I took my place at the other end of the table and turned so that I wouldn't see every time Allison put her hand on his arm or laughed at his jokes.

The bar got livelier as the night wore on, and I loosened up as I continued drinking. We ordered food and more drinks. After a lively debate with Jeremy (thankfully someone had finally said his name!) about the rights of women around the globe and whether the US should be so actively involved in helping, I checked the time. It was almost 9 p.m. and poor Philippe looked like his eyelids had weights pulling them down.

I stood and moved toward Philippe to see if he was ready to go. His relieved expression told me everything. Philippe and I said our goodbyes to everyone, and Allison pulled him into a tight hug, slipping a piece of paper in his hand. As we stepped out into the cool night air, I saw Philippe put the paper in the garbage.

Relief flooded through me, followed by a pang of guilt. Allison was my friend, after all.

Philippe yawned. "Your friends are lovely, but that was exhausting."

"I know exactly what you mean. Tomorrow, we can do some sightseeing, just the two of us, if you want?"

"That sounds great. We didn't really see much on the last trip." Then he turned to look out the window.

The cab ride back to his hotel was much faster without all the traffic, and neither of us said much. "I'll meet you in the lobby at 11 a.m., okay?"

He stepped out of the cab, his eyes heavy with fatigue, and

closed the door. He gave me a wave before entering the hotel. As the taxi pulled away and the city lights blurred past, I realized I hadn't thought about Sam all night. Nor did I feel guilty about that. There was something so freeing, and so unlike me, in letting things unfold in their own time and own way.

18

MY ALARM DIDN'T HAVE the chance to jar me out of sleep. I woke up early, struggling to make sense of my feelings. I'd realized somewhere in the middle of the night that I didn't want to invite Sam to join Philippe and me on our tour of the city today. That was completely contrary to everything I'd worked out with myself yesterday.

You're being an idiot, Lila.

I'll just see if he calls me and go from there. I guess this was the compromise I'd come up with. If Sam called, then we would obviously get together. If he didn't call, maybe that was a sign that I should spend the day with Philippe alone.

I met Philippe in his lobby. My stupid tell tale heart did a little jump for joy at the sight of him. *Seriously, Lila, what is your deal?*

He embraced me enthusiastically.

"Ready to explore the best of DC?" I asked, my nerves dancing at the edge of my voice.

"Lead the way," Philippe replied, his smile reaching his

eyes, and evoking that stupid fluttering sensation in my abdomen.

"I mean, it's not Paris, but it's a pretty cool city all the same."

We set out, flagging down a taxi to make things easy first thing in the morning, to one of my favorite places.

"Welcome to the National Mall," I said, as we approached the Lincoln Memorial. I loved just sitting on the steps and looking over the reflective pool toward the Washington Monument. As we ascended, I glanced at Philippe. Like a little kid on Christmas, his eyes were lit up, and seeing things through his perspective reignited my own sense of wonder.

"It's massive," he breathed out, his gaze sweeping from the towering figure of Lincoln to the inscriptions on the wall. Much as he'd done for me in Paris, I shared tidbits of history related to Lincoln and his achievements. We stood for a moment, looking out over the reflecting pool. Philippe had a lot of questions about the start of the Civil War and slavery, which I answered to the best of my ability before we wandered down the path to the Washington Monument, taking our time to stop at the Vietnam Memorial, and the World War II Memorial at the end of the reflecting pond. I enjoyed watching his facial expressions change throughout the tour. Curiosity, excitement, and other emotions. Something churned inside of me that I fought to suppress, but no matter how hard I tried, I could not stop the thoughts of what it would be like to explore the world with Philippe.

We stood looking toward the Washington Memorial. "Interesting facts about the Washington Monument. It was designed to look like an Egyptian obelisk, and until the Eiffel Tower was constructed, it was the tallest building in the world."

"Hmm," Philip looked up at the monument. "You know,

the French always must be first when it comes to phallic symbols."

I snorted laughing.

"Are you getting hungry?" I asked.

"Starving," he replied. "I'd love to see what you consider real American food." He raised his hands and twiddled his fingers together in front of his face, like a villain scheming up a plan.

I giggled at his silly gesture. "I think you got a good sampling the last time you were here, but I'll do my best to find even better stuff." An idea came to me. "Food trucks!"

"Food trucks?"

"Oh yes," I grinned devilishly, leading him toward Capitol Hill.

We found a good selection of trucks, and despite the variety of Tex Mex and other options, he chose a cheeseburger. After all, he explained, it was what the rest of the world considered "American cuisine." I had to admit that I'd certainly never turned down a good cheeseburger.

"Mmmmm," Philippe bit into the cheeseburger. "Way better than McDonald's."

"Obviously!" I snickered, grabbing a napkin to wipe the ketchup and mustard from his chin. My hand lingered a little longer than necessary, and he stopped chewing as his eyes found mine. We held the gaze for an uncomfortably long moment. As he moved his head a little closer, I became aware that my hand was still on his face. Snatching it away as if his skin had burned mine, I buried my face in my own burger. There was no doubt something had transpired between the two of us, and we'd both felt it. I think. But we continued eating, neither of us mentioning it.

After hours of walking and touring the most iconic sights—the Capitol Building, the US Botanic Garden, and finally taking a cab back to the lovely Georgetown area, we enjoyed some hot chocolate from a street vendor. Thankfully it wasn't as cold as it could be in mid-February, and today was actually perfect weather. We walked on with no particular destination before finding a bench next to a water feature in a park where we sat in comfortable silence, sipping on our drinks and taking in the sights around us.

Finally, Philippe turned to me. He stared intently at me for a moment, before reaching out and slowly pushing back a wisp of hair that had blown over my face. I caught my breath and held his gaze, afraid to move. His fingers were warm on my cheek, and I wanted nothing more than to lean into him, to hold him.

My body said *yes* to exploring this further while my heart and mind scrambled to build walls, wanting simultaneously to fall into him and also shove away and stand up, leaving him behind on the bench, wondering what just happened. This didn't make sense and a relationship between us couldn't end well. I had no intention of moving to Paris, and how could he move here? Even though Callie and Julien had managed to make it work, it had not always been an easy road for them.

As if he could sense my internal panic, he placed his hand on the nape of my neck, gently stroking under my ear. I released the air I'd been holding, tension dissipating as I leaned into his hand. Eyes closed, my imagination drifted to a place where we could run off happily into the sunset and there were no roadblocks to us falling in love.

My eyes popped open as reality set in. I stared directly into his eyes, seeking answers to questions I didn't dare to ask aloud. While I knew the best answer was to stand up and pretend like this moment had never happened, other questions ricocheted through my head. Should we kiss? Would we ruin the lovely friendship we were building? What was the point of starting something that could never come to fruition? Were either of us the type who could have a little fling that we picked up whenever we found ourselves in the same place? Was that what he wanted? I shifted closer to Philippe and ran my hand down his arm, desperately wanting him to understand my signals that I wanted him to kiss me.

He leaned toward me, lifted my face toward his, and brushed his lips across mine, ever so gently, eliciting a shockwave through my body. I pulled away briefly, then grabbed him by his jacket collar and brought him toward me, my lips anxious to find his. Our tongues danced gently together as he ran his hands through my hair, and I wrapped my arms around him as tightly as I could over his winter coat. If we hadn't been on a park bench in public, I might have straddled him, wanting so badly to be as close physically as we possibly could.

This was the reaction I had expected to have with Sam and hadn't. My eyes opened, and I broke the kiss. "Oh my God."

Sam.

I pulled back breathlessly.

"What's wrong?" Philippe asked, confusion clouding his expression as he reached out to touch my face.

I stood up, pacing back and forth in front of him. I threw my hands up and huffed. "We can't do this. I can't do this." I moved out of the way for a group of tourists on the sidewalk, grateful for the moment to regroup my thoughts. "Philippe, I need to tell you something."

"I know already."

"What?" How could he know what I was about to say?

"Callie told me you are dating someone."

"What?" I repeated, wondering why Callie would have shared this with him and why he hadn't mentioned it to me sooner. My emotions bounced between relief, confusion, and a little anger. What if he was just playing with me right now because he knew I was dating someone else? The appeal is always stronger for something that's out of our reach. My anger and doubt grew as he continued.

"Well, actually, she told Julien. I just happened to be there."

"So, why would you...?"

"Kiss you?" he asked.

I nodded.

"I couldn't help myself. Tell me you don't feel this, Lila?"

I sighed. Maybe his feelings matched mine. Maybe it wasn't a competition as much as it was his attempt to show me what he wanted before I developed real feelings for Sam. "Of course I feel it. But there's no hope for us, Philippe. This is an impossible situation." I sat back down on the bench, pulling my knees up to my chest and staring out at the water.

He placed his hand on my knee. "Callie and Julien succeeded."

"I'm not Callie. I don't intend to move to France. *This* is my home."

He nodded, removing his hand and adjusting his position on the bench. He also stared intently at the pond in front of us, as though he would somehow find the answers floating on top of the frigid water. He mindlessly zipped and unzipped the outer layer of his coat.

After eons of silence, I turned to him. I'd only found one possible solution, even if I didn't like it. "Can we just stay friends?" I asked. "We get along so well, and I don't want to make things any more awkward. I like you."

"I like spending time with you as well, Lila." He paused, and then opened his mouth as if to say more but was interrupted by my phone.

I knew it was Sam before even looking at it.

"I've got to get this," I said to Philippe, whose face fell in disappointment.

"Hello," I answered, standing up and walking slightly away from Philippe.

"Hey, pretty lady," Sam greeted me. "How's the sightseeing going?"

Guilt rushed through me, my lips still tingling from the shared kiss. Subconsciously, my fingers raised to my lips as I tried to calm myself and answer Sam. My voice was about two octaves higher than normal as I exclaimed, "Great! It's going great!"

If Sam noticed anything weird about my response, he didn't indicate it. "Did you two make plans for dinner? If not, I have a place I'd love to take him."

I looked over at Philippe. "Sam would like to take us to dinner. What do you think?"

His eyes pierced mine. "Sure, *friend,* I would love to go be a third wheel on your date with *Sam.*" He made no attempt to shield the disgust on his face.

He was right. This was a terrible idea. My mind whirred, thinking about how I could make this better. An idea crossed my mind. "How about if we invite Allison?"

A look I couldn't decipher crossed his face, before he nodded slowly. "Sure. Certainly better than returning to the hotel by myself."

I returned to Sam, and we made plans. A quick call to a more than enthused Allison confirmed she'd be joining us.

Philippe and I walked in silence to the meeting point Sam had established, and my gut roiled in discomfort.

W*HAT HAD I DONE?* Allison breezed into the restaurant, removed her overcoat, and handed it to the hostess. The red dress she wore had a very low neckline and accentuated her lovely shape. She had applied just the right amount of makeup to make her green eyes and her plump lips pop. Her blonde hair, pulled up into a casual ponytail, bounced along with her bubbly personality. I tried to ignore the once-over Philippe gave her as he leaned in to embrace her, kissing both cheeks. She looked and smelled fresh, and I silently cursed myself for not insisting on a later meeting time so that Philippe and I could have also changed clothes and freshened up after our day traipsing around. I subconsciously smoothed my hair.

"I'm so glad you called!" she gushed at me, before glancing coyly back at Philippe. "How has your day been?"

"Super," Philippe said, in a slightly sarcastic tone. "Lila is a full-service tour guide."

My face heated instantly, replaying the kiss.

Words poured out of Allison's mouth as she asked Philippe for specifics on what we'd seen, piping in when he mentioned her favorite places. Standing a few feet away from the two of them, I watched the door for Sam, shifting from one foot to the other as bubbles of anxiety brewed in my belly.

Sam strolled in confidently and walked directly up to me, looking incredibly attractive in his lightweight cream sweater and khaki pants. Grinning devilishly, he planted a soft kiss on my lips. I avoided looking at Philippe, who turned away from us.

"Sam, this is Philippe and this is Allison."

He shook both of their hands, smiling. "Lovely to meet you both. How do you all know each other?"

"I met Philippe while I was working in Paris. He's my best friend's husband's best friend." Sam nodded, sizing Philippe up. "And Allison and I work together. They met last night at the outing with my colleagues, and really seemed to hit it off." Philippe shot me a warning look, which I ignored.

Sam didn't notice. "Another WaterCorps gal! Lila's told me so much about the meaningful work your organization is involved with."

Allison beamed. "Yes, it's a wonderful place to work. What about you two? Lila hasn't mentioned you to me."

My cheeks burned. "Well, we have only gone on two dates."

"Three," Sam interjected, putting his arm possessively around my shoulders, as he pulled me in for another kiss.

This was a bad idea. But neither Sam nor Allison seemed to notice the tension between me and Philippe. A hostess escorted us to our table and seated us, and asked if we'd like to start with drinks.

"Yes!" Philippe and I both stated.

"This is my favorite sushi restaurant," Sam said to Philippe. "Have you had sushi before?"

"Yes, we French don't just eat baguette and *fromage*," Philippe said, frowning. He rolled his eyes. Great start.

Sam shrugged his shoulders, giving me a questioning glance. "Just asking, man."

Trying to save this before it devolved further, I plastered a smile on my face. "Actually, I ate some of the best sushi at this place in Paris that my friends Callie, Emilie, and I used to go to regularly," I said enthusiastically.

Sam nodded and I shoved my face in the menu. I chewed nervously on my thumbnail, barely able to focus on any of the printed words. Food was really the last thing I was thinking about, and I took a large gulp of my wine.

"So how did you two meet?" Allison asked, sipping on her glass of white wine and looking back and forth between me and Sam.

Sam chuckled. "The gym."

"That doesn't sound very Lila-like," Allison chuckled. I wanted to kick her under the table. What did that mean, anyway?

"I joined a gym. I'm trying to get healthier," I said flatly.

Sam wiped his mouth with a napkin. "Lila was on this treadmill at an incline so high I assumed she was training for Mount Everest! But what got my attention was when her Walkman shot off and crashed into the wall, and she was so dedicated to finishing her workout, she kept going. I knew I had to meet her. Then when I found out she'd been held hostage by a broken treadmill and refused to give in, my admiration only grew." We both laughed at the memory.

"Hey, I had two minutes left. I wasn't stopping!" Sam squeezed my knee under the table. I fought the urge to jerk my leg away from him, but the laughter eased some of the tension overall.

Allison turned to Philippe. "I'm more of a yoga girl. I find it's useful to be very flexible," she said, staring at Philippe like a lioness with a fresh piece of meat.

The intensity made me blush. "Way to be subtle," I murmured into my wine glass.

All eyes zeroed in on me. *Woah, Lila, back down. Where was this even coming from? You're on a date with your potential boyfriend, and Allison has every right to flirt with Philippe.* And yet, it wasn't settling well at all.

"What was that?" Allison asked.

They all looked at me expectantly. I took another gulp of wine and placed my glass on the table slowly, desperately seeking a way out of this one.

When I just shook my head, coming up with nothing, Philippe turned his gaze to Allison. "Flexibility is certainly a good quality."

Allison beamed.

I wanted to crawl under the table in embarrassment, but Sam saved the day. "I've always admired people who can do yoga. I'm about as flexible as a two-by-four."

I had to hand it to him. Either he was completely unaware of what was happening, or he had a knack for rescuing people from uncomfortable situations. I smiled his way, and he squeezed my knee again under the table.

The waiter arrived, delivering platters of sushi. We all *oohed* at the presentation; the previous conversation forgotten for the moment. As we dug into the food, my maladroit attempts at using chopsticks sent a piece flying. It landed with a thud in the soy sauce, sending a splatter of brown droplets all over the tablecloth and a few droplets on my dress.

Sam quickly offered his napkin with a grin. "You've got a knack for launching objects, don't you?"

A tinge of guilt hit me like a rock. He was being so lovely, and I was a terrible person.

"Practice makes perfect," Allison said, demonstrating the proper employment of the chopsticks with annoying perfection to Philippe, and giggling as he fumbled with picking up his own sushi.

This is going to be a long night. As we ate, I took inventory of our foursome. Sam, who touched me at every opportunity, marking his territory (thank God we weren't dogs); Philippe, the enigmatic French connection who didn't even attempt to hide his disdain toward Sam, yet seemed to enjoy flirting openly with Allison; and Allison, the unwitting pawn in my game of emotional chess, who giggled at every word that came out of Philippe's mouth. Finally, there was me, Lila, the conductor of a train speeding toward a high-speed crash.

Somehow, we made it through dinner with no further issues and relatively pleasant conversation. I excused myself to go to the ladies' room, and upon my return, found the three of them chatting as if they were old friends.

Sam insisted on covering the bill, despite our protests. "Trust me, it's not a problem," he said. "Salaries in your line of work definitely suck."

The three of us stared at him, wondering if we should be insulted by the comment.

He paused before blurting out, "I just meant, you all work so hard and for such good causes, but the compensation is not what you deserve."

"Money isn't my driving factor," Philippe said dryly.

Before things could devolve further, I placed my hand on Sam's arm and said, "Your generosity is much appreciated."

He nodded, embarrassment still pinkening his cheeks.

As we exited the building, Allison asked Philippe if he'd like her to escort him back to his hotel, so he didn't get lost. He agreed, causing a painful and acidic bubble to climb my esophagus. Swallowing hard, I embraced him, kissing both cheeks, but avoiding eye contact. "Call me if you'd like to spend some more time together before you leave." The words hurt as I realized I might not see him again before he left.

He nodded, expressionless, and shook Sam's hand. "Thank you for a lovely dinner." While his words were kind, his tone was flat.

I watched Allison thread her arm through his as she echoed Philippe's sentiments to Sam, and then they turned and began walking in the opposite direction. A pang of jealousy tugged at my heart.

"Whew. We dodged a bullet tonight, didn't we?" Sam asked, laughing.

"What do you mean?" I turned toward him, pulling my scarf tighter against my neck in the cold breeze.

"Er, just that it started off kind of rough, but we managed to end well."

"Oh, yeah, sure," I agreed, jamming my hands in my pocket.

"Would you like me to walk you home?"

I smiled at him, trying desperately to shake off my mood and focus on this moment and this man. The choice had been made, and I would give this a chance. We'd been having a great time, and I didn't want to ruin that over a silly fantasy. Pulling my hand out of my pocket, I reached for his. He gladly accepted, kissing my hand before lacing his fingers through mine. As we walked in the direction of my apartment, I tried to push all thoughts out of my mind about the French man walking away from me.

19

"Hm?" Embarrassed that I hadn't heard a word Sam had said for the last five minutes, I turned to face him.

"Where did you go?" Sam asked, head tilted.

"I guess I just spaced out. Too much wine and sake after walking all day in the freezing cold." I hoped he'd buy that.

"I should have gotten us a car."

"It's okay, Sam. If I didn't feel up for a walk, I would have said something." We arrived in front of my building and stopped walking. The tiredness crushed me, but it wasn't just physical fatigue. It was the weight of the emotional internal battle I was having, trying to suppress the strong attraction to Philippe and increase the intensity with Sam.

Sam placed both hands on my shoulders, and leaned down, placing a kiss on my lips. I didn't respond. I tried to, but my lips rebelled. This was nowhere near the same explosion that had coursed through me when Philippe kissed me, and I hated myself for thinking about Philippe during this moment. Pulling away, Sam's confusion registered on his face. "What's going on Lila?"

I stepped back, needing more space between the two of us, and looked up at the stars, praying for the wisdom to handle this situation, or to be suddenly hit by Cupid's arrow. Life would certainly be less complicated if I could fall in love with Sam. He'd been such a great date tonight. He'd crushed all of my stereotypes about the kids of millionaires, unless he was putting on a huge act. But to carry it on this well for so long, he'd have to be a sociopath.

Maybe he was a sociopath. And I should just run away.

He's not a sociopath, Lila. He's a great guy. But he's not Philippe.

Boom. As hard as I tried, I couldn't suppress my growing feelings.

"Lila?"

"Sorry, Sam, I was trying to gather my thoughts. You're such a great guy..."

"Oh boy, here we go," Sam interrupted.

"I don't know what I want right now." *That was a lie.* "I think it's just too soon for me to get involved in a relationship. You came along so unexpectedly. So *wonderfully*," I added quickly.

"Lila, I like you. I think you like me."

I nodded. I did like him.

"Isn't that enough to give us a chance?" he asked, his eyes pleading with me.

I reached out and grabbed his hands. "I need some time to process everything. Make sure I'm ready."

He nodded, although it didn't appear he truly understood. It was a feeling I definitely understood. Being left at the altar gives you a new perspective on pain in relationships. And that's exactly why I knew I needed to give this some space and make sure if we continued dating, it was for the right reasons, and that my head and heart were at least open to the possibility. But who was I kidding? My hesitation had nothing to do with the previous pain I'd experienced, and a lot more to do with my confused feelings for Philippe.

"So what's next?" Sam asked.

"I'm not sure." I paused, taking the time to choose my next words very carefully. Truthfully, I didn't want to end things entirely with him. But I also knew I couldn't throw myself fully into Sam and ignore what had just happened. I squeezed his hands, which I was still holding in mine. "I think I just need a little time to process. It's not fair of me to ask you to wait while I get my head and heart sorted out."

"I'll wait, Lila," Sam interjected seriously, rubbing his thumb gently on my back of my hand.

I nodded. He didn't know I had kissed Philippe earlier or had these tangled up feelings, and it didn't feel good to keep things from him. "I can't promise you anything, Sam."

"I understand. But I'm willing to wait for you anyway."

I hugged him. He held me tightly against him, nuzzling his nose into my hair. We stood there for a moment, holding each other.

"Go get some rest, Lila. Call me when you're ready to talk." He placed a soft kiss on my lips, waited for me to get safely in my building, and gave a wave as I closed the door behind me, a sad smile on his face. A million daggers stabbed at my heart.

SLEEP EVADED ME. I tossed and turned before clicking on my lamp. I sat up in bed, sighing. My journal, the gift from Callie, sat on my nightstand. Grabbing it, I penned all the thoughts I'd had over the last few days. The journaling didn't have a magical effect of helping me find the answers to everything, but it did feel good to get everything out, and the fatigue was taking over. Turning the lamp off, I finally fell asleep around 4 a.m. When I woke up, it was after ten. I made coffee, took a quick shower, and got dressed. I'd made a decision. I needed to go talk to Philippe.

Guilt rippled through me when I looked at my phone and saw a text from Sam.

> Sam: Just checking in on you after last night. Doing okay?

> Me: I'm doing okay, thank you. That's really sweet. Thanks again for walking me home, and for your sweet words last night.

> Sam: Any time. I meant what I said.

> Me: Thank you.

I PUT the phone in my purse. Sam's text didn't irritate me, but I couldn't keep my head in both worlds. Setting thoughts of Sam aside, I wondered what I would find when I got to Philippe's hotel room. Pulling my coat tight against the brisk air, I focused on not tripping over the tree roots that jutted through the side-walk. Despite my efforts to shove them away, my thoughts were consumed with the imagery of Allison touching Philippe at every possible moment at the restaurant. I really hoped he had no interest in her. Pretty selfish thought, considering I had no desire to be in a relationship with Philippe. I strongly disliked the jealousy coursing through me. And so what if Philippe wanted to have a little fun while he was here? Maybe I just wished that fun was with me.

The front desk attendant greeted me warmly as I entered the hotel. The elevator door dinged open almost immediately, and I pressed the button for the fourteenth floor, my nausea growing with each floor we passed. I took in a deep breath as I exited the elevator.

Marching down the hall, I stopped in front of his door. The fake bravado I'd summoned up on my way over fizzled away. My hand raised to pound on the door, a wave of anxiousness kicked in. What would I say? Smoothing my hair once more and praying that the right words would find their way to me, I knocked.

"Room service is here!" I heard Allison's voice from inside the room.

Oh giant monkey balls. Oh fudge. Panic engulfed me and I did a weird dance as my body tried to decide whether to go left, right, or stay put and confront them. Ultimately, I decided to run to the elevator. Smashing the button did nothing to bring it faster, and I begged it to come before Philippe opened his door and saw me. Relief spread over me as the doors opened.

"Lila?" Donkey balls. *Please no.* I could just disappear into the elevator and pretend like I hadn't heard him.

Again. "Lila?"

Shoot. I turned slowly and plastered the biggest smile I could muster on my face. "Well, hi! I was just stopping by to check in on you."

"Then why are you getting on the elevator?" Philippe asked. He stood there clutching a towel around his waist. My heart dropped to the floor. They'd spent the night together, and clearly, it had been a fun one. Tears pricked at my eyes as I fought to control a deluge.

Allison peeked around the door. She only wore a T-shirt. Her hair, messy, fell around her shoulders.

"Hey Lila! How's it going?" She waved cheerfully.

"I, uh, didn't realize you were here. I'll leave you two to, er, do whatever you were doing."

"Lila, wait!" Philippe insisted.

I gave a weak little smile and stepped into the elevator.

TEARS BLURRED my eyes as I walked-ran back to my apartment and threw a change of clothes and my computer in a bag. I didn't want to be alone. I entered the garage and found my car. I needed my parents. The radio blared with my favorite '90s alternative rock, and I smashed the button to kill the sound. I wanted silence for the twenty-five minute drive home. The houses and lawns got much bigger as I got nearer to the house I'd been raised in, and my anxiety lowered as I passed familiar sights. The trees I'd played in as a kid, the neighbors outside, chatting on the sidewalk. I waved and smiled as I drove by. As if I didn't have a care in the world.

My mother was alone in the kitchen when I walked in, and the moment she saw me she rushed over and grabbed me into her arms. "Hi baby! I was not expecting to see you this week-end." She pulled back and assessed me. "Are you okay?"

"Mama." I hugged her tightly as sobs racked my body.

"Lila? Oh baby." She held me, stroking my back.

"It's okay, Lila. Let it out." We stood there for what may have been only moments or could have been hours. I noticed nothing except the gentle strokes of my mom's hand sliding up and down my back until the cat rubbed against my leg, as if she also knew the pain in my heart.

Mom released me. "I'm making lunch. Your dad's bowling. Wanna talk about it?" Mom was always good about giving me space to process my emotions, but also letting me know she was there to listen if I needed it.

Nodding, I sat down at the table.

"You remember Philippe, right?"

"Of course. Julien's friend."

"He's in town. We spent the day together yesterday. He kissed me."

She stopped what she was doing, wiped her hands on a towel, and set about making tea as she listened.

"What about Sam?"

I filled her in on the details. She didn't interrupt, just listened, occasionally nodding. The tea pot boiled, and she prepared us each a cup, bringing them to the table.

"I don't know what to do." I blew on the steaming tea and wrapped my hands around the cup to warm my cold fingers.

"Give yourself time, hon. It's only been a few months since Matt. Maybe you're not ready to be with anyone yet, and you've leaned into Philippe to protect yourself from falling for Sam?"

I shrugged. "Maybe."

She looked at me for a moment. "You've just had a terrible heartbreak. You can't fix that by throwing yourself into another relationship."

Sucking in a deep breath, I tried to find the words to explain. "I don't think that's what I'm doing. I feel very ready to move on from Matt. My time with Sam has been so fun. And he's here. And he offers so many... amenities."

My mom chuckled at my silly statement. "But obviously you're struggling because of these feelings for Philippe. Which, I don't blame you for," she added.

I cocked my head questioningly in her direction.

"I noticed him at the wedding. He's quite the cutie."

"Mom!" I reddened at the idea of her checking out the men my age.

When my mom stopped laughing at my response, I said, "Sam's the obvious choice. And he's not a bad choice. I just…"

"I know you think you're ready to move on, but the heart takes time to heal. It *does* heal, sweetie, but you must give it time. And I wonder if this situation you've placed yourself in is your subconscious creating obstacles to you moving on with anyone."

I wondered what my mom could possibly know about heartache. She'd been with my father since college. But I sensed she was speaking from experience. Maybe there'd been someone else.

As if she could read my thoughts, my mom said, "Believe it or not, your father wasn't my first love."

I looked up, surprised.

"I had a high school sweetheart. He was my first everything. I thought we would get married. We went to different colleges and our freshman year we did what we could to stay together. But then, I went to surprise him for a weekend visit, and he told me he wanted to see other people. I was crushed."

"Oh Mom. I didn't know."

"Well, if that hadn't happened, I never would have accepted a date with your father, and I wouldn't have you. So sometimes the best things come from the worst pain." She came around the table and gave me another hug. "You just have to give yourself time to make sure you're ready to move on."

Squeezing my eyes shut, I tried to force all the conflicting thoughts away. My mom was right. Matt's painful actions had saved me from an unhappy marriage and likely a divorce. But despite feeling like I was healed, was it possible these feelings for Philippe were some weird protection mechanism? I admitted the possibility, but the pain of seeing Philippe and Allison together had caused a very deep wound. There was no denying the pull I had toward him. Perhaps it was his moody demeanor or his mysterious nature. Perhaps it was the kindness under the shy exterior.

"Tell me about him, Lila. If you'd like to talk it through."

Turning to look out the window, I struggled to find a starting place or the right words. "Philippe is different, Mom. He's protective and funny, and I thought he was aloof and didn't like me, but I know that's not true. He just... he makes me feel something that I can't explain."

"Hmmm," my mom twisted the tea towel in her hands. "Is there any chance it's just the allure of him being French? You've had some life experiences others only dream about attached to spending time in France. Is it possible you're feeling a connection to the special experience, not just him as a person?"

That was a good question. Pondering whether my mom could be right, I thought about the way my whole body lit up when Philippe's tongue found mine. I didn't believe that level of electricity could be created by nostalgia.

"I think it's more, Mom. I can't explain it. It's a strong connection. I think about him nonstop. I want to learn everything about him. I've got this absolutely gorgeous, kind, smart man interested in me, who should be the obvious choice, and I can't stop wishing it is Philippe that I'm with when I'm with Sam. What should I do, Mama?"

"Oh honey, I wish I could give you the answer. Falling in love, if that's what this is, would be a real predicament. Darn Paris and its love allure!"

I giggled.

"But in all seriousness, I think you know already that Sam might not be the one for you, and if you want to avoid hurting both of you until you figure out what you want, you should probably end things with him. Whether or not Philippe is... well, you'll have to figure that one out. Obviously, I dislike the idea of you being swept off your feet to Paris."

"I have no intention of moving to Paris. My life is here."

My mom sighed. "You're young. You have a lot of life to live and so many opportunities in front of you. But at almost fifty years old, I wouldn't want you looking back on your life and having any regrets. Especially not of this nature. We don't need another Sally situation."

Sally had been my mother's best friend ever since they were in pre-K. She had been madly in love with her high school boyfriend but dumped him because her parents didn't think he was good enough for her. They each went their own ways, got married, and had some kids. They reunited at their thirty-year high school reunion. And both of them realized they had made the biggest mistake of their lives by walking away from each other. Two divorces and a lot of heartache later, it did wind up being a happily ever after for Sally and her beloved Dave, but a lot of carnage was left in their wake.

I understood exactly what my mother meant. If there was any chance this could be something, I should at least consider seeing it through. The image of Allison standing in the doorway in nothing but a T-shirt crossed my mind. Was it already too late?

I took a nap on the couch and woke up when my dad arrived. "Lila bug!" he practically yelled. "I didn't expect to see you." He pulled me in for an intense squeeze. "What's new?"

I didn't tell him the details of the Philippe/Sam drama, but I did tell him about the gala, the people I'd run into, and the progress we were making on my project before disappearing up to my room for some solitude. My mother kept my room exactly the same as when I'd left home, but she'd thoughtfully cleared out all memories of Matt, much as she'd done in my apartment. However, she'd replaced them with pictures of my closest friends. I smiled at a picture of me and Callie on the Champs-Élysées.

The album from my time in France sat on my nightstand, and I crawled onto the bed, pulling it onto my lap, and spent some time looking through it. Most of the pictures were of my adventures with Callie and Emilie and our travels. The last few pages were of New Year's Eve 1999. I stared at a photo of me and Matt, smiling like the happy fools we were at that time. In another, he must have been in the middle of saying something, and I was looking adoringly at him. Callie had probably taken the picture.

I missed Callie. She would have the right advice. I kept flipping through the album and found other pictures I'd completely forgotten about. Group photos of all of us. I laughed at one where Callie had inserted herself right in between Julien and Philippe, and she was beaming. Julien had an amused look on his face. I'd instinctively known from the moment I saw them interacting that something would come out of that night. I'd assumed it would just be a really great experience for her to have in her memories, not a marriage and an apartment in Paris, but I was glad that was the way it had turned out for her. I turned the page and saw another picture. It was our whole group except for Fred, a friend of Julien and Philippe's. He must have been the photographer. Matt and I stood on the far end, but what grabbed my attention was that, at least from the angle this picture was taken, Philippe seemed to be looking right at me. That couldn't be right. It clearly had to be my imagination. But I was laughing and looking at Callie, who had her arm wrapped tightly around Julien's waist, and I swear, Philippe was staring right at me.

Must just be a coincidence. Maybe I'd said something right before the picture was taken?

I put the album away, grabbed my laptop, and settled onto the bench of my window seat. I stared outside, watching the clouds on this gray day, and collected my thoughts.

Finally, I fired up the computer, opened my email, and composed an email to Callie.

> Subject: Free today?
>
> Hi Callie,
>
> Any chance you'll be on AOL today? I really need to talk to you.
>
> Xo, Lila

Callie typically caught up with friends and family on Sunday afternoons and evenings, so I hoped she'd see the email.

> Re: Free today?
>
> Is Philippe okay? I'm logging in now.
>
> Callie

Whoopsie. I should have figured she'd worry something had gone wrong with Philippe. But I guess, in a way, it had. I logged into AOL, waiting for the shrieking and songs that reminded me of the Atari game with the pinging balls to subside before I waited for a message to join her. AOL provided a much faster solution for us than email, and calling was so expensive. I was anxiously awaiting Julien's predictions of the day we'd get to video chat.

A ping announced a new private chat, and I joined Callie.

Callie: What's going on?

Lila: Philippe's okay. He's fine. But I messed things up.

Callie: WHAT happened?

Lila: Philippe arrived safely, I picked him up, and we had a nice evening together at one of my favorite bars. Before my friends got there, he stepped in as my "pretend boyfriend" again. He spent a lot of time with one of my colleagues, named Allison. We spent the next day sightseeing around DC, and, well, we got a little carried away and he kissed me.

Callie: HE KISSED YOU?

Lila: Yes. Actually twice. He kissed me when he was saving me at the bar as my "pretend boyfriend." But the kiss is not the biggest part of this story. There's more.

Callie: What could be bigger than a kiss? Go on! (Julien's with me FYI, he heard me scream when Philippe kissed you.)

Lila: It didn't end well. Here's the thing—it was a great kiss. I got all the feelings I've been struggling to feel with Sam.

But it all went downhill from there. We wound up going to dinner with Sam and invited Allison. It was weird and awkward. Philippe was upset with me. He left with Allison.

I went to his hotel to check in on him this morning and she was there. It was clear she'd stayed the night. So, I guess he's moved on from whatever happened when we kissed.

I waited anxiously for her reply to all this information, pacing the room. A ding announced her reply.

Callie: That's a lot to process. Let me recap:
Philippe kissed you before you met up with
Sam? You liked it. You invited him on a date
with your boyfriend, but also invited a date for
Philippe, and then he left with her? And you
left with Sam, and you're upset?

Lila: When you put it that way...

Something about the way Callie recapped all of this made it seem... silly.

Callie: Just trying to understand the situation.
And... PHILIPPE? Are we sure we're talking
about OUR Philippe?

Lila: Yep. You got the details right.

Lila: It shouldn't be a big deal—it's not like
Philippe and I are, or ever can be, a thing. But
for some reason, it crushed me.

Callie: Do you have real feelings for him, Lila?
Because I'm living proof that it can work, if
this is what you really want?

Lila: I'm very confused right now. My head
and heart don't agree, but my heart is not
willing to shut up about this. And I don't even
know how Philippe really feels. He seemed
interested, but maybe he was just overcome
by the moment? He certainly didn't waste
time moving forward with Allison.

Callie: Lila, did you really not see it?

Lila: See what?

Callie: I figured you already knew this, but Philippe's had a thing for you basically forever. I'm just dumbfounded that he'd sleep with someone else. You're all he talks about. And now Julien's trying to pull me away before I can hit send!

Lila: Huh? He's had a thing for me? All this time?

Callie: uh yeah!

I sat there, staring at her words, stunned. How was this even possible? We had just started developing a fun friendship, and he kisses me. But he takes another girl home in protest? None of it makes sense. Then again, it became pretty obvious Philippe liked me when his lips were on mine yesterday.

Callie: So, what are you going to do? You're moving forward with Sam? You going to just let Philippe have his fling with Allison or...?

Lila: Our kiss was explosive, Callie. And then I shut it down because of my guilt over Sam. But I'm struggling to understand my feelings too. My mom thinks I'm inventing feelings for Philippe so I can protect my heart from anything going south with Sam. But truthfully, I've been fighting feelings for Philippe since Paris. Even though it is such a bad idea considering our geographical locations. But when he kissed me, it was like the world stopped. And it REALLY bothered me to see him with Allison.

Callie: I KNEW IT!!! Julien owes me 50 euros. I told him you and Philippe were vibing in a big, big way. Now, how do we fix this?

This is what I was worried about. I'd known the instant I

admitted my feelings to Callie that she'd roll straight into matchmaker mode, wanting nothing more than a fairy-tale ending where her best friend and her husband's best friend fell in love.

Lila: There's nothing for you to do, Callie, and please, leave this one alone. I've got to figure out what I want with Sam, where my feelings stand, what I want long-term. Why is this is bothering me so much?

Callie: Do you want to be in a relationship with Philippe? All the challenges aside, if the world were perfect, would you choose Philippe?

Lila: I don't know. And the world isn't perfect. He lives in France. Why can't I just fall for Sam and do this the easy way?

Callie: Philippe's a great guy.

Lila: So is Sam.

Lila: I have no idea what I'm going to do, but for now, I'm gonna let my parents take care of me. I love you.

Callie: I love you too. And you don't have to make a decision today. Tell your parents I said hello.

Lila: Give Julien my love. Bye!

Callie: Bye! Keep me posted!

FEELING NO LESS confused about my feelings or next steps, I disconnected and followed good smells wafting up the stairs to the kitchen, where my mom was busy preparing dinner.

"Smells good, Mom." I hugged her and wandered into the living room.

"Want a beer?" my dad asked, barely glancing away from the Yankees game. Baseball wasn't really my thing, but nothing seemed better than spending the evening watching it with my dad.

"One step ahead of you," I said, tossing him one of the two cans I'd grabbed on my way through the kitchen. He smiled and patted the couch next to him.

It wasn't the Sunday I had envisioned, but it was exactly what I needed. I let my parents pamper me like I was still a child, comforted by Princess Purr, who was curled up in my lap, purring loudly.

20

My work-life balance definitely teetered in favor of the work side of the scale that week, which didn't bother me at all. Plunging myself into the demands of the office, I pushed aside any personal decisions for the time being. The gala produced a full calendar of meetings, plus we were busy planning our annual spring fundraiser. This was my shtick. When life gets too heavy, I like to keep as busy as possible, so I can shove down all uncomfortable emotions and feelings.

Until someone forces the issue.

By midweek, enough new tasks had been added to my plate that I had to reassess my priorities. Perusing the meetings on my calendar, I updated my list.

To do:

- Get new suit (or two)
- Organize travel for the trip to India (yay!) I just got added to
- Go through notes from the gala meetings & schedule remaining meetings

- End things with Sam

Writing that last one surprised me. Up until now, the waters had been murky. I had pro'd and con'd the heck out of it, still unsure of how to move forward. My mom was right though. Even if I wasn't going to pursue Philippe, or anyone else for that matter, the connection I sought with Sam just wasn't there. No matter how incredible he was.

Allison wandered into my office. As usual, she looked more like she should be doing a photo shoot for the front cover of *Hottest Working Women in America* than working the daily grind of a nonprofit organization. I whistled as I eyed her from head to toe. "Wow, you look great."

Allison twirled around, her finger at the lapel of her light pink, multi-tweed jacket and (short) skirt suit. The neckline and arms had a raw edge, a unique flair. She wore pink heels. My outfit paled in comparison. I was sporting my normal uniform of black slacks and an undistinguishable black blouse. "If you were a dude, I'd report you to HR for the way you just stared at me." She laughed.

"Well, you look really nice, Allison." I had been avoiding her to the best of my ability the last couple of days. All of our out-of-office meetings made it pretty easy, but by Wednesday, it was unavoidable. I just decided to avoid any talk about Philippe, if that was possible.

She shrugged her shoulders, as if she was unaware that her fashion style put the rest of us to shame. Picking at something on her jacket, she said, "How was the rest of your weekend? How's *Sam?*"

"It was nice, and he's great, I guess." I obviously didn't want to share I was breaking up with Sam because of my confused feelings about Philippe, when Allison had just spent at least one night with him. But I had the urge to talk about my confused feelings for Sam.

"What do you mean, you guess?" Allison asked, forgetting about whatever was on her jacket and giving me her full attention.

"I'm just not sure he's the one for me," I admitted.

Surprise covered her face. She sat on the edge of my desk, legs crossed. "Do you want to talk about it?" she asked.

We weren't that close of friends, and it felt awkward, all things considered, but I was still tempted to get another perspective. Leaving out the Philippe part, of course.

"Well, I made my pros and cons list, and neither side really won."

"Hmm." She looked at me thoughtfully. "My mama used to tell me if there's a situation I needed to create a pros and cons list for, I already knew the answer."

"What do you mean?"

She hopped off the desk and started toward the door. Looking back over her shoulder, she said, "If it ain't all pros at this stage, honey, why are you wasting your time?" With that, she practically skipped out of the room.

There was some logic to what she said, and although I didn't wholeheartedly agree with the sentiment—for example, with Philippe, despite all of the pros, there was no denying the Atlantic Ocean as an obvious con—but I got the gist of what she was saying. On date three, we should be blinded by the love goggles. The cons make themselves obvious later on, but if they're present this early, it's probably a kiss of death.

"Lila!" my boss bellowed from down the hall, interrupting my thoughts.

I grabbed my bag and ran out to meet him. "Coming!" We had meetings to attend, and I pushed all thoughts of Philippe and Sam to the back of my mind.

Thursday morning I woke up early, picked out my cutest workout clothes, and even threw on a little lip gloss. I hoped I'd run into Sam and wanted to look my best. True to his word, he was giving me the space I'd requested, and he hadn't reached out. Despite all the hemming and hawing, I still wasn't sure what was about to happen with us. I needed to see him.

Entering the gym lobby, I scanned the small area and didn't see him, so I moved straight to the torture device, a.k.a., treadmill, my arch nemesis. Thirty-minutes still seemed like six years, but at least I wasn't climbing a mountain this time. I wiped down the machine, sucked down some water, and walked into the lobby. And there he was. Looking like Ken Doll himself, flirting with Front Desk Girl. He leaned over the counter and said something to her that made her laugh out loud as she twirled her ponytail with her finger.

He looked up and saw me. "Lila!" Forgetting all about Front Desk Girl, he rushed over and, much to my surprise, wrapped me up in a big hug. "How was the rest of your weekend?"

Some part of me had hoped that when I saw him, I'd feel a surge of excitement. Instead, dread filled me about what I had to do next. "It was good," I said. "I went to see my parents, and they always spoil me."

He nodded. "That sounds nice."

"What about you?"

"I played golf with my dad on Sunday. That's about it."

"Ooh, it was a cold one on Sunday. Where did you play?"

"We flew down to South Carolina," he said casually, like everyone had the means to just hop on a plane for a day of golf. He shoved his hands in his pocket, and avoided eye contact.

We were both avoiding the question I knew Sam wanted the answer to.

"Listen, Sam..."

"Lila..."

We both started speaking at the same time, and then laughed. "Please, you first," Sam insisted.

Wiping my sweaty hands on my pants, nervous as heck, I tried to form my words carefully. I didn't want to hurt Sam, but I also knew I couldn't continue this when my heart was in flux. I moved toward the door and he followed. This conversation definitely could not happen within earshot of Front Desk Girl, who glowered at me.

Bile rose in my throat. Difficult conversations were not my strong suit. I took a long pull from the water bottle. Clearing my throat for the third time, I began timidly. "Sam," I looked up to see her staring at us. I wanted out of her view too. "Let's go outside."

He nodded, and held the door open for me. The bright sun gave me a little courage. I took another sip of water and began again. "These last couple of weeks have been wonderful. You're funny and generous and everything a girl could want."

"But?" As I'd been speaking, his smile had vanished, a deep frown creasing his face.

Ironically, a cloud covered the sun at that exact moment. Just perfect.

"But I am not ready to move forward yet, and it's not fair to you to keep you waiting."

He shook his head back and forth. "I told you I'd wait as long as you needed."

"That's not fair to either of us. I don't want to lead you along, and right now, I can't move forward with us."

Sam stared down the street. He said nothing, and I fidgeted in the silence. While I was relieved that I had told him the truth, a tiny fear pricked at the back of my neck. *What if I never found anyone else? What if this was it? Should I take it back?*

No, Lila, a fear of being alone is not a valid reason for staying in a relationship.

But a bigger fear pushed through. *What if he is the one, and I was just sidetracked by this silly obsession with Philippe?*

If it's meant to be, it will be, right?

After what felt like forty-four days, he turned his eyes back away from whatever it was that he'd been staring at while processing this information and looked straight at me.

"Well, it's been fun." And then he turned on his heels, reentered the gym, and strolled right back up to the desk to continue flirting with Front Desk Girl, as casually as if I'd just given him the weather report, not broken up with him.

Wow. Guess he wasn't as attached as he originally proclaimed.

His reaction, although likely out of hurt, only confirmed that I'd made the right decision. I'd stood up for my own needs and wants, followed my intuition, and even if ending things made me sad, my shoulders lifted as the extra weight of anxiety finally lifted.

MID-AFTERNOON, my office phone rang. I didn't recognize the number on the caller ID and assumed it was one of the staffers returning my call about some upcoming meetings.

It was Philippe.

Thump-thump. Thump-thump. My dang telltale heart nearly beat its way out of my chest at the mere sound of his voice.

"Lila, I'm leaving tomorrow, and I don't like the way we left things. Any chance you're free for dinner tonight?"

"Hold on a minute." I covered the phone mouthpiece with my hand and exhaled a huge breath. Waiting for another moment to compose myself (and not wanting to appear too eager), I said, "Yes, I can meet you tonight. I should be done at work by about 5:30."

"Great!" and he sounded like he really meant it.

We made plans for where to meet and what time and I hung up the phone, smiling. I knew he was choosing to spend his last evening with me, not Allison. That made me really happy, for reasons I refused to dig into. It also made me feel petty and a little bad for Allison.

We'd chosen a very casual venue, not far from his hotel, but it still offered some of the best burgers I'd ever had. I arrived a few minutes early and ordered a dirty martini. Still in my work clothes, I hadn't had time to do much other than brush my hair and reapply some lip gloss. I smoothed down my blouse and removed, put back on, and finally removed my blazer, deciding it was too much.

Philippe walked in, looking around for me. I watched him for a minute. He wore a blue polo shirt and baggy jeans, a look I'd always appreciated. Butterflies flitted in my stomach as I watched him scan the room. Not wanting him to think I'd stood him up, I called out his name, waving him over to the bar.

It was still early, so the bar was mostly empty. Without bodies to absorb the sound, the music seemed extraordinarily loud. The wait staff was busy prepping everything for the crowd that would begin arriving after six. The smell of burgers and fries wafted out from the kitchen, and my mouth watered. I hadn't eaten lunch. Not intentionally.

"Drink?" I asked as I leaned in to kiss each cheek, pretending as though our last encounter had not been me running away while he stood next to Allison in only a towel. He smelled really good.

Philippe nodded and gave his order to the bartender.

We found a table in a back corner and settled in, both of us immersed in the menu. I didn't know about Philippe, but I was happy to just pretend the other day never happened. He didn't seem too eager to replay it either.

The waitress took our order, and we laughed as we both ordered the exact same meal: a burger with Swiss cheese, mushrooms, and bacon.

Silence. Discomfort. I shifted in my seat, taking another sip of my drink. "So, are you all packed and ready to go home?" *Now that's a brilliant conversation starter, Lila.*

He nodded his head, then took a sip of his beer. "I packed before leaving to come here, that's why I was a little late. Just in case I am out late or something." He looked down into his beer, wrapping his hands around the mug, suddenly shy.

"Well, I'm not going to beg to take you dancing tonight." I laughed, but my joke came out sounding very flat. No repeats of the clubbing night in Paris. And then, it dawned on me that maybe he was going to be out late because he had plans with Allison after this. I gulped down the rest of my martini and caught the eye of the waitress, indicating I'd like another.

Philippe laughed. "Please don't try to take me dancing. It didn't end well last time."

We had a habit of our time together not ending well. "I was surprised you wanted to have dinner with me tonight," I admitted, suddenly very interested in the olives in my refreshed drink.

"Why?" He removed his hands from the mug and placed them in his lap. A few seconds later, he coughed, and then placed his hands on the table, interlacing his fingers and twiddling his thumbs.

I took a deep breath, scouring my brain for something to say. This was painful. How would I answer that question?

"So when do you—" I started.

"Are you going to—" he started at the same time.

We laughed. "You first," Philippe insisted.

"I just thought you and Allison would see each other again. Tonight. It seemed like you two were getting along well."

He put his hands back around the beer mug, swirling the remaining content. "Allison is a nice girl. We've had some fun days touring the city, and she's decent company. But I'm not interested in pursuing anything else. Especially not since I'm leaving tomorrow."

I nearly choked on my drink. He had seemed interested enough to pursue getting naked with her. And did he not want to pursue anything further because of the distance, or just not with Allison?

Unsure of what to say, or how to feel about everything he'd just said, I changed the subject. "So, what did you go see?"

"I will give Allison this. She's a great tour guide. We went to the Air and Space Museum at the Smithsonian, and strolled by the White House. That was neat." His voice was flat as he rattled off the places he'd been with little enthusiasm.

I should have given that tour. I squirmed.

"Anyway, it wasn't nearly as fun as the tour you gave me." Philippe looked out into the restaurant, avoiding eye contact. Then he continued, "I made sure Allison knew last night that I had no intention of pursuing anything."

Now that was interesting news. Allison sure hadn't given that impression when I'd spoken to her earlier.

"How's Sam?" he asked, avoiding eye contact.

Now it was my turn to hide details. "He's great." Slight white lie. I wasn't ready to tell Philippe I'd broken up with Sam.

He nodded. "Are all American girls so anxious to get married?"

My eyebrows shot up at the unexpected question. "What does that mean?" I fired back, defensive on the behalf of American girls as a whole.

"Well, my experience thus far is you, Callie, and Allison. Callie managed to hook my best friend into marriage after only four days, and I swear, Allison had the same game plan." His voice was sour. This was a side of him I hadn't seen before.

"Ok, well that's just not fair. You know that there's never been a couple better suited for each other than Callie and Julien."

Philippe nodded. "That's true."

"And Allison, well, she's just apparently really into you. But I'd be surprised if she's looking to jump straight into marriage."

He chuckled, relaxing his shoulders a bit. "She asked last night when she could come to visit me, and that's when I knew I needed to set the story straight."

A pang of sadness for Allison shot through me, but it certainly relieved my guilt about being here. "She's a nice girl. Just a little, well..."

"Overenthusiastic?"

"Yes, she is high energy. But fun." It felt safer to defend her now that I knew he wasn't interested. However, I wasn't sure how this made me feel about him and his treatment of women. I also desperately wanted to ask him about what happened the other night. I guess I'd have to wait for him to tell Julien and Julien to tell Callie, and then I could easily get it out of her.

"Well, you've lumped all of us American girls into one category, and I certainly have never tried to do anything even remotely close to..."

"No, no you haven't," Philippe jumped in. "Relax, it was just a joke. A lousy one, apparently."

Only his voice had no indication that he was joking when

he'd made the statement. We fell into another awkward silence. Why couldn't we settle into a normal conversation?

Thankfully, our food arrived and he bit into his burger. A moan escaped, and despite my irritation at myself, the sound made me feel all tingly. Involuntarily, of course.

"You were right, this is delicious," he stated, his mouth full of food.

I giggled. "You have mayonnaise on your nose!" I fought the urge to wipe it off for him.

Philippe grabbed his napkin, wiped his nose off, and said, "You can recommend food for me anytime, Lila."

If there's ever another opportunity, I thought.

BOTH OF US groaned as we stood up from the table. "I never stop when I should," I whined, in pain from overeating.

"We can walk it off," Philippe suggested. "Shall I walk you home?"

I nodded. It was warmer than expected for the season.

"What time is your flight tomorrow?" I turned to face him. There was a comfortable space between us, despite my desire to close the gap and reach for his hand.

For some reason he looked at his watch before saying, "I need to be at the airport by 10 a.m."

As we walked slowly toward my place, I filled him in on the best way to get there. We seemed to have gotten past the weirdness and were settling into a more comfortable groove. Maybe it was because I knew he was leaving tomorrow and all of this tension would just go away. Who knew when we would even see each other again?

Approaching my apartment building, I stopped, looked up toward my floor, and stated the obvious. "Well, this is me."

He nodded. Hands crammed in his pockets, he looked at the ground, shuffling his feet. "I'm sorry we didn't get to spend more time together, Lila." He raised his eyes to look into mine, and I had to avert my eyes.

So was I. "Maybe you'll be back sometime soon?" I busied my hands by digging in my purse for my keys.

"No plans for any meetings here in the next year. But maybe you'll come see Callie again soon?"

"I don't know about soon, but I'm sure we'll see each other again." Having found the keys, I pulled them out and stood in silence, trying to figure out what to do next.

"I guess I should get back to my hotel."

"Okay."

He stepped toward me, and I caught my breath as he closed the distance between us. "Lila?"

"Yes?"

Philippe took a deep breath. "About the other day... the kiss. It was a mistake. I shouldn't have let it happen. You have something with Sam, and I shouldn't have done it."

I stood there, stunned into silence. My mind raced to process his words, to find a way to tell him that I had ended things with Sam, that I had been absolutely blown away by his kiss, that I desperately wished there was a way this could be something more. But I said nothing. He'd said it was a mistake.

He leaned toward me, and I thought he might kiss me, but instead, he kissed each cheek. "Take care, Lila," Philippe said softly, and turned and walked away.

I guess there'd be no Paris predicament after all.

21

Late March 2002

"Lila!" my boss bellowed. "We're waiting for you in the conference room!"

I startled. I'd been lost in my thoughts about Philippe. Despite my best efforts to push him out of my mind, thoughts of him still consumed me. The way he smelled, the feel of his lips on mine, how I desperately wished our last moments together had been different. But that's not what had happened. Even throwing myself into my projects and the legislation we were working on had not helped me forget the whirlwind of my recent emotional turmoil.

I joined my colleagues and tried my best to focus on my work. It was going to be a long week if I couldn't get myself together.

After our long Monday staff meeting, during which I struggled to stay focused, I avoided everyone and returned immediately to my office. Not ready to dive into work, I opened my email, hoping that maybe somehow he'd written, expressing his undying love for me. I could find a way to make this work. Seeing nothing from Philippe, I opened a new email and started typing. I had no intention of sending it, but I hoped it would help me sort through my feelings and bring closure if I typed it out.

Subject: Update

Dear Philippe,

There's so much I want to say to you. I can't stop thinking about our kiss and the way I feel when we're together. You asked me if I feel it too, and I do. And that's confusing and crazy because I shouldn't want to be in a new relationship now, certainly not with someone who lives on the other side of the Atlantic Ocean!

I broke up with Sam. It wasn't fair for me to continue with him when all I can think about is you.

I don't know what to do at this point, but I needed to tell you how I feel.

I WAS INTERRUPTED by my boss, who startled me. "Lila, we have a situation," he said, storming into my office.

His unexpected and loud arrival caused me to jump, and in my attempt to hide what I was doing, I accidentally hit SEND instead of SAVE on the draft.

"Nooooooo!" I yelled.

Now he looked startled. "It's not *that* serious!"

Red-faced, heart beating a million miles a minute, I stood, breathing deeply to avoid a panic attack. What had I done?

"Are you okay?" Tom asked.

I nodded, unable to speak yet.

"Here's the situation. There's a critical meeting in Paris next week with our European partners. It's about the new clean water initiative we've been working on. Sally was supposed to go, but the legislation she's been working on is being fast tracked, and I need you to go instead."

"Huh? Paris? Next week?" I squeaked.

"Are you ill? What is happening to you?" He placed his hand on my forehead in an oddly parental gesture. "Are you feverish?"

"No, I just... well, this is surprising."

"I thought you'd be all over it, with your Paris connections and all. And I trust you to handle this."

My heart skipped about fourteen beats. "Okay. I've got this."

Tom thumped my shoulder, said, "I knew I could count on you," and turned to leave.

"Um, Tom, is it okay if I make my travel arrangements to leave Friday? I'll stay with my friend Callie, so there won't be hotel costs."

"Sure, I don't care when you leave."

I sat back down at my computer and timidly opened my inbox, praying that somehow I had not actually sent the email. My hands shook as I clicked on the folder for Sent messages. There it was. I had sent it.

Subject: Help

Dear Callie,

Two things. One, I'm unexpectedly coming to Paris for a meeting. Arriving Saturday morning. Can I stay with you and Julien?

Two. I accidentally sent Philippe an email I never intended to send him, telling him I broke up with Sam and can't stop thinking about him.

Help!

Xo, Lila

I EXITED THE PROGRAM, and set to work rescheduling all of my appointments for the following week. Reality settled in. I was going back to Paris. And I would undoubtedly see Philippe. What had I done?

I SPENT the afternoon meeting with Sally, who filled me in on all of the pertinent details of her project, and finally braved reopening my emails. Saying a silent prayer that Philippe had never received the email, I was both relieved and disappointed to see he had not replied. But there were four somewhat frantic emails from Callie.

Re: Help

You did what?!

Callie

Re:Re: Help

Yay! You're coming! Yes, of course, you can stay with us! I'll see if Emilie's available for a girl's night on Saturday!

Re:Re:Re: Help

I need more details on what you sent him. How did you accidentally send him an email? And you broke up with Sam? What is going on?

Re:Re:Re:Re: Help

PLEASE tell me what happened with Philippe. I'm dying over here!

Xo, Callie

Re:Re:Re:Re:Re: Help

Hi Callie,

I'm so sorry—that wasn't nice to drop a bomb like that and disappear! I've been in meetings all afternoon. To fill you in: I decided it was unfair to Sam to continue on when my feelings are confused. I had dinner with Philippe before he returned to Paris, and he was friendly and lovely, but made it clear our kiss was a mistake. I had already broken up with Sam, but I didn't tell him. I thought I could just move on, get past this silly obsession, but I can't stop thinking about him.

I thought I could write out my feelings in an email and just not send it. That it would help me process and move on. You know, kind of like Monica, Rachel, and Phoebe burning the old ex-boyfriend stuff?? But my boss startled me and I somehow managed to hit send.

I'm so embarrassed. How will I face him? Is there any way you can not tell Philippe I'm coming next week?

Xo, Lila

THE REPLY CAME ALMOST INSTANTLY, as if she'd been refreshing her email a thousand times just waiting for my response.

Re:Re:Re:Re:Re:Re: Help

Uh, sorry friend, that cat's out of the bag. He was here when you said you were coming. Don't worry, I didn't say anything about the email. He's been with us all evening, so I know he hasn't seen it.

The Paris Predicament

Callie and I finished making arrangements. I'd take the train and Metro to her apartment on Saturday morning, and she'd do her best to keep Philippe away. Trembling, I checked my email one last time before packing up for the day. Still no reply. Grabbing my purse and coat, I left the office, trying to ignore the gnawing in the pit of my stomach.

BY THE TIME I got to the airport on Friday, I was a jumpy bag of nerves. I snapped at the poor gate attendant and then tried to apologize for my rude behavior. Philippe had never replied, and I was torn between feeling anger, hurt, and disappointment. Maybe he hadn't checked his email. Maybe he had and wanted nothing to do with me. Maybe he was angry. So many maybes.

Once I settled in on the plane, I put in my earbuds, still feeling a twinge of guilt about Sam every time I used the MP3 player, and closed my eyes, hoping to sleep.

I did not. My stomach was in knots, anxiety tore at me, and to make the trip even more fun, a family with two very unhappy children sat behind me. Every few minutes, my seat jerked with one of them kicking it or pushing into it. There was not enough red wine in the world to make this trip bearable. However, not wanting to arrive in the state I had last time, I did not drink that much, and just watched the movie until the kids settled down. I slipped into quasi-sleep at some point and awakened an hour before landing when the breakfast of a cold croissant and jelly, yogurt, and fresh fruit was served. Clearing customs was a breeze, and I arrived quickly at the train station for the forty-five minute trip into the city.

22

The train rumbled stop by stop on its way to Paris. They were always packed to the gills, but I managed to basically wrap myself around my small suitcase and squeeze into an open spot, grateful for the space that opened up more and more with each stop. I dozed off once or twice but the closer I got to the city, the worse the pain in my abdomen became. Had Philippe seen my email? Would he want to see me, or would he stay far away while I was in town? Would Callie and Julien be upset with me for upsetting him? Was he even upset? The questions just flowed through me. This uncertainty was darn near paralyzing.

The increasing amount of graffiti on the stone walls separating the train tracks from housing indicated we were getting closer to the city. My anxiety subsided slightly as I lost myself in the familiar sights, happy as always to be back in Paris. As we approached the Gare du Nord, I hefted up my bags and moved toward the nearest door. While I knew my way around the transit system pretty well, it was always more stressful to navigate with luggage. Thankfully, the congestion was much lighter at eight in the morning on a Saturday than it would have been on a workday. I maneuvered through the Gare down to the Metro station, running to catch a train that arrived seconds before I reached the platform. It was mostly empty, so I claimed one seat for my bags and a seat for myself. Traveling through a crowded public transport system in Paris with multiple bags was one of my least favorite things to do, so I was grateful not to be squished in like a sardine.

The walk from the Metro to Callie's apartment took almost no time at all. The morning was quite warm for March and sweat rolled down my back as I lugged my suitcase down the street. The massive red door loomed in front of me, and while I knew the code for entry, nerves knotted my stomach. Was this trip to Paris fate's intervention? Had it been thrown in my lap as an opportunity to see if this was real between me and Philippe? Or was it just the Universe's sick sense of humor? Maybe there was no reason for anything, and it was simply the cards I had been dealt and Philippe had nothing to do with it. I didn't want to get my hopes up, but it was darn near impossible to stop the constant flow of thoughts that maybe, just maybe, Philippe wanted something more.

Entering the courtyard, I heard a squeal and "Lilaaaaa!" hollered at me. Glancing up, I saw not only Callie, but also Emilie, standing on the small balcony of Callie's apartment, waving and hooting. They disappeared, and shortly after reappeared at the main door. Running at me as if we hadn't seen each other in decades, they engulfed me in their hugs.

"I'll take this," Emilie insisted, relieving me of my small suitcase.

"Let me look at you," I said, checking Emilie out. "Still as gorgeous and punk rock as ever. I'm so glad you're here!"

Emilie smiled appreciatively. "You were lucky. I just happened to be back for this week, tying up a few loose ends." I followed them into the building as they bombarded me with questions about my flight, my parents, work ... all the inconsequential things, skirting the topics of Sam and Philippe. Emilie filled me in on her parents and some of our mutual friends from Uni. I knew that would come eventually, probably over some wine.

"I'm so tired. I barely slept a wink on the flight. I want a nap." I whined.

"Absolutely not," Callie replied. "You know the rules. Stay awake or you'll be miserable the entire time."

My bottom lip popped out in a pouty protest.

"How about a hot shower while we make brunch?" she asked kindly. "I assume you haven't eaten?"

"That sounds lovely."

Grabbing a change of clothes and my toiletry bag, I entered the bathroom, stripped down, and stood in the hot shower until the hot water ran out. Toweling my hair, I cracked my neck from side to side, trying to stretch away some of the pain from the eight-hour flight.

The sight in the living room warmed my heart. Two of my best friends, happily chatting on the couch, mugs of tea in their hands, with a spread of fresh croissants, *pain au chocolat,* of course, and fresh baguette with an array of jams. Saliva immediately pooled in my mouth at the spread.

"Let me make you a cup of tea!" Emilie volunteered.

"Where's Julien?" I asked.

"Saturday morning is football training," Callie said.

"Oh yes, of course." Julien was quite the soccer player, or footballer, as they called them in France. As a former soccer player herself, Callie loved the fact that he continued to play.

Emilie returned with the tea, and sat, patting the couch beside her. I knew the time for the inquisition had arrived.

"So, shall we start with Sam or Philippe?" Callie asked, crossing her legs and shifting so she was facing me.

"Philippe?" Emilie asked, surprised. "What's he got to do with anything?"

Clearly Callie hadn't filled her in on that part.

"Oh, we'll get there," I assured her. "Sam's the easy one, so let's start there." Over the next hour, I told them all the details. How we'd met (they got a good laugh at my rocket launch of the Walkman) and the short whirlwind relationship. They were enthralled that he had taken me dress shopping.

"Just like in *Pretty Woman!*" Emilie said.

"Without being a prostitute!"

Emilie snorted. "Obviously! And you let this guy go? *Why?*"

Callie smiling mischievously, leaning in toward Emilie, clearly enjoying the fact that she had insider information. "That's the Philippe part of the story," she said, putting her pointer finger up to her mouth, like a detective working through a crime.

"What?" Emilie's eyebrows nearly shot off her head in surprise.

"And that's where the hard part starts. So, let's get back to Sam." They nodded, waiting for me to begin. "Sam's great. Dating a guy that could spoil me like that all the time is certainly appealing. But no matter what, I couldn't shake the feeling that he was just a placeholder. No passion or chemistry. And I knew I needed to end it."

"Wow, you're a stronger woman than I am, Lila. I'd be all about dating for money." Emilie winked.

"On that topic," I turned to her, suddenly very tired of telling my own boring story. "Any men in your life these days?" We hadn't been very good at keeping up with each other.

Emilie wasn't exactly one to email, and I had been, well, distracted.

"You don't get off that easily," Emilie said. "I've been waiting this whole time to hear what on earth is going on with Philippe. And now you just go and change the subject?" She shook her head back and forth in dismay.

I laughed. "I've been completely dominating the conversation. I wanted to let someone else talk a little bit about their life. We have all day to hear the rest of my story. There's not much to tell anyway."

"Well alright. I'll share my news quickly, and then it's back to the Philippe saga," Emilie stated, placing her hand on my knee, leaning in attentively.

"So you *do* have news?" I asked. Callie and I looked at each other. Callie looked as surprised as I felt.

"You do?" Callie asked, hurt registering on her face that Emilie hadn't shared this information with her. My lips turned up in a slight smile at Callie's response, considering she'd not had the chance to tell Emilie about Philippe either. "I guess I've been so busy working that you and I haven't even properly caught up. That's a crime considering we live in the same country! I have to wait until our friend comes all the way over from the United States to catch up on your love life?"

"Don't be dramatic," Emilie said dryly, picking up her teacup. "This is a very recent development. I haven't been keeping anything from you."

Relief showed on Callie's face. I had forgotten how easily her feelings could be hurt. It was both a sweet and annoying quality. "Do tell!" she said.

"Okay, well it's obviously not a local guy. We all know how those Parisian men are." She rolled her eyes and we all laughed.

We both nodded. "That's probably better anyway. Who

wants a long-distance relationship anyway?" I stated, realizing how ironic the words were that came out of my mouth.

Emilie and Callie turned to me, looked at each other, and shrugged.

Emilie continued, looking directly at me. "Do you remember JP from Uni?"

I scrunched my nose, trying to remember which one he was. "The tall guy with all the tats and piercings?"

"Yep, that's the right guy."

"Ooh, he's hot!" I set my teacup on the table, shifting myself so I could look directly at her.

She nodded, her face flushing slightly. Embarrassment was not an emotion Emilie wore often, which caused me to really pay attention.

"Agreed. He just moved back to Strasbourg too. We hung out a couple of times with our mutual friends, but then started hanging out just the two of us. One thing led to another and we've been going out from time to time."

Callie stood up, collected the empty cups, and moved toward the kitchen. Over her shoulder she said, "Um, I hate to break it to you, but something that's been going on for over a month is not a recent development in girl time! I can't believe you've been secretly seeing this guy and didn't share the news?"

"You slag," I chided Emilie.

We all giggled.

"It's not that I was intentionally trying to keep it a secret," Emilie admitted. "But, I do have to say that with him I wasn't sure if it was just fun and games, and I didn't really want to act like it was something more than that until it was."

"So, is it? You're telling us, so, yes?" I asked.

Emilie smiled slightly. "I'd say it's on its way to becoming something, yes."

We all squealed.

"Okay so now that you're caught up on my news, back to you, Lila. Tell us all about Philippe!"

I shifted positions on the couch. "Well that's just it," I started. "There's really nothing much to tell. Except we spent the day together—he was in Washington, DC for a conference—and we had what started out as an amazing day together. We walked around, had a fun time seeing different monuments. He's interested in so many of the same things I am." I turned to Emilie. "When I was in Paris last time, we also spent a really incredible day together, and well, I started to develop some rather confusing feelings. Especially since it was so soon after the breakup."

Emilie nodded.

"And we might have kissed," I added quietly.

Emilie's eyebrows did that thing again. She had an excellent surprised face. "Way to bury the lede!"

"Okay," Callie said, "Now we're getting to the good part." She crossed her legs and leaned toward me. "Spare no details. This is what I've been waiting for."

So I didn't. I filled them in on every detail of our day together and the kiss that made me swoon. "So, at the end of this day together, we were sitting on a park bench drinking hot cocoa, and when we'd finished, we were just kind of... magically pulled together." I shrugged my shoulders.

Emilie giggled.

"What's so funny?" I asked.

"I just have this vision of you two staring at each other, and your lips being pulled together like magnets."

Admittedly, the vision was funny.

"It did feel somewhat like that. And once it started, I didn't want it to stop. Y'all, he is an incredible kisser."

"Ew, I don't know if I want to know that. Now I'll just be looking at his lips next time I see him," Callie said.

"Well, it's true. More importantly, all the ooey gooey feelings and the flash bangs and fireworks I'd expected each time I'd kissed Sam and never experienced—they sure kicked in this time." I sighed and touched my lips, remembering the moment.

Emilie and Lila were both leaning into me, dreamy smiles on their faces, like girls do when we hear stories of new love.

"Aww, that's so sweet," Emilie crooned. "So what's the problem?"

Callie giggled.

"What?" Emilie asked.

"You'll enjoy this part," Callie assured her.

"If you're a masochist!" I quipped.

Callie put her hand over her mouth, trying not to laugh.

"Please continue," Emilie begged. "I'm in agony."

I told them the details of the whole night. The call from Sam, the quick decision to invite Philippe—"Oh no! Why would you *do* that?" Emilie asked, only to be followed by, "Are you insane?"

"It gets better," I said, filling them in on the double date. As good girlfriends do, they both criticized poor Allison and her attempts to woo Philippe.

"Aw, don't be too hard on her. She didn't realize I was bringing her into my spider web of lies and confusion. She's a nice girl."

"Mm hmm," Callie agreed with a sarcastic tone. Emilie and Callie looked at each other and nodded their heads as if agreeing telepathically that even nice girls get trashed if they're imposing on our territory. At least, that's what I imagined that look between them meant.

Then we got to the part about Philippe and the towel.

"What? He *slept* with her?" Emilie exclaimed, hopping off the couch. "That jerk!"

"I mean, I didn't forensically examine the situation, but it sure seemed to be the case. And he's not a jerk. Can you blame him?"

She shrugged her shoulders. In reality, Philippe could not be blamed for that. I'd thrown him at her.

Callie shifted uneasily on the couch.

"What do you know?" I asked.

"Julien's going to kill me." She paused, and Emilie and I stared at her expectedly. After a dramatic silence that nearly killed me, she finally said, "It's time for a stronger drink." She stood up and moved to the kitchen.

I sprang up from the couch, following her into the kitchen, with Emilie on my tail. "You cannot leave us hanging like this! And it's only 11 a.m."

"Puh-lease, sorority girl Lila. Like you've never day drunk. That's why God invented Bloody Marys and Mimosas!"

Emile and I laughed.

"Fair point," I agreed.

Callie retrieved three glasses, the vodka, and some cranberry juice and pulled tiny little ice cubes from a tray in the mini freezer on top of the miniature fridge. She turned and looked solemnly at us before returning to fixing the drinks while she spoke. "I eavesdropped on a conversation between my husband and a certain best friend of his. And I didn't hear everything, but I'm fairly certain that Philippe and Allison did not, in fact, sleep together. Apparently she got really drunk, and passed out in his room."

"Cheese and biscuits," I hollered, throwing my arms in the air. My two friends looked at me in surprise, and then busted out in laughter.

"That's my line!" Callie joked.

"But why was he there in a towel? And why was she in his shirt?" I demanded.

"I don't have all the details, but I did hear him say that he got up to take a shower, and when he came back out, she had apparently misread the situation and disrobed. She'd ordered room service, and when you knocked, thought it was them. Maybe she grabbed his shirt to answer the door?"

Callie shoved a drink in my hand, we clinked our glasses together, and I knocked back a big gulp before wandering back into the living room. I had completely misread that entire situation. Thank goodness I had not reacted by running straight to Sam to get even.

"That's a lot of supposition," Emilie chimed in, "but I suppose it's a possible theory."

Pacing the small living room, my thoughts wandered all over the place. I'd been so hurt about the fact that he'd allegedly jumped into the arms of someone else—despite the fact that I was with Sam—that this new information wasn't settling well. After another sip of my drink, I placed my glass on the table and continued to pace.

Callie and Emilie followed me into the room, and Callie placed her hand on my arm. "Nothing has happened that you can't recover from. Depending on what you want the outcome to be. That's the first thing you have to decide."

"Oh this is tragic," Emilie said. "It's like a Danielle Steel romance."

"Oh, the story is not over yet, girl," Callie piped in, unable to control herself at this point from sharing probably the worst, if not funniest, part of the entire story.

"There's more?" Emilie squeaked.

Callie nodded and continued. "Then she *accidentally* sent him an email professing her feelings."

"You did *what*? How do you accidentally send an email? And what did it say?" Emilie sat forward on the couch. "Girls, why on earth did we quit smoking? This is a cigarette moment."

Instead, she reached for the baguette and slowly chewed on a piece.

I settled on the couch and told them the rest of the story.

Callie nodded. "So this is where we stand. We know they both have feelings for each other—"

"Wait, how do we know that?" Emilie asked. "Because of the kiss, or is there more?"

Callie and I exchanged a glance. She shrugged her shoulders. "Well, I might have some insider information on Philippe's feelings, but..." she put her pointer finger over her lips in the universal sign for *keep quiet about it.*

"Okay, so you both *allegedly* have feelings for each other, you sent an email a few days ago, and Philippe never replied. He was under the impression you were still with Sam up to that point, right? Is that it, or do I need more information?" Emilie asked me.

"That's the gist of it," I replied.

Emilie chewed on her bottom lip, hands on her hips. "Are you sure you have more than just a crush on him?" she finally asked.

"I don't know," I moaned, suddenly interested in the food on the table. I scooped out a bit of jelly and spread it on half a croissant. "I know that I can't stop thinking about him, even when who I'm with might have been the hottest guy on the planet, and seeing Philippe with someone else seared my insides. Kissing him felt like, well, *home.* But with fire." I stood up again, not able to sit still.

"She's got it bad," Emilie said to Callie, who nodded her head in agreement.

"This is not good!" I insisted. How could I think that trying to move forward with Philippe could result in anything good? Long distance would be hard and painful. Why couldn't I just be satisfied with the guy who lived in my city? Was it actually about Philippe, or some weird self-defense mechanism? After all, if I chose to pursue a relationship with someone who lived 5,000 miles away, would I really be in a relationship? Or would it be a situationship—in which I was involved with someone "on paper" but still lived a life alone. That didn't seem healthy. I returned to the kitchen and refilled my drink.

"Love is *always* good," Callie said, following me.

"Except when it has the potential to destroy you," Emilie said. There we go. There was our dark spirited girl. "I think I need a shot. You got something other than vodka?" Emilie asked Callie. "Tequila?

I nodded in agreement. Shots seemed appropriate, despite the fact that we hadn't even gotten to lunchtime.

"I haven't had time to get to the store yet. I thought we'd do that this afternoon." Callie stated. "Shall we hit the store now?"

The three of us agreed, grabbing our purses and jackets and exiting the apartment. It was probably a good idea to break up our drinking as well. A small grocery store was within a ten-minute walk, so I continued to spill the details as we walked. We loaded our shopping bags with the essentials. Booze, more booze, and snacks to go with the booze. By the time we'd finished shopping and walked back to Callie's flat, I'd told them everything I could think of to share and answered all the questions that arose.

Callie shoved open the large outer door to her apartment complex, only to run smack into Philippe. Of course. "Oh cheese and biscuits!" Callie exclaimed, nearly losing her balance. Philippe reached out to steady her.

"Hi Callie." He kissed her cheeks, then saw Emilie. I, at the back of the crew, stood frozen in place, praying for some miracle that I had just developed the superpower of invisibility. Searching for any large potted plants or trees I could try to hide behind, and coming up empty, I tried to get out of eyesight.

"It's good to see you, Emilie," Philippe said warmly, leaning in to kiss her cheeks. And then he saw me. He froze. "Lila, what are you doing here?" His voice was anything but the warm, friendly tone he'd give the other two. He shook his head back and forth. "I need to go. I'm, um, late for, er... something," and he brushed by quickly.

Emilie and Callie turned to look at me. I shoved past them into the apartment building, and started climbing the stairs, hot tears running down my cheeks. Hustling behind me, our booze bottles clinking away, Emilie said, "Are you okay?"

"I am so very not okay," I mumbled through sobs.

"Yeah, that was not pleasant."

Emilie took the bags I was carrying, and we entered the apartment.

"Hello, *les filles!*" Julien greeted us enthusiastically. "Lila, so good..." he stopped mid-sentence as he saw my face. Looking quickly to Callie and back at me, he asked, "*Qu'est-ce qui c'est passé?*" *What happened?*

"We just ran into Philippe."

"*Oh, non!*"

"*Oh, si,*" Emilie said, traversing the living room and depositing the bags in the kitchen. She immediately retrieved three glasses, dropped two ice cubes in each, and we picked up where we'd left off, only with a larger supply to draw from.

Callie ushered me to the couch and sat next to me, rubbing my back, similar to how she'd comforted me on the night of my failed wedding. "It's okay, Lila."

"He obviously wants nothing to do with me," I moaned, my chest heaving with panicked, shallow breaths.

"I'm sorry for that poor timing," Julien said, a deep frown on his face. But he offered nothing else. I knew this was an impossible situation for him. Philippe was his best friend, and no matter how much Julien cared for me, I knew where his loyalties lay.

Callie shot him a look that he clearly understood.

"I'm going to go take a shower and then um..." his voice trailed off.

Callie nodded and I buried my head in my hands, embarrassed at the position I'd landed in. "I'm such an idiot."

"You are not an idiot. You could have never foreseen that run-in, and I'm sure you surprised him as much as he surprised us."

"What do I do?" I begged for advice.

No one had any answers.

23

Sunday morning I awoke to the delicious smell and sizzling sound of *lardon*, small chunks of pork that are similar to bacon bits, and onion, frying in a pan. I went to the bathroom, brushed my teeth, and wandered into the kitchen.

"Good morning!" Julien greeted me cheerfully, setting down the wooden spoon and turning to kiss me on each cheek.

"Morning. Where's Callie?"

"She went to the bakery to grab some fresh bread. She should be home any minute." He returned to stirring the mix, then pulled eggs from the fridge, cracking six of them into a large bowl as I made myself a cup of coffee.

"Mm, that smells so good. Whatcha making?" I peered around him to see what he was cooking.

"A quiche Lorraine for lunch. Will you hand me that bowl please?" Julien pointed at the counter next to me.

"Sure!" I handed him the bowl. "Lunch? What time is it?"

"It's almost eleven."

"Wow, I never sleep that late!"

He stopped what he was doing and turned to me. His expression was grave. "Listen, I did something."

My heart rate quickened. I set down my coffee cup and leaned against the counter. "What did you do?"

"I asked Callie first!" he said, defensively, taking a step back.

"Okay. What did you do?" My imagination was in full overdrive at this point, guessing at the many things he could have done.

"I don't normally like to get involved in situations like this. But I can't stand to see two people I care about suffering. Especially when..." his thoughts trailed off. He grabbed a towel off the counter, wiping his hands.

"Yeah..." I knew what he was insinuating. Especially when they might be falling in love, but neither one can seem to take the right actions.

"So, I called Philippe this morning."

Now my heart beat as fast as if I'd just run a mile at a full sprint. "And?" I managed to squeak out as I braced myself against the counter. My knees wobbled.

"I told him you two needed to talk and asked if he'd consider having you over this evening."

I sat down at the small table, trying to digest this information. On one hand, I couldn't wait to see Philippe. On the other, fear filled me. Sometimes it's better to live in the *What if?* than to be rejected.

"He agreed," Julien continued quickly. "If you want to see him, he'll be expecting you at five at his place."

I buried my head in my hands. Julien stepped toward me, placing a hand on my shoulder.

"Should I have not done this?" Julien asked, a concerned look on his face.

"No, it's okay. It's better that we clear the air."

Relief washed over his face, and he stepped back.

"Julien?"

He looked over at me. "Yes?"

"Thank you."

He nodded, closed the space between us again, and patted my head like one would a child.

"I hope for the best for both of you, Lila."

DESPITE HAVING VERY LITTLE APPETITE, I ate two pieces of Julien's delicious quiche, showered, and got ready for the day. I had several hours before I needed to leave for Philippe's apartment, and despite Callie's efforts to keep me engaged in small talk, I had a hard time staying in the present moment. The anticipation was driving me crazy, so I pulled out my clothes for the conference and ironed them. We turned on some music, Callie and Julien kept themselves busy doing laundry and their weekly apartment cleaning, and I tried to focus on anything other than the impending discussion coming with Philippe.

A knock on the door interrupted my thoughts.

"Are we expecting someone?" Callie asked Julien.

He shrugged his shoulders, a confused look on his face. He opened the door wide. Philippe stood there.

My heart leapt at the sight of him and those adorable hazel-green eyes, although they avoided me, staying glued on Julien. My stomach immediately dropped, dread running through me. It was not a good sign that he had arrived here, was it?

"Uh, I thought we were meeting in an hour?" I stammered. My knees quivered and I struggled to hold back tears. There could be only one reason why he'd come here now, and that was to tell me to leave him alone, that he didn't want to see me again tonight.

"Can we talk now? I couldn't wait." His pained expression told me everything. He did not have the feelings I did, and there was no need to spend an uncomfortable evening together hashing it out.

"Uh, sure, let me put on my shoes." I slowly slipped on my sneakers, dragging out the process like I was about to begin my march to execution. A firing squad stood at the ready to take down my heart.

Callie and Julien exchanged concerned looks, and Philippe gave them a small smile before exiting the apartment. "I'll wait for you downstairs."

Trembling, I tried to brace myself for what was coming. I blinked hard to keep the tears at bay.

Callie placed her hand on my shoulder. "No matter what happens, you're going to be okay. I'll be here."

I hugged her tightly.

Dragging my legs, because they resisted forward movement, I made my way down the hall, and the stairs. Why was I such an idiot? Who falls in love with essentially a stranger who lives across the ocean? Well, besides Callie. But she didn't do it within months of being left at the altar. Clearly Philippe had come to the same conclusion, and just wanted to get it over with sooner, rather than later.

Exiting the building, I found Philippe leaning against the side wall. He gave the smallest smile. He didn't look angry, but he also didn't look like someone who was madly in love, ready to jump into a transatlantic love affair.

"This," Philippe started, pointing at me and then back at himself, "is the worst idea ever."

I sucked in a deep breath. *Here we go.* At least I would have closure this time and he was man enough to end things (before they ever really began) to my face instead of taking the cowardly way out.

Tears pooled in my eyes, and I fluttered my eyelids, trying to keep them from falling. I shoved my hands in my pockets and nodded, staring down at the ground. Way to rip the Band-Aid right off, Philippe. I admired him for not beating around the bush.

He reached out, gently cupping my face in his hand and making me look at him. His expression softened. "But screw that, Lila. I haven't stopped thinking about you since the moment I saw you at that New Year's Party. I've tried to keep my distance because you were with Matt, and then Sam. And I literally keep my distance because we live so far apart!"

He laughed at his own joke, and I smiled, desperately wanting him to continue his thought. Confusion coursed through me. Was he saying he wanted me? Or was he saying that he wanted me but this couldn't work?

"You didn't reply to my emails. I thought you didn't want to see me, and then you literally *ran away* from me yesterday." My chin quivered and I tried to hold back the tears.

He dropped his hand and stepped back. "I wasn't prepared to see you and certainly wasn't ready to talk to you. I panicked. I don't know how to do this, Lila. There are just so many obstacles in our way," Philippe said.

He paced back and forth on the sidewalk in front of me. Stopping, he turned to face me. "I'm terrified, Lila. It hasn't even been a year since your relationship with Matt ended. A relationship that was supposed to end in marriage. Despite my feelings for you, I can't help but wonder if I'm a rebound? If I'm just a placeholder until you figure things out. I don't want to be a rebound. And more importantly, I want you to have the time and space to make your own decision." He took a step back, shoved his hands in his pockets, and stared down the street.

Why did everyone keep saying that? Why did we need time if we knew deep inside that the other person was the wrong fit? It made no sense that I'd need mourning time. Matt hadn't died. Our relationship had ended because it wasn't right. "Maybe you're right," I whispered.

Surprised, his head snapped back in my direction, his brow creased in either pain or fear, maybe both. I had the urge to place my hand on his face.

"About the short time," I added quickly. "It hasn't been very long. But if I'm being honest with myself, Matt and I hadn't been in love for a long time. We were good friends, companions, who were comfortable staying together because it seemed like the right thing to do. But it wasn't much more than that. We never should have planned a wedding. I don't think either of us wanted it. Well," I added, shrugging my shoulders, "Matt made it very clear by not showing up that he didn't want it."

Philippe looked at me with deep compassion and pulled me in for a big hug. His hands ran over my hair and down my back. "What about you? I saw you on your wedding day. You looked like the most radiant princess, whose dreams were all coming true."

"It's true. I planned the perfect wedding. I thought Matt would be one and done for me. That we could live happily ever after."

Hurt crossed Philippe's face.

"But I quickly realized I'd been living in a world where moving forward, as long as it wasn't bad, was better than upending our lives. I was taking the easy route because I thought that's what I was supposed to do. But Matt and I didn't have a whole lot in common. We lived parallel lives, together, if that makes sense?"

He nodded but his eyes didn't fully register comprehension of the idea.

I tried again. "He did his thing, I did mine, and we did

some things together, but we weren't really a team. We coexisted, fairly happily because we were good friends. But there was no spark. No magic. I didn't really understand what I was missing until I spent time with you."

Philippe stared intensely at me. "Lila, I have loved you since the moment I first saw you. And I had to hide it for so long."

A whirring sensation grew in my ears as blood rushed to my head. I turned, staring out into the street, afraid to look at him. I didn't know what to say or do in this moment. While these were exactly the words I'd wanted to hear from him, all the questions I had ran through my mind. I was suddenly scared senseless. It was one thing to dream about this, to have a crush on him, to email and have a fun play relationship, to spend time together when we were in the same vicinity, but would that translate once we were really in a relationship?

"But you never answered my email," I said softly, hands jammed in my pockets, still not looking at him.

"I am so sorry, Lila. I didn't want to hurt you. It surprised me so much. Until that moment, I'd believed you were happy with Sam and had no interest in me beyond a friend. I did not know what else to do. Like you, I didn't know about your feelings, and I was trying to just find happiness and move on with my life." He reached out for me, pulling me to turn to face him.

I looked up at him. He pushed his glasses up, leaning toward me while he waited for an answer. I wanted nothing more than to pull him into my arms, but I stayed rooted in place.

"Like you said though. This," I repeated his gesture from earlier, pointing at him and then at me, "makes no sense. It's impossible." And yet, that was definitely not what I felt inside.

"It's certainly not easy or ideal," he admitted. "I want to be able to be with you every moment possible. Are you willing to see where it leads us? No promises at this point, other than we want to be together and see if we can make it work?"

Sighing, the thought of spending time with him, and being with him at every possible opportunity, made me lightheaded. Though we'd never be able to be the couple who could go out on regular dates, spend lazy evenings watching TV together, or see each other whenever we wanted, I started to think that might be ideal. I was gone so much with my work travel schedule anyway. Could we do this?

Philippe, sensing my hesitation, took both of my hands in his. "I don't want to do life without you. You make me smile and feel so good, and I promise, I will do my best to never hurt you."

"That's a big promise," I whispered, inching toward him. Could I promise the same?

"We can't promise each other we know how this will go. But I at least want a chance. I think we deserve a chance."

I looked into his eyes, my heart racing. His eyes searched mine for an answer. And I leaned in. "I think it's time for you to kiss me," I whispered in his ear.

He stepped in and put his arms around my waist, pulling me in closely. Kissing my neck first, then my chin, and then moving up to my mouth, he kissed me softly three times before flicking his tongue gently against my lips. I opened mine and touched my tongue to his. I melted completely into his arms, moaning softly. This was a new sensation where I melted into his body, wishing this moment would never stop. I didn't care where we lived or what we did, all I cared about in this moment was being with him.

Whooping and applause sounded in my head at the magnificence of this moment.

Philippe released me and started to laugh. He looked up, and Callie and Julien attempted to duck out of view.

"I *thought* the applause I heard in my head was real," I said, laughing.

Philippe smiled, waving off our lurking audience. He turned toward me. "Now what?" he asked.

"I suppose I should invite you up?"

"I'd like that," he said, and we entered the building, holding hands.

I had no idea of what would come after this. I'd make the most of the next week in Paris and we'd figure out the rest from there. I decided to shove all the fears aside, and let my heart have a win. No one is promised anything in this life. Not a tomorrow, not with any certainty. I was certain if I walked away from this moment without at least giving it a try, I would live with regret the rest of my life.

This situation no longer seemed like a predicament; rather, it was the beginning of something beautiful. It felt like love.

THE END

Epilogue
Christmas 2002

"We're here!" Philippe nudged me gently, pulling me out of sleep. "Wake up, sleepy head!" He was giddy like a small child and kissed me on the nose.

Stretching, I looked over at Julien and Callie, who grinned like two kids on Christmas morning. I was the only one who had never been to Strasbourg. This was Philippe and Julien's hometown, and I couldn't wait to see where Philippe had grown up. I'd been imagining what the house looked like and sending up many prayers that the most important people in his life would like me. Despite the gnawing nerves in my belly about meeting his mother, which terrified me, I hoped she would open her heart to me. Philippe's mother was very important to him, and it didn't sound like she was exceptionally thrilled about the fact that her son had fallen in love with an American.

As if he could read my thoughts, Philippe wrapped his arm around me and pulled me in for a hug. "*Maman* will love you!"

I sure as heck hoped so! I glanced at Callie and she smiled knowingly, having been through this two years before.

The train lumbered slowly into the station in Strasbourg, unsteadying us as we stood and gathered our belongings. As we came to a stop, I saw Emilie on the platform, jumping and clapping her hands. It was a dramatic contrast to her head-to-long black peacoat, Doc Martens, and spiky black pixie cut. I giggled as I watched her hop up and down as she awaited the doors to open.

We had barely cleared the stairs of the train when she threw herself at us, and Callie, Emilie, and I hugged tightly. "Welcome to Strasbourg!" Emilie said. It was the first time any of us had seen Emilie since the big trip to Paris when Philippe and I expressed our love for each other.

Since March, Philippe and I had emailed each other daily, chatted live in AOL chatrooms whenever we could, and we'd managed to coordinate to attend a Human Rights conference together. Philippe visited me in the United States over the summer, and it had been a long five months before I'd finally arrived in France several days ago to spend two weeks over the holidays with him. We were spending Christmas in Strasbourg with his family.

And I was terrified.

From what he's shared so far about his mother, she's a force to be reckoned with, and very picky about who Philippe spends his time with.

There was no time to be concerned about that. We maneuvered our luggage through the train station, where we found Julien's father, waiting to take Callie and Julien home. He hugged and kissed both of them, giving Callie a tenderhearted glance, and relieving her of her bag. That was the reception I prayed I would receive as well.

The next big stage of our relationship was now beginning. I grasped Philippe's hand tightly and looked up into his eyes. He smiled at me, before bending down to kiss me softly on the nose and then on the lips. "I can't remember the last time I've been so happy," he whispered in my ear.

I hugged him tightly. "Me either," I admitted. I shrugged away any fears about meeting his parents and basked in the happiness of the current moment.

Acknowledgments

A Note to the Reader & my thanks!

I'm so excited and grateful to you for reading Lila's story! I hope you loved this story as much as I loved writing it.

I know many fiction authors don't write an acknowledgment page, but I have so many people to thank. While I wrote the book, I couldn't have done it without my amazing support system, and I believe they deserve to be mentioned.

A special shout out goes to my friend Emma St. Clair who writes series based on the point of view of all the friends. *The Love Cliché* series is one of my favorite and inspired me to make a series following the friends from *4 Days in Paris*.

Other people I want to thank:

My beta readers and fellow authors. Michelle Oucharek-Deo, Elizabeth Ducie, Carol Amorosi. These ladies really went above and beyond to help me after a grave sickness nearly kept me from finishing this book on time. I'll never forget your willingness to jump in and provide feedback on a whim.

Emma St. Clair, Jenny Proctor, Victorine Lieske, Kasey Kennedy, Savannah Scott, Savannah Carlisle, Lindsay Gibson, Catherine Michaels, Michelle Oucharek-Deo, and so many other romance writers – thank you for inspiring me, supporting me, entertaining me, educating me, and being great writers!

Dakota Nyght and Jennifer Milius – the two best editors a gal could ask for. Thank you for your hard work on this!

Honorée – you've been such a great mentor and supporter. And the "eleventy-billion miles" came from her. Thanks for your encouragement and funny expressions. When are we going to Paris?

My community. The Women in Publishing Summit continues to fuel me and provide support and encouragement and love. THANK YOU.

My family and friends. 2024 was an incredibly challenging and scary year. Your support has been amazing. And to my kiddos. You're the best. Love you!

Lisa, Tia, Kerry, Charlotte, Smail, Stef, Dan, Seb, Ludo – this book literally wouldn't exist if it weren't for our friendship and time together in France. Love you all and I miss you so much.

I want to thank YOU, dear readers, for all the outpouring of love through reviews and social media. It means so much to hear from you!

And Nick... thank you for all of your love, support, and encouragement. And for reminding me that it's never too late for a good love story.

If you aren't already following me on Instagram, please do! @lexi_haddock. I post about my books, travels, and lots of videos and pictures of Paris!

The website is my travel blog and reviews of my travels tips for visiting Paris and France, and more. https://lexihaddock .com